Sign of a Promise

SIGN
OF A
PROMISE
AND OTHER STORIES

James C. Schaap
Dordt College

Dordt College Press
Sioux Center, Iowa 51250

Mandate Series

The Unity in Creation   *Russell Maatman*
The Armor of Light   *Merle Meeter*
Sign of a Promise   *James Schaap*

Published by Dordt College Press
Sioux Center, IA 51250
Printed and bound in the United States of America

ISBN 0-932914-02-0

Contents

VI   Contents

Author's Preface

Two years ago I stumbled on an old unkept cemetery, miles from any main road, surrounded by Iowa corn. Few stones remained upright, many were gone. But the stones that were there and still readable told an incredible story of children and tragic death, and I knew at that moment that a significant, unrecorded human drama had once occurred here, far from the cities, at this isolated spot in the garden of America. But I knew also that just as the stones themselves had been lost, many of the old stories would not last the passing of a generation, unless someone tried to give them the life they deserved, not only as interesting tales, but also for the strength they illustrated and the wisdom they carried.

The purpose of this collection is to keep some of those stories alive for my own children and my grandchildren, not only for their entertainment but for their understanding of themselves, so that they too can be enriched by a sense of who they are, where they originate, and what they inherit from their ancestors, lest they, like so many others, fall into the bland flow of American life, shallow and weak, bereft of the sustaining strength which tradition maintains.

Each of the stories in the collection is based on an actual incident or story. Some come from regional histories, some from diaries, some by word of mouth, but all are rooted in historical fact. None of the stories is meant as history, however, for all of them are embellished in varying degrees into a kind of fiction. Names have been changed, settings altered, characters added, dialogue created, motivation supplied. I have, in short, subordinated the historical reality to the imaginative reality, because I am convinced that poetic truth is, at times, more revealing, more powerful, even more interesting than fact. Fiction is, I believe, a potentially stronger medium than history for my purpose, which is to illustrate the beauty of an ethno-religious heritage too grand to be sacrificed on the altar of American homogeneity.

With this objective in mind assembling a group of stories is no easy matter. One could simply trace those sketches in which the Dutch-Frisian pioneer attains success, fervent prayers are answered, heroism is unexcelled, or God acts in an easily explainable manner. Such a collection would certainly be appreciated by many who need only sentiment to feel fulfilled. On the other hand, it would be quite possible to collect the opposite—stories which reveal only stubbornness, pride, greed, rebellion, or hypocrisy. Such a book would satisfy those whose own rebellion needs fuel.

What sharpened my discernment for making such choices was the newspaper. There is, during any given month, in any locale, a full repertoire of comedy, tragedy, and farce. To choose only the sentimental is to neglect the bitter; to choose only the ugly is to forget the beautiful. Neither type alone exhibits truth. Therefore this collection, like the news, includes some sweet stories, some vile stories, some comedies, and some tragedies, in the hope that together they capture at least something of the reality of my heritage, for its beauty is illustrated only by complex truth.

At the core of my heritage lies a deep belief in the doctrines of John Calvin, whose dogma of depravity and election is often caricatured. Less emphasized but equally important is the idea of calling—that every Christian has a God-appointed task to use his abilities to glorify his Creator in whatever field he works. This has been, to me, a vitally important idea. For in my work as a writer, I am covenanted to my work as a Christian. My writing will, therefore, reveal my Christian heritage and commitment. But to do this is a complex and difficult task, and the degree to which I succeed will vary with the expectations of every reader. The stories do, however, express the beginnings of my concern with the relationship between faith and work. May both writer and reader grow in understanding.

I am indebted to many for the publication of this volume. To my parents, who exercised their covenant responsibilities in a manner which led me to understand the beauty and truth of that very heritage. To my wife and children for understanding and patience. To Dordt College for an education that directed me into the work I am now doing. To my colleagues, especially Hugh Cook, whose many hours of reading, discussing, and editing were no small sacrifice. And, finally, to Merle Meeter, whose interest and concern as teacher and friend have been constant, and whose commitment to Christian literature has been a source of strength and a standard by which I can and will judge my own success as a writer.

jcs
july, '78

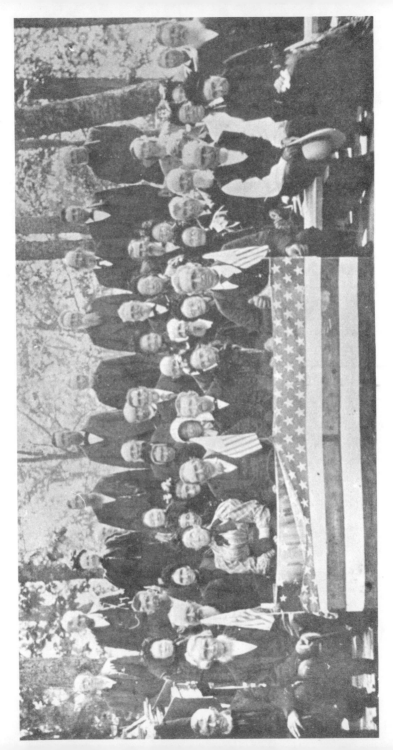

Independence

Johannes clung to the rail with his blistered hands, but relaxed his body as if he were in a saddle, absorbing the lurches of the ship in his knees as he stood, dumbfounded, staring out at the wind-driven schooner scudding across the waves. The winds had subsided as the storm passed, and the ship had responded, its creaking muffled in relief. But the ocean had continued its frantic throbbing, as if the entire drama had been staged in a theater of measurable proportions. Then, suddenly, its labor peaking, the sea had borne this ghastly three-masted schooner, torn and battered, its ragged sails flapping from what masts still stood on her decks.

Johannes watched, silent. The others stood beside him on the deck, quiet, eyes focused on the ship that rolled, dipped, and rose with the swells of the ocean. Jagged wooden frames rose statue-like from the deck, and the base of one thick mast jutted skyward like a broken spear, its shaft snapped by the storm. The schooner danced like a spectre, so close now that they could hear its shrieking timbers; then it jigged aimlessly into the purple horizon until it disappeared as suddenly as it had come, its past—its crew, cargo, even, perhaps, its emigrants—as enigmatic as its destiny.

Johannes was awed. Two ships had been so close here . . . nowhere, yet he knew nothing of the other, nor would he ever. He couldn't help remembering Zeeland and Middleburg, the town, the house and shop. It was all so close, so warm, he knew everyone; the very streets seemed like family now. "But the new country!" people had said,

"America!" When he heard them, the streets, the village, the house and shop, had all become so close, so confining, so colorless.

And what of the people who had once stood on those decks, he thought, watching and waiting, their eyes straining constantly toward the fickle horizons? Johannes kept looking west, following the trail of the schooner, even though the ship had already passed into the mist. That was all he would ever know, he told himself again. No names, no faces, no hump-backed trunks, no lives, no souls. Had the storm flung them all into this endless rolling sea? Had their lives been simply swallowed up by the malevolent ocean? His own ship surged beneath him, floating like some trifling pendant on the breast of the ocean.

His steps were cautious but weak as he left the deck. He moved slowly down the stairway, his left arm braced against the wall to steady himself. German emigrants moved carefully throughout the lower quarters, speaking very little. Children cried—they never seemed to stop; at least the passing of the storm would quell the rage of sickness among the passengers. For several days the hold had been littered with bodies and trunks, the floor coated with vomit, the halls cluttered with anything that couldn't be secured. In Johannes' mind, listless bodies sprawled there yet, for he had seen it all and would always remember. No dominie could preach human depravity and dependence on God so clearly as he had seen it, had heard it, had smelled it, had even felt it. But the halls were cleared tonight, and the storm had broken.

He stopped at his berth and felt the dampness in the curtains that he had specially hung about his quarters. He had tried hard to make it livable. The sailors had smiled when they saw him decorating, preparing the berth for Maria and his Geesje, but it was so useless. His wife and daughter could appreciate nothing since their departure. First there had been the nearly constant quarreling with the Germans, then the disregard and cynicism of the crew, and finally the storm. He lifted the canvas. Maria lay motionless in the berth, her mouth gaping, her face sallow and drawn. Geesje lay at her breast in a gray pallor, cramped and weak, thin and tiny for her nearly fifteen months. She would still take nothing but her mother's milk. Johannes backed into the berth, swung his aching legs into the bed, leaned back slowly, and pulled the cover over the opening behind him. The berth was dark and damp. He reached over, almost as an afterthought, and felt for his daughter's pulse, then his wife's. He found them both alive, crossed his arms over his chest and tried to relax. From within the hold the ocean felt smooth, finally, as Johannes Remeeus said a silent prayer.

The sun rose above a calm ocean. Johannes' family had slept well, their strength returning in a tide of repose, when they were awakened by shouts from the deck and a cannonade that boomed like thunder through the sleeping quarters.

Johannes turned on his side, drew back the canvas, and looked down the narrow hallway. All down the line heads popped out in similar fashion, searching for some explanation for the unusual noise.

"What is it?" someone gasped.

More curious questions—a waking babble of voices.

In a moment Johannes swung himself out of the berth and stood, his legs stiff, his knees full of pain. He held up the blanket and saw his wife sitting up, her elbow propped beneath her for support.

"How is it, Maria?" he asked.

She swept her tangled hair from her face with her left hand and drew it back behind her ears.

"Good," she said. "I feel better. And you?"

Johannes saw a slight smile, warm like a summer morning, break from the unfamiliar creases that lined her face. But she was still beautiful. Two weeks on board had robbed her face of its youthful sheen, but her blue eyes, glazed by sickness during the storm, were now bright and clear. Geesje turned slowly in her sleep, her mouth puckering as if she were already nursing.

"Ja, good." Johannes ran his fingers through his hair and smiled back at his wife. "I will go up to see what is happening here."

The ocean was still, the sky broadly blue, and the deck as full of activity as it had been during the fury of the storm. But Johannes knew that it was not yesterday. A box of firearms stood opened on the deck and multi-colored flags festooned the rigging. Crew and passengers alike were firing round after round, hooting and shrieking in unrestrained celebration. One by one the passengers had left their berths and were joining the fest.

Johannes found some Hollanders standing amidship, watching and laughing. He hesitated momentarily at the stairway, then walked quickly over to join them.

"What is it?" he asked.

"It is a holiday! July 4. It is the Day of Independence for Americans."

The men watched closely as the crew sang and drank and ate in unchecked celebration. Johannes enjoyed the spectacle, but unlike the Germans who participated more readily, the Hollanders were reticent; they stood apart, laughing and joking with each other for the first time in days.

Johannes ran back to the stairs and descended in a flurry, rushing to his berth. He found the canvas open and Geesje awake and nursing, Maria lying comfortably on her side.

"It is the Day of Independence, Maria. You should come above."

"What is that?"

"Independence—the Americans celebrate every year today, July the fourth. It was their War of Independence."

Maria's smile changed into a hesitant laugh, as her brows hunched in confusion. "So they shoot guns?"

Geesje, unwilling to give up her mother's breast, also turned her blue eyes toward her father. Johannes Remeeus simply shrugged his shoulders and turned back toward the stairway.

By the time Johannes had returned to the deck, his Dutch friends were shooting and laughing and dancing like the rest. The morning passed quickly, full of the gleeful charm of a new and unexpected holiday, celebrated by adopted children only beginning to sense the ardor of a changing life. By noon all were on deck, even those who had suffered most during the storm, and all were served from a delicious pig prepared specially for the holiday by the crew. The Hollanders watched the crew hoist their tankards and sing strange lusty songs.

Maria approached her husband soon after their dinner. The men sat like birds in a circle; the women also sat together.

"Johannes," she said quietly over his shoulder, unwilling to break the spritely mood of the conversation. "Johannes, we would like to sing the Psalms. The women said."

Remeeus looked up at his wife, her blue eyes shining from a face flushed with pink. He saw the round-faced women behind her and paused only momentarily before moving from the circle and running toward the chartroom to look for the captain, a burly man whose skin was as weathered as the boards on his ship.

He found him sitting at his desk, a map before him, roast pork still steaming on the plate to his left. The door was open to the warmth of a July morning. Johannes knocked.

"Yes?" The captain turned in his swivel chair and looked over his shoulder at Johannes Remeeus. "What is it?"

"Captain, my people—the Hollanders—would like to sing Psalms today. Would it—"

"Psalms!" the man blurted, puzzled, unbuttoning the top button of his coat. Johannes waited quietly. "Psalms, you say? But today is the Fourth. Nobody sings Psalms today—Christmas, Easter, sure, but the Fourth? You don't know some other songs?" He leaned back toward the emigrant.

Johannes noted the furrowed brows that framed the

captain's deep brown eyes. "We would like the Pslams, sir."

"You would sing Psalms, eh?"

"We would be happy like the rest. When we sing the Psalms, we can be happy. We too can celebrate."

The captain put his hands on his thighs and rose from the chair. He walked to the doorway, past Johannes, and surveyed the deck. Most of the crew, and many emigrants, were still eating. He stood a head taller than Johannes, his thick black hair falling nearly to his collar. With his back to the visitor, he spoke again. "It will make you happy then?"

Johannes stepped closer, still facing the Captain's back. "Ja, it would make us happy."

"Then you will. It is not usual, you know, this psalm-singing on the Fourth, but if it will make you happy," he swung his arm toward the emigrants, "then you may sing your Psalms."

The firing continued until the ammunition was spent, but the emigrants, adding their own bit of celebration and their own vision of Independence, raised their voices in the long droning notes of Psalm 68. Remeeus himself was the *voorzanger*.

Geloofd zij God met diepst ontzag!
Hij overlaadt ons, dag aan dag,
Met zijne gunstbewijzen; ———

Shaking his head, the captain strolled over to the assembly of Hollanders, his hands clasped behind his back. The crew, nearly exhausted from the hours of celebration, listened and laughed, while some Germans joined the chorus, their own language almost harmonizing with the Dutch.

——— *Die God is onze zaligheid!*
Wie zou die hoogste Majesteit
Dan niet met eerbied prijzen?
Die God is ons een God van Heil;
Hij schenkt, uit goedheid, zonder peil,
Ons 't eewig zalig leven:

Hij kan, en wil, en zal in nood . . . .

Remeeus smiled. The people sang with enthusiasm not seen for days, the notes moving much faster than normal. He had only to determine pitch, for his people moved independently at a pace too strong and joyous to be tempered by one man.

Zelfs bij het nad 'ren van den dood
Volkomen uitkomst geven. *

The ship moved slowly through calm seas, pressing ever closer to the Newfoundland banks.

---

*Let God be praised with reverence deep;
He daily comes our lives to steep
In bounties freely given.
God cares for us, our God is He;
Who would not fear His majesty
In earth as well as heaven?
Our God upholds us in the strife;
To us He grants eternal life,
And saves from desolation.
He hears the needy when they cry,
He saves their souls when death draws nigh,
This God is our salvation.

A Vision of the Kingdom

Lamert van der Jagt faced the lake breeze, grasped his lapels with both hands and watched the dredge fade into the blue horizon. Digging out a harbor had been an expensive undertaking, and difficult. The government men had laughed when he told them of his plans, but when they saw the money, they consented to make the eleven-mile trip up the shoreline and dredge out the heavy sand according to van der Jagt's orders. Now they were through. Not even a week, just as he had planned.

He turned in the soft sand and looked south down the beach, a smile curling his tight-drawn lips. Already he could see them coming to his Amsterdam—ships, big ships from Milwaukee, stopping here at Lamert van der Jagt's new seaport, loading the logs and leaving quickly, bound for other ports, for far-distant markets. They would be here shortly, he told himself. And others would come, from the north, from Buffalo, slow line boats and flatlined steamers, their decks festooned with the red faces of immigrants, looking as he once had, for a new home, a good home. More Hollanders—his people.

The sun still topped the deep forest that rose above the lakeshore. He started to walk back toward his cabin, slowly in the dry sand, past pine uprights marking lots he himself had plotted. This was his land, his beach, and soon, he reminded himself, log cabins and fine frame homes would line the white sands and turn the nearly vacant shore into a busy frontier village. Already he had sold some of his plots; already he had named the streets—Lake, Holland, Cedar, Maine—streets that yet existed only on his parchment. There were special acres for a school and a church. Soon children would play in this sand. Their mothers would watch them from windows facing the lakeshore, while their fathers would work for him on the pier, or fell trees in the broad forests that stretched for miles inland.

Lamert van der Jagt breathed hard as he walked in the sand. Now the dredge was gone—Amsterdam harbor had been dug. The cool lake water lapped at the beach. This lake would bring him new life and prosperity, a solid community in this rich country, a home to be proud of. It was his vision. Others stayed in Milwaukee or moved inland to farm. But Lamert had bet on the lakeshore. There were many forests to be cut—birch, oak, maple, pine—and always there were uses for the wood. In Sheboygan they talked of plank roads, more building throughout the county, wood for fires. And the water would bring them ships, here to this town—good, cheap transportation.

His pier had been constructed for several weeks already. It was broad and smooth, jutting out into the surf like a long, indomitable warship. He stopped again for a moment to catch his breath, and gazed down the planks that lay motionless above the undulating lake water. He himself had set the pilings, deep within the shifting sands. Nothing could move them, he was sure.

Henry te Ronde was first. His oxen had pulled a load of cord wood to the beach nearly two weeks ago, and ever since that day other Dutch settlers had followed, from sunup to sundown, aboard wagons of varying shapes, lugging their wood to exchange for grain or seed at the new pier. Wood was already piled high; te Ronde's load lay beneath tons of logs stacked high on the new pier, awaiting the ships. For van der Jagt was one of them, an immigrant; they trusted him, and he had always been fair with them. He was so proud of that reputation.

He turned away from the pier and the lakefront and walked up the beach toward the stand of triangular pines surrounding his cabin. He was a strong man, shoulders wide as an axehandle, legs like fence posts, and arms thickened by nearly forty years of heavy labor. But the slow grade to the end of the beach was always wearying, for the dry sand gave way beneath each heavy step. He stopped when he reached the edge and turned for a last view. He grabbed the chain on his vest and pulled a large silver watch from his pocket. Already late for supper. Janncke would be *pruts*.

He surveyed his kingdom once more, from the bleached pole that marked the southern limits, to the oak stump thrust up from the forest line far to the north. A gull floated lightly over the squared plots of his land, and before him the mighty pier stretched like a giant through the deep blue-green water, on its back a yoke of cord wood awaiting departure. It was a grand sight! Lamert van der Jagt laughed instinctively, irrepressibly, then turned into the house.

"It is done, Janncke," he said, hanging his coat over the wood peg at the door.

His wife looked up from the table and smiled, shaking her head. "Late again! What must we do with you? Send you to bed without supper?"

The children laughed at the jest. They sat around the table, waiting.

Lamert pulled out a chair and sat slowly, exhaled long and hard, and watched his wife. "What have we here?"

Janncke stood over the table, ladling out equal portions to the two children.

"Stew, with a rabbit." She looked up only momentarily.

"Janncke, everything is ready now. The dredge is gone back to Sheboygan. The port is dug. It is finished."

She used the ladle to pour some of the thickened stew. "Ja, ja, good, good. Now we must eat."

"But will you listen, Janncke?—tomorrow, perhaps tonight yet—"

"Lamert, *laat ons bidden!*" she said, folding her hands as an example to her children.

He watched his wife closely. She lowered her head, expecting to be led in prayer. The logs in the fireplace shot sparks over the wide floor planks.

"Dirk," he pointed to his son, "you, eh?"

The boy rifled through the Lord's Prayer, eager to eat. When he finished, there was no conversation for several minutes. The family ate heartily. Then Janncke took the pot and hung it from the iron crane set into the wall by the fireplace, the only source of light for the one-room cabin.

"When will the first of the big ships arrive, *Vader*?" Dirk looked into his father's eyes.

"Tomorrow, *jongen*, if we're lucky."

"Will they be big ones?" Dirk's eyes widened. His arms stretched into a gesture.

"*Ja*, big, very big! Maybe not as big as some in Sheboygan, but bigger than any we see here."

The rabbit was tough and salty. Lamert ate quickly, hardly tasting the meat.

"I wrote to the *Nieuwsbode*, you know, Janncke. Quintus says we will be reading the letter with the next issue." He wanted his wife's attention. She responded with a smile. "Soon Hollanders will be coming to Amsterdam—new Amsterdam!" he said.

Janncke's resistance was melting in the heat of her husband's enthusiasm. Her smile widened. "Then maybe you come once on time to supper!"

"*Ja, Vrouw*." He looked back down, smiling.

Dirk and Christian ate steadily, watching their father race through his meal.

"We will have friends then, *Vader*?"

"*Ja*, sure, Tina, many friends. Soon there will be a village, like Sheboygan. Many people. Many Hollanders." Lamert bit the stubborn meat off a leg bone.

"And you will have done it—ja, *Vader*?"

"With the Lord's help, *jongen*!" Janncke answered before her husband could reply.

He reached for more bread.

"*Ja*, with the Lord's help alone," he admitted.

"We must remember who sends all our blessings."

Janncke spoke with authority to her children.

Lamert spoke with his mouth full of bread.

"Ja, ja, you listen to your mother."

He never tasted the food; in fact, he felt no particular hunger, but he knew he should observe the ritual for the sake of the family. His mind was afloat with the tall ships already bound for his Amsterdam.

"Laat ons lezen, Vader?"

"Eh?" van der Jagt's head snapped back.

"Lezen!" Janncke repeated, looking directly at her husband for the first time since he had entered the cabin.

Lamert was struck by the look, for there was no bitterness in her face, no anger in her eyes. But he had no time for such things. "Ja," he replied slowly, shaking his head.

Janncke motioned to her son. "Dirk—"

"No, Janncke, I will get it." He restrained his son with an upraised arm, pushed back his chair, and rose, turning toward the buffet. He opened the cabinet and lifted the Bible from the shelf it shared with Janncke's good dishes. Then he stood, slowly, and looked out of the window above the oak cabinet.

"Janncke!" He turned momentarily, then looked back out the window. "They are here!" He dropped the Bible on the buffet, ran to the door, grabbed his coat, and turned back to his family.

"There it is—a ship . . . here!" he shouted, pulling on his coat. Then he was gone.

The children ran to the window. A two-masted schooner rose like a dream on the darkening horizon.

"Can we go, too?" Dirk turned, like his father, his face alive with the excitement.

"Read first," she said.

"But *Vader*—"

"Read first—"

Dirk dropped his head and hobbled back to his chair. His sister followed reluctantly.

Lamert ran down the beach, kicking up little tongues of dry sand with each step. He waved both arms over his head, trying to signal the ship. Without breaking stride, he mounted the broad pier and galloped down the planks, never looking down, his eyes fastened on the ship whose bow already pointed toward the jetty, perpendicular to the broad stretch of lake horizon.

He stopped at the edge of piled cord wood, still waving frantically, his face aglow with anticipation. Then he climbed high onto the pile, still waving, still watching the merchant ship from Milwaukee as he scrambled madly up and over the eight-foot logs.

Then, suddenly, his foot twisted and caught in the uneven pile. Pain shot through his leg as the cord wood jumped beneath him, pinning his ankle and buckling his back. His body caromed off the avalanche of logs, and plummeted, with tons of cord wood, into the cold lake swells beneath the pier.

Soon after dawn the next day, the men from the schooner spotted his body bobbing in a tangle of logs that rolled gently in the tranquil morning waters.

Redskins!

For September it was plenty hot. But it got much hotter when John te Slaa stormed into town, knocking fat Anna Nyhof, face first, into the soft dirt of the main street.

"*Verrekte jongen!*" she screamed, wiping the dust from her face. But when she turned to him, she looked straight up at the nether side of his mount. She mumbled some Dutch words, more suitable to the barnyard than the village street, then rose, awkwardly, rump first, retrieving her flowered hat as an afterthought.

Johnny was already gone, bounding over the wooden walks until he stopped, momentarily, and steamed down the path to the blacksmith shop. Already panting like a locomotive, he could barely yell; but somehow, prompted by the fear that shook him, he managed a muffled yelp—something between a cough and a hog snort.

"Injuns!" he meant to say, but when he stopped again and squinted into the deep darkness of the shop, not one of the men who daily gathered there rightly understood the message.

"Injuns!" He spit it out again, puffing like an overworked hound.

"Whatcha say, son?"

"I said . . . Injuns! We got us some Injun problems!"

The shop was quiet except for the soft snapping of the fire.

"Heck, son, we ain't never had no problems with Injuns."

Johnny te Slaa swallowed hard and tried to get his breath back. "I'm tellin' ya," he said, pointing north, "they're comin'."

"Who says?"

Te Slaa looked around at the old men. Their wide eyes slowly became visible in the dimly lit shop.

"Heck, everybody!"

"Well who's everybody?" The voices still grumbled out of the darkness.

Startled at their disbelief, Johnny stammered and shook like he was on trial. "Well all them people!" He pointed again, northward.

"Now settle down, son, and tell us what this is all about." Zwerink, the blacksmith, walked over, pointing a hot pincers at the sweaty youth.

"Well, see, I was out in the field, you know,"—he stopped for a breath—"and I'm seein' all these wagons movin' south, movin' fast like they're crazy or somethin'." He wiped his arm across his wet forehead. "So I ask 'em, one of 'em, I yells at 'em as they're a-goin' by, I says, 'Where ya goin'?' *'Injuns!'* they says, just like that, 'Injuns is on the warpath!' "

Zwerink took three long rooster strides past the youth, then turned and pushed hard on his bellows. Somewhere in the darkness an old man burped.

"Close to a hundred, they said. Already burned Two Rivers to the ground. Killin' and stealin'—murderin' and burnin' everything they can get their hands on. Comin' through Man'towoc right now, leavin' a path a fire!"

"Ach, we ain't had no proof."

"You'll see 'em! Mark my words. They'll be through. It's somethin' awful!" The boy scooped a drink from the cooling tank and looked up, wiping the water from his face. "We gotta' *do* somethin'. Pa sent me in to tell ya."

"What do you say, Abram?" someone asked.

"There's lots of 'em, te Slaa?" Zwerink faced the boy.

"Close to a hundred, they say."

"No, not Injuns—people, in the wagons, runnin' away?"

"Ja, you wait, you'll see."

Abram Zwerink dropped his hammer on the anvil and

stared into the darkness. The men watched and waited, eyes focused on the smith. Johnny leaned up against the cooling tank, hands on hips, confident and proud as a barnstorming preacher after an altar call.

Suddenly, before anyone could as much as spit, dust rolled up and into the shop like lake fog, and there, right before them, was Tone Lammers, still mounted, his horse dancing excitedly in the doorway, its thighs bumping the wall, making the winter shoes hung from the ceiling clang like church bells.

"Get that blame animal—"

"*Verdrommel*, Lammers!"

Lammers squinted into the darkness. "Zwerink," he said, "you here?" The horse stamped and pawed in the dirt, and men coughed hard in the thick dust.

"Ja, ja, here Tone."

"Abram, we haf Injun trouble!"

"You, too?"

"Vatcha mean, 'me, too'? Course, me too. Unt you, too, Abram. Ja, everybody. The Injuns ist here—over a hundred, the people say. Just plain viped out everyting to de nort. In Manitowoc now—on their vay sout'!"

John te Slaa smiled broadly as he straightened his collar.

"See 'em yourself, Tone?"

"Course not, tink I'm crazy? But de people move sout', boys. People from Sheboygan—everybody gettin' out!"

Abram Zwerink removed his apron. "Well, we better talk this over. Let's get out on the street and figure out what we can do." He led them toward the door.

"Get that horse outta here, Lammers!"

Lammers reined the mare and galloped off toward the street, throwing more dust in the men's faces as they surged toward the door.

"I told you, Abram, didn't I? I was first, eh?" Johnny nipped at Zwerink's heels like a dog chasing a wagon.

"Ja, ja, now settle down!" Zwerink led the men quickly into the main street where they stopped and half-circled in front of Winklehorst's store. Dust hung in the air.

"Everybody, come over now! *Subiet!*" Women stepped from the sidewalks and gathered like sheep in the middle of the street. Shopkeepers peered from their windows, craning their necks at the commotion. Dogs barked and howled, sensing the excitement. In a few minutes, a crowd of close to fifty had assembled, muttering and poking at each other for answers.

"Vat is it, Anna?"

"Ja, I don't know, Dina. Somebody died maybe?"

Anna Nyhof spotted Johnny te Slaa, but she had sensed that something bigger than her insulting plunge into the dirt was happening here, so she sneaked over behind him, determined to vent her outrage when the gathering broke.

"Now listen, people!" Zwerink took charge. "There's been some talk—"

"*Spreek Hollands!*" someone yelled.

"No, English!" another shouted back.

"Will you be quiet and listen!" Zwerink's tone was as effective as his hammer. The people hushed. "And shut those dogs up!" He pointed down the street.

"John te Slaa and Tone, here, heard some news this morning that we should talk over. John, tell us once." He grabbed the boy by the shoulder and hoisted him up on the plank steps. "Now calm down, son, and tell all the people what you told the men before."

Johnny proceeded to relate the story, as well as he could, to the crowd. With each sentence the people grew more quiet.

"Thank you, Johnny," Zwerink said when he finished. "Now you, Tone," he directed, pointing at Lammers.

Antonie Lammers cleared his throat and surveyed the crowd that continued to grow. "*Verschrikkelijk!*" he said.

"Speak English!" someone yelled.

"I say, it's terrible. I also have seen many wagons rushing sout'. I asked the people, too. They spoke of Indians—"

Suddenly there was a rumble down the street, and three mounted farmers, pitchforks raised in their hands, raced into the crowd, scattering people like flies.

"Injuns, Abram!"

It was Gerrit Brasser and two neighbors. Gerrit was an elder in the Dutch church, well-respected. The men stayed on their horses, and the crowd drew close once again.

"There's Injuns up to Manitowoc! On their way south. Heard it from people movin' away. Must be somethin' awful!" Gerrit's horse dodged and jumped, puffing and snorting from the strenuous ride.

"They're scalpin' and burnin' everything in sight. Those savages are killin' even the little children, and takin' the women-folk."

Anna Nyhof staggered and fell like a stuck sow, knocking the farmer behind her to the dirt, where he sat, dumbfounded, Anna's head in his lap. Dina rushed quickly to her side and fanned her face with her hat.

"Now listen, folks," Zwerink continued, "there's no cause for alarm—but we'd better not panic!"

"Vat is dat—*panik*?"

"Ah, ja—what you say? *schrik*?"

Zwerink went on, "Nobody even *seen* an Indian yet! Far as I know, all you people what know anything at all just saw some people on the run—"

"Abram, you crazy? If my windmill blows down, I don't have to see the wind to know it been there! What about all them people?"

"Well, Gerrit, from what you and Johnny and Tone say, none of them seen any Indians either—least-wise that's what I understand you to say."

Tone Lammers kicked into the dirt, then kneaded the ground. "Well, no, but ya tink de 'id all run like dat if day had no goot cause? Tink der *gek,* Zwerink?"

"Just let me finish now!" Zwerink stood up on the step to Winklehorst's store. He stretched out his arms to the crowd, begging for quiet. "This calls for a plan, people—we got to plan this thing out!"

Murmurs rose into near chaos.

"I'm leavin'."

"Me, too."

"I ain't stickin' around."

"Now hold on!" Zwerink was a forceful speaker. "There's something we can do before we all up and gallop off to Milwaukee. If them Injuns is still up to Manitowoc, they're not going to be here for some time. You can figure that much. What we got to do is warn the others. Bring all the farmers into town so we can plan this thing proper!"

There was some approval for the idea.

"That's right!"

"Zwerink's got it!"

"Dat's goot, Abram!"

"Now, I think everybody ought to go back home and get their families and neighbors. We'll meet here again, say, two this afternoon." Abram grabbed for his watch. "Don't have the time. Who's got it?"

"Quarter of eleven, Abram."

"Good. Two o'clock we'll be back here. And bring weapons, anything you can get." He turned to his left. "Ed, we better have yer guns."

Ed Winklehorst assented.

"And where's Pieter Ramaker? He sells guns."

"Ramaker's enlisted," someone yelled.

"Ain't that just like him? Never around when you can use him."

"What about the cannon, Abram?" A sharp voice came out of the tangle of people.

"Ja, the cannon!" others echoed.

Zwerink scratched his head. "That thing ain't been used in years."

"Still works every Fourth!"

"But we got no shot."

"What cannon you talkin' about?"

"The cannon by the bandstand."

"Oh, that cannon."

"Maybe she'll shoot nails or something."

Zwerink shook his head. "All right, all right. Joe, take some a these men and see if you can move that thing. But the rest of us better go out to the farms."

"What about the women?"

"What women?"

"The *afgescheiden kerk.* They got their Mission Fest today—started this morning."

Tone Lammers, pulling at the ends of his mustache, stood next to Abram. "Vell, you'll haf to tell dem dat they can haf der gatherin' not today. They vill be real disappointed—"

"John!" Zwerink looked for te Slaa.

"Ja?" The boy was trying to pull Anna Nyhof's shoes off, while a half dozen women brooded over the lump of flesh on the street.

"John, let the women handle her—you get yer horse and go to yer church. Tell the other women," Zwerink commanded. "And don't get so terrible upset there, or you'll have 'em all crazy. Just tell 'em to get home to their husbands—and tell the widows to get to town. Tell 'em the Mission Fest is over for the year."

The crowd disappeared almost as quickly as it had formed. Some townspeople stayed in the street, of course, talking excitedly to each other and warning other farmers who came to town late.

John te Slaa never did find his own horse. He grabbed a drab-looking mare that sagged through the middle like a drainage ditch, mounted, and thundered heavily past the shops and stores of Main Street, south out of town.

It wasn't far away, so it took only a few minutes for him to reach the sandy knoll that overlooked the old wooden church. The moment he lumbered over the hill, he spotted the congregation of black-draped women sitting in the shade of the elm grove north of the building.

The sway-backed mare rumbled down the road, but when Johnny arrived, no one even raised her head. The women sat perfectly still in prayer. Johnny stood in the stirrups and coughed, trying to draw someone's attention, but every head was bowed, every eye closed. Leading them was their short, stocky dominie, whose splendid Dutch phrases flowed like sweet music. Johnny coughed again, almost gagging, but no one stirred. He saw his own mother seated in a tall consistory chair, her hat tipped forward. Then the dominie's voice started to drone into a low monotone, and he knew it was nearly over. Finally, he amened, and the women turned in unison.

"John, do you have someting for our gathering?" the dominie asked.

John dropped from the saddle. "Ja, Dominie!" He glanced from side to side. Zwerink had said to be calm, but his heart raced in his chest.

"Ja? Is it someone in particular you would like to speak to? Your mother perhaps?" The dominie cocked his head.

"Ah, no, sir, Dominie, you see, ah . . ." John licked his lips quickly and ran to the front. "May I—" he leaned towards the preacher, whispered, and the dominie's face paled in the mid-morning sun, while his burly head nodded in machine-like jerks.

"Ah, ma'ams . . . ah, ladies—" Johnny quickly snatched his hat from his head, "I . . . that is, Abram Zwerink, the blacksmith, you know . . . Abram Zwerink told me to come and tell you that, ah . . ." he struggled for the right words, "that, ah, that there is probably some Indian people around here." He tried to smile politely. "Heh, heh, and he said to tell you that you should probably go home now."

The women gobbled in low-toned whispers.

"He says that the widows and the old maids—ah, well, those who don't now have any husbands—should go to Oostburg right away. He says to tell you that the Mission Fest is over for this year."

The dominie stepped quickly in front of Johnny. "Fellow Christians, my friends, vee vant to thank this courageous young man for coming into our midst this morning and bringing us this news. Unfortunately, vee didn't get to hear Dominie Bylsma and his mission report—" he nodded to a distinguished looking man seated behind him "—but vee must do as John says. Shall vee rise?"

Scattered whispers grew into a low murmur. The

dominie held Johnny's arm as the ladies got to their feet. Then he laid his arm around Johnny's shoulder, holding him close.

"Shall we sing *Dat 's Heern zegen op u daal*?"

Johnny looked at the preacher, amazed. "da-da-da-da-da-da-da- . . ." on and on the prolonged whole notes plodded like an old cow to pasture, and he was trapped; he felt the dominie's stiff woolen sleeve against his neck.

"*Loof, loof nu aller Heeren Heer. Amen.*"

When it was over, he ran from the front, down an aisle, and to his mother. "Tell *Vader* that we're all to meet in town at two o'clock. He's waiting for you at home. I'll go back now—got to find my horse in town." He waited for no reply, but in one fluid motion turned back to the mare and ran to the back of the assembly. He jumped aboard the mare, slamming his heels into her ribs. The horse stood motionless, chewing on some long grass that sprouted near the steps of the church.

"Hey, giddap!"

She turned her head to look unhappily at the rider.

John was not to be denied. He bounced and kicked like a spoiled baby. Finally, she walked grudgingly up the hill toward the village.

By two o'clock the village swarmed like a prairie ant hill. A constant stream of wagons from all directions poured into Main Street, each holding its hallowed cargo of household treasures and food. The dominie wheeled in with his oak pulpit—no one could guess how he had handled it alone. Arie Joose hauled in a full load of firewood aboard a wagon already filled with furniture; even his feather bed was packed against the bangboard. Some brought very little with them; only the fearful eyes of children peeked over the sides of the wagons. Emma Westerbeeke brought her silverware, and Gertrude Veldboom her whole crop of green beans.

Men shouted and gestured, waving axes and scythes, even spades. Old man Navis puffed his long pipe bravely, armed with an old, fancy sword from the wars of Napoleon, and looking for all the world like a Knickerbocker knight. When he walked, the sheath scraped along behind him, drawing a kind of moat in the loose dirt of Main Street. Ed Winklehorst's store was alive with activity; a line had formed at the front and was moving slowly inward. One by one others left, holding shiny new shotguns and rifles, emptying ammunition into their pockets.

Abram Zwerink held his double-barreled weapon in his left hand as he walked through the people, stopping occasionally to give encouragement or further orders.

"Got my piece, Abram. No redskins gonna touch my missus!" Seine Le Mahieu brandished his flintlock, older even than his wrinkled spouse.

"Got any ammunition?"

Le Mahieu sat back in his wagon, his eyes checking through his possessions. *"Verdraaid,* guess I don't have none."

"Better see Ed." Zwerink took the old rifle from his hands. The pan was gone and there was no flint in the hammer. He looked back at Le Mahieu.

"They're gonna get her sure if you have to use this!"

Vrouw Le Mahieu broke into obvious grief.

Those who didn't have guns or axes held pitchforks, which stood like saplings above the crowd. The women bunched together like cattle in a storm, their heads bobbing under their bonnets as they talked and cried, while trying vainly to hold their excited children.

Abram Zwerink pushed through this confusion and stood once more on the front steps of Winklehorst's hardware store, surveying the throbbing multitude which had gathered at his instructions. He hadn't seen so many Hollanders since he emigrated. The town was jumpy with fear and excitement; Dutch and English words were everywhere to be heard.

"All right!" he yelled, but even Zwerink's boom could not quell the bedlam. *"Monden dicht!"* he tried again. Still there was no response. He thrust his double-barreled ten gauge into the air and fired.

Women screamed and children cried. Men grabbed for their guns and craned their necks like chickens, looking for Indians.

"Up here!" Zwerink yelled again.

Slowly the crowd responded.

"I think Abram wants to speak."

"Must be two o'clock."

"Shush up now, everybody!"

Quiet returned, and the people turned to the blacksmith.

"Folks, we been talking here, now, for an hour or two, and we got us some plans drawn up. Now, listen. First thing we want to say is that if some of you people want to pull out, you can go. Ain't nobody goin' to be stoppin' you."

Some people responded audibly.

"Not me."

"No, we're staying—this here's our land!"

"We're fightin' for the *kolonie!*"

"Nobody push us off what's rightfully our own!"

There was some cheering, few dissenting opinions.

He started again. "Nobody'll be mad if some want to leave. So once this meetin' adjourns, be off with ya!" Zwerink shifted his weight on the step, preparing to explain the carefully drawn plans. "Now, those of us that's plannin' to stay are goin' to have to do some special things."

The crowd grew silent.

Zwerink spoke. "First, we want to use all these wagons here for a barricade."

"Vat is dat—*barricade?*"

"Barricade? Ah, what would that be in Dutch?—ah, *muur?*"

"Oh, ja, . . . ja, goot!"

"So let's see . . . Tone, take your wagon and three or four others and block the road to the north."

Tone Lammers shrugged his shoulders and whined like a

homeless dog. "Ach, but Abram though, my wagon is yust new dis spring!"

Zwerink stood, astonished. "Your wagon or your wife, Tone?"

Tone Lammers pursed his lips and twirled the ends of his mustache once more. The crowd waited, silent. Zwerink shifted his weight from side to side, uneasy in the prolonged silence.

"Ja, ja, good, the north road?"

The people on the street breathed a collective sigh of relief.

"Ja. Take men with guns and set up a station." Zwerink sent out three more groups in other directions, then waited for the dust to settle. "Now, we will need fast riders for the advance pickets. John te Slaa, you take two or three more boys—be sure you all have guns—and move about two miles north. Keep your eyes open. When you see something, ride into town quick—and don't fight!"

The crowd murmured its approval of Zwerink's strategy.

"Now, those in town—" the crowd hushed again. "The men with rifles will man a line on the outer perimeter of the town."

"Vat is dat vord—*perimeter*?"

"Ach, ah, *rand*—something like that."

"Next, the men with shotguns will form another line, and then those who hold hand weapons will stay here in the middle of town." Zwerink pointed at the imaginary lines the men had designed.

"What about us, Abram?"

"What do you have?"

A short, old farmer held up his hay fork.

"That's a hand weapon—you stay here."

Ed Winklehorst nudged Abram from behind and whispered in his ear. Zwerink nodded and started again.

"The women will be in charge of the cooking and the children. All the children must be kept off the streets."

"Is that all we gotta do?" a woman's voice came out

from the crowd.

"Ja, I think—"

"Abram, some of us can handle guns as good as the men. Why can't we—"

"Abram!"

"Ja, Joe?"

Some of the men grumbled about "women doin' the men's work," while Joe te Linderd elbowed his way through the people, moving toward the speaker. When he reached Zwerink, he pulled him down and whispered in his ear.

"Ja, ja, that is a good idea!" Zwerink stood again, looking over the crowd. "The women can, ah . . . well, since we will be needing . . . ." It didn't come easy. Abram rocked back and forth in his boots. "Te Linderd says the women should rip up their pettycoats—"

"Eh? Vat is—*pettycoats*?"

"Oh, ja, how must one say dat?—*ondergoed?*"

"*Ondergoed*! Oh, no, what have we here?"

Zwerink continued, "—and they can make bandages since we may need them later." Zwerink looked quite sheepish, his cheeks flushed. He pointed toward te Linderd who had moved back into the cover of the crowd. "By the way, Joe, how did you do with the cannon?"

"Can't budge the thing." Te Linderd raised both hands and shrugged his shoulders.

"Did you try oxen?"

"No, we tried with four or five strong men."

"Well, plenty of oxen around here now. Try it."

"Where do you want it moved, Abram?"

"Up on the front line—with the sharpshooters, to the north!"

"Sharpshooters?" Te Linderd's brows furrowed in confused unbelief.

"The men with the rifles."

"Oh, ja, those sharpshooters. Ja, ja, good—we'll try to move it again."

Zwerink turned back to the crowd. "That is the plan. Now, we've heard some more reports from the north since this morning. People say there's near a thousand Injuns. They said they left Manitowoc burned to the ground. Sheboygan is expecting them, but they haven't seen them yet. Nobody knows what tribe this is, or what caused them to go crazy with killing. And no one that I've talked to has even seen them yet!"

"But the people keep moving, Abram!"

"Ja, Seine is right. A steady line is moving south along the lakeshore."

The two dominies came up to the front; sober and reflective, they represented the community churches. They stopped respectfully at Zwerink's feet and asked for his ear. "Should vee haf some prayer, Abram?" they asked.

"No, I think we better get about our business. But I will remind the people of their spiritual duties."

"Just a few more things—" he started again. "Ike Hartman will show you men with hand weapons how to use them. He will meet you by the livery right now. And the dominies remind us all to be praying for ourselves and our children."

"Perhaps we could sing, '*Getrouwe God de heid'nen zijn gekomen, en hebben stout Uw erfland ingenomen,*' Zwerink—it would be fitting?"

"Dominie, we must be about our tasks now!"

Abram Zwerink turned abruptly and walked into the hardware store to talk to Winklehorst. The crowd slowly dispersed, a few families piling into loaded wagons and leaving town, most others taking the positions that Zwerink had directed.

Ike Hartman was a paunchy old man with a thick silver mustache that stuck straight out from his upper lip. When he was younger, he had fought Chief Black Hawk in the Indian wars to the south, and he was sure now that his expertise could be of help among his fellow Hollanders. He notified Zwerink much earlier that he could sharpen the combat techniques of the farmers. It was, to him, a calling.

He stood before a ragged crowd of field hands,

bellowing like a lighthouse horn. "All right, men, war is a helluva dirty business, and these savages are damn good fighters!"

His men straightened up quickly, forming a line that ran before the commander like a bolt of lightning.

"Now, we're moving to the bandshell to go through maneuvers, y'hear? I want everybody moving, runnin' like mad!"

"Ach, why must Ike cuss like that?" someone asked as they ran.

"Got to in the army," came the reply; "it's regulations."

The men trooped off quickly, jogging behind their sergeant. The bandshell was nearly a quarter mile down the street, and short men, tall men, tubs of blubber, and bags of skin and bones all moved down the road, each holding his own peculiar weapon, all grunting like farrowing sows as they closed in on their destination.

"Companyyyy—halt!" Hartman commanded, almost ready to collapse himself. "We'll rest us some here, men."

When they finally arrived, Hartman lined them up in a row, then paraded up and down the ranks, strutting like a general. "Men," he said, "this is damned dirty business. What we gotta do is learn to kill or be killed." He drew his black cap low over his eyes, twisting the ends of his mustache as he leaned his left arm on the sword at his side.

"But Ike, though, must you do so much swearing?"

Hartman's head jerked. "Who said that?"

"I did. I said must you swear so much?"

Ike's jaw dropped. " 'Course I gotta swear. Whatcha think? War's *man's* business!" He turned again and moved up and back along the ragged row.

"We gotta learn to kill, men!" He turned suddenly, as if furious, and stared into Edgar Wieskamp's face. "We gotta learn to stab em—here!" He jabbed at Wieskamp's rib cage, nearly knocking his feet from under him.

"Now, let's see those weapons. Hold 'em out straight, thisaway, like the Injuns are comin'."

Hay forks and manure forks rose slowly from the ground and jutted out straight, waist level.

In a half hour, Hartman had them thrusting and parrying like ancient French noblemen.

By the middle of the night, there was still no sign of Indians. Johnny te Slaa and two friends manned the forward pickets nearly three miles north of the village. The September night was cool and quiet, and the excitement of the day had wearied them so much that only Johnny could hold his eyes open. They lay under cover of a stand of cedars, waiting. Once again he scanned the horizon. Johnny was sure he should be able to see the glow of Sheboygan in flames, but once again he saw nothing at all, certainly no Indians. The cool lake wind pestered the yellowing leaves of the trees above them.

Then he heard rustling in a nearby thicket. Or did he? He thought he did, but, he told himself, it might have been a dream, his imagination maybe. Again, the leaves crackled—more noise than could have been made by the breeze. He was sure this time, but no one else had heard it. He reached down to one of his friends.

"Ed!" He poked the boy carefully as he whispered.

"Wha—!" The boy awoke, but John slammed his hand over his gaping mouth to quiet him. In the commotion, Jake ten Pas also opened his eyes. Johnny let up on Ed's mouth slowly, raising his finger to his mouth.

"Something's in the bushes."

"Injuns?" Jake ten Pas's eyes rolled in their sockets.

"Don't know!"

"Should we get back to town? Abram said no fightin'."

"We gotta see what this is—we gotta know 'fore we can go back."

Johnny drew the handgun he was issued from Winklehorst's hardware, and pointed it into the dark night. There was no further sound just then.

"I'm goin'. You guys stay here. If I don't come back, high-tail it for town, ya hear? Tell them the Injuns is here finally!"

Jake glared at his friend. "We ain't goin' without you!"

"You gonna have to, maybe."

"Watcha mean?"

"Well, stupid, what if there's Injuns in there?"

Suddenly the bushes rustled again. All three heard it; all three knew.

"You mean you might get caught by 'em?" Jake held close to Johnny's arm, staring his friend in the face. "Your old man'd be really mad—who'd he have to do the chores?"

"Look, I got to go, see. There ain't no other way."

"Heck, you might even get yerself killed, Johnny; what then?" Jake was adamant. "What then, Johnny, eh?"

In the clear moonlit night Johnny could see the leaves of the bushes move. He pulled his arm away from Jake's grasp and took two long steps on his haunches before dropping down to his belly, his pistol held out in front like a light.

"Johnny!"

He turned back toward his friends, his head barely raised from the ground.

"Do you want me to tell Emily 'bout what you was saying about her before? I mean, if we don't ever see ya again?"

"You crazy, Jake? I don't plan on dying."

"Ja, ja, good, but you be careful!"

John crept ever so slowly forward, his belly snaking through the twigs and leaves. There was no sound anymore, but he still could see the bushes move unnaturally where he first had heard the rustling. He moved slowly, like a turtle, the dampness soaking his shirt.

Still the bush kept moving. Closer and closer he crept, watching the bush like a hawk, but still he saw nothing. He glanced back momentarily. There, in the moonlight, he could catch the glint of a rifle barrel where his friends waited, guns raised. Johnny's heart pounded; he could feel the blood, the pulse throbbing in his throat and forehead.

He raised the gun slowly toward the bushes and waited, daring to go no further. The rustling continued, louder now, but he heard no talking, no horses. He drew back the hammer slowly, until the metal clicking seemed to scream out through the silence. Then he held the pistol with both hands, ready to fire, closing one eye, putting a dead aim on the moving bush. He felt ants crawling on his neck and a strange wet warmth through his body.

Then he heard breathing, heavy breathing. He was sure. More breathing and more rustling. Then a grunt. More rustling, another grunt, almost a burp. Something was coming now, coming much closer, out of the bushes. The pistol aimed straight for the target, held tight and straight by both of his hands. The bush moved aside; he saw the leaves part clearly and cleanly down the middle. His finger perspired on the trigger. His hands were icy with fear.

"Roooinnkk!" A deep belch trumpeted from the bushes and out stepped a sow, turning her thick head left and right, sensing the danger around her. Johnny saw her reddish hide clearly in the moonlight and dropped his gun, his head sinking into the wet grass.

"It's only a pig!" he said, exhaling.

"What ya say?"

"A pig—"

"A pig?" Well, what's a pig doin' out here?" The boys moved forward to be with their Daniel, guns still raised.

Johnny te Slaa sat up slowly. "Eatin' I guess. Must be Jan de Koter's. He probably went to town without locking anything up."

The sow shook her huge head once or twice, watching the boys closely. Then she buried her nose in the sweet grass, worried about nothing at all.

The boys settled back into their position. In little more than an hour all three fell asleep.

The sun rose bright and shiny over the lakeshore, and found the village intact, sparkling under a quilt of autumn dew, its inhabitants motionless. And it was early when two riders rode up quietly from the east. The boys might have seen them first if they hadn't been sleeping, but their late-night adventure had been far too much for them. The two riders appeared suddenly on the hill, silhouetted against the pastels of the early morning sky.

"Abram, who is it?" The men were awake, at least some of them. The north line of sharpshooters looked fearfully toward the mysterious intruders, shouldering their weapons as they watched.

"It's not the boys." Abram himself seemed worried.

"Is there just two?"

"Ja—"

"But there's three boys."

"Ja, that's right—it can't be the boys, eh?"

"Sure don't look like no Injuns, though."

"Can't rightly tell."

Rifles cocked, the men positioned themselves for an assault.

"Think we oughtta let 'em have it, Abram?"

Zwerink didn't like the looks of things. There was nothing in the riders' dress or demeanor to suggest that they might be Indians. Yet, everyone had said that the Injuns were coming. People were running away, weren't they? The riders were closing in on the village—he had to make the decision. Everything he felt told him that shooting was stupid, but a deep and sharp emotion made his own fingers tingle with a vivid sense of urgency. He looked around quickly and saw the cannon. Nuts, bolts, nails, even old mower teeth had been jammed down its ancient throat. The riders came ever closer, still unrecognizable against the dawn.

Abram pointed to the cannon. "Maybe we oughtta let out a warning."

Joe te Linderd lit the end of a long stick. When it finally popped into flame, he held it near the homemade fuse they had wound the night before. The fuse sputtered into flame, crackling and spitting out sparks as it burned slowly down. The men waited, standing straight or lying on the ground, hands clasped firmly over their ears.

"Kaaa-boooooommm!" The old fieldpiece sounded off, setting dogs wailing throughout the village.

Ike Hartman sat up in his blanket and reached for his sword. "What the hell was that?" he sputtered.

Almost a minute passed before the smoke cleared. Nuts, bolts, shards of metal lay scattered like acorns no more than fifty feet in front of the big gun.

"Guess she didn't work, Abram. Should we try 'er again!"

But the warning had been heard. The two riders stopped abruptly, waving their hands in the air. Suddenly three horsemen rushed past them toward the village, dust kicking up beneath them. They raced in and dismounted quickly, running, until they stopped, ducking behind the wagon barriers.

"What is it?" Johnny te Slaa's eyes were round and glassy.

Abram Zwerink was astonished. "Who was it you passed out there on the road?"

"We didn't see nobody."

"Those two men—out there." He pointed.

"Those two? Heck, never saw 'em before. How we supposed to know 'em?"

"But they're not Injuns?"

"Those guys?" Johnny nodded towards the riders.

"Ja!"

"Course not—they're just like us."

"Hold your fire, men!" Abram yelled immediately.

The men on the horizon soon became visible once more. One man waved his hat frantically. The other flagged a long red handkerchief through the air until both men reached within fifty feet of the wagons.

"Gonna shoot?"

"Course not, c'mon." Abram put the pistol back in his holster. "Where you boys from?" he yelled over the open field.

"Green Bay." They walked forward very carefully, still

apprehensive. Finally, their faces became clearly visible.

"Seen any Indians?"

The men shook their head and laughed. "Oh no—you, too?"

"What are you talking about?"

"This whole darn country's done turned into an army camp, I swear." They stopped again, directly before the first line of defense.

Zwerink stepped out to meet them; the others followed like sheep.

"I mean everywhere we been, people're standing around with guns, talkin' like they're crazy—yellin' about 'Redskins'!"

"You mean you haven't seen none?"

"Aw, heck no!"

"Is Manitowoc still there?"

"Still where?"

"Where it always was?"

"Sure is."

"And no Injuns attacked Sheboygan?"

"Nothin' attacked Sheboygan 'cept chicken skin. Don't know how all this started, but it's just so much hogwash!"

"Vat is dat—hogwash?"

"But what about all them people we seen on the move—goin' south?"

"I know it, we seen 'em. We heard about it, too. But it's all for nothin'. There ain't no Injuns—least-wise none what's gonna give you any trouble 'round here."

The whole town gathered quickly at the northern perimeter. They all stared, astonished by the revelation.

Ike Hartman kicked at the dirt.

Johnny te Slaa's mouth gaped in disbelief.

Abram Zwerink took his hat from his head and scratched his temple.

"No Injuns?" he asked again.

"Nope."

"Well, I'll be jiggered!!"

"Vat is dat der vord—jiggered?"

"Ach, Johannes—*nu breekt me de klomp!*"

"Ja, ja, me too."

The dominie tugged at Abram's arm, begging his ear. "Abram," he asked, "Abram, how about *'t Hijgend hert der jacht ontkomen?*"

Abram Zwerink never heard the question.

The dominie climbed aboard Brasser's new wagon, his back to the strangers.

"Friends, just one verse of Psalm 42—"

Johnny te Slaa, remembering the pinkish sow, rubbed his tired eyes, jerked the pistol from his pants pocket, and emptied the bullets into his hand.

"So Gallantly Streaming"

"Yesterday morning a live Yankee was caught on our streets and placed in jail. He is a Dutchman affecting craziness and refuses to give any account of himself. He cannot tell what regiment he belongs to and says the Yankees picked him up and forced him into the army. We think such characters ought to be hung as spies, as it is not likely that the Federal government would enlist idiots into its army.

Vicksburg *Citizen,* June 23, 1863

"No, Isaac, I say we can't be here too long. At least that's what the men up front are saying."

The wagon rolled along easily behind the mule team, one of hundreds that snaked through the long, low cotton fields of the delta, moving south towards Vicksburg.

"I heered they's makin' bread outta peas now." Henry Zimmerman turned his head and laughed, incredulous.

"Ach, Henry, certainly—"

"I'm tellin' ya, that's what I heered. They grind up peas into a kinda meal, then make bread outta it. Supplies is gettin' short in the city."

"From peas?"

"Well, that's what they said."

"Who?"

"Some troops. Saw 'em last night near the woods by that creek, ya know? Said they heard it from some Reb deserters. Said there's lotsa deserters, too. That's another sign."

The sun was hot. Isaac Te Kolste held his rifle in his left hand and used his right sleeve to wipe the sweat from his eyes.

"So you tink it won't be long?"

"Course I *tink* it won't be long. How long you reckon you could eat pea bread?" Henry Zimmerman's bearded jaw opened wide as he threw his head back in laughter. Isaac simply nodded.

"I'm tellin' ya, Isaac, this whole thing will be over in a little while. Why, Farragut's got the river all the way to New Orleans. Grant'll get 'em, you can bet on it."

"Where?"

"New Orleans, fool, down on the Gulf. Them Rebs only got Vicksburg. That's all they got." Zimmerman raised both hands above his head, holding the reins between his knees.

"Ja?"

"Ja!" Zimmerman looked sideways at his shotgun guard. "Where the hell ya been, Dutchman, yer finger in a dyke or something? Jeez! Listen, fool, you gotta keep them ears a yerz open, hear? Us privates is low men around here—we don't learn nothin' lessen we watch out for ourselves. Tobacco?"

"No."

Henry jammed the plug in the side of his mouth and bit off a hunk. "Damned skeeters. What a swamp down here, eh? Look at them poor mules." He put the plug back in his shirt pocket.

Isaac watched the mules, their tails in constant motion, swatting away the insects.

"Gotta be comin' to a river soon, I'd judge. Woods is gettin' thicker. Must be the Yazoo. Can't be the Mississippi."

Their wagon tailed another, following blindly along the old rutted river road that meandered through the flat land and into a dense stand of oaks and hemlocks. Henry used the hand brake skillfully, holding the heavy rig from rolling too fast down the grades.

"There! Told ya, Isaac. See that?" He pointed to his left. The wagons skirted a river all right, a deep blue, wide, almost motionless river. But the wagons kept rolling along its bank.

"Must be lookin' for a landing or something." Zimmerman craned his neck trying to see past the wagon in front of them to the head of the train. "Say, listen, Isaac, kin I call ya, 'Ike'?"

"Ike?" Te Kolste squinted at the sharp syllable.

"Yeah. Had a friend in Manitowoc named Isaac. A tanner. Good man. Called him 'Ike.' That okay?"

"Ja, that's goot then."

"Ya ever get up to Manitowoc? Nice town."

"No. I vas at Sheboygan once." Isaac smiled proudly.

"No?" Henry slapped the reins over the mules. "What do you Hollanders do down there—work all the time?"

Isaac looked puzzled. "Ja, we work a lot," he admitted.

"Well, that's the way to make money, I guess." Isaac watched Zimmerman closely. "Listen, when we get our butts outta this swamp and back home, you'll have to come up some time. We can drink some beer—I'll show you 'round some."

"Ja, that would be goot," Isaac smiled.

The wagon in front of them stopped, slowly. Henry shouted at the mules and used the brake to bring their wagon close to the one in front. The woods had nearly broken to their left; the edge of the river was within fifty feet.

"Now what?" He climbed up on the seat, still trying to catch a glimpse of the lead wagon. "Suppose the front is at the crossing. We gonna be here for a time, sure." He sat back slowly, wound the reins around the seat, and spat tobacco juice onto the road.

"Hey, what do ya say we get us some water?" Henry was down in a flash. He jerked the brake hard, locking it. "C'mon, Ike! Thirsty?"

"But what if the wagons—"

"Them mules ain't goin' nowhere, and we gonna be sittin' here for awhile anyhow." He pointed to the nearby river. " 'Sides, we can get back quick. C'mon!"

Isaac stepped down from the wagon, looking left and right. Then he followed his driver through the tangled underbrush along the bank, tramping down the chest-high foliage until he reached the water. He looked back again. Drivers and guards, even regular troops, had dropped from their wagons and headed for the water.

The river was broad and blue; it flowed slowly westward, its motion barely visible. The water was clear. Zimmerman crept close to the edge on hands and knees, then dropped his face into the river, drinking deeply. When he came up for air, he looked back, water dripping from his thick beard.

"C'mon, Ike." He motioned with his head, then dropped his hands into the river, leaned over, and took another long drink.

Isaac knelt in the spongy bank. His knees were soon wet, even though he was more than a foot from the edge. Water spiders flicked like shooting stars over the surface. He reached down carefully and scooped a mouthful up toward his face.

"Tastes kinda strange, but it's wet." Henry's shirt was soaked in a V, all the way down to his belly. He pulled his hands from the river and brushed the mud from his fingers.

Isaac drank only one more mouthful. "Is there many floods here?" he asked.

"Damned if I know. Why?"

"Look at the trees."

Grayed, lifeless stumps grew out of the water, twenty, thirty feet from the edge, almost to the middle of the flow.

"Yer right. Never seen no stumps like that before."

Gray-green moss clung to branches of trees all along the edge and hung in long beards toward the ground. Isaac had never seen anything like it, not in Holland or in the new country. There was no wind here, no motion, no sound, except for the babble of troops up and down the river's edge. It seemed that time itself had stopped, as if he were in a huge room, full of water and trees, cut off from real life.

"*Wat benauwd,*" he said quietly.

"What's that?" Henry looked back.

"Ach, I said it is *benauwd,*" he repeated slowly.

"What the hell is that? Would you speak English? Gosh sakes, how you expect me to know what yer talkin' about?"

He couldn't begin to explain it to Henry Zimmerman, but the people back home would understand. The undergrowth framed huge hardwoods that exploded into the sky, barely visible from the floor of the woods. And the river, quiet, serene, broken here and there by ageless stumps, moved with a mysterious grace that seemed at once heavenly and demonic. He wanted to run, to feel the cool lake breeze against his face, to dry the sweat that ran constantly into his eyes. He gasped for air, inhaling deep and hard, hoping to fill an emptiness in his lungs.

"Damned greenhorns! Get back to your wagons! Don't drink that damn water! You all crazy?"

Both men looked up quickly.

A cavalry lieutenant, sword bouncing at his side, came riding along the wagons, his horse jumping and prancing as the man yelled at his troops.

"Looked good to me," Henry whispered. He rose from all fours, replaced his cap on his head and started back through the underbursh. "See what I mean, Ike? They don't tell ya nothin'!"

It was nearly noon the next day when they reached the camp northeast of Vicksburg. All night long Isaac had heard the rumble of distant thunder but had felt no rain nor seen any lightning. Not until morning had he realized what he was hearing, for the closer they had moved toward the front, the louder the thunder had roared.

The roads soon filled with men and wagons, veteran troops, some bandaged or on crutches.

"I reckon we're nearin' the front, Ike," Henry said. "We gonna get us a piece of the action now. You can bet on it!"

Isaac sat quietly on the wagon, the rumble deepening.

"Must be big guns, I'd say—an' doin' a lot of shootin'!"

The mules held the wagon to a steady pace, bringing them through backwoods country turned suddenly into a city of movement. Battle-worn soldiers stood beside the road, allowing the fresh troops in the column to move forward to the front. They waved and smiled at Henry's greetings.

"Gonna see what's goin' on, Ike," he spoke excitedly to his companion. "Hey, soldier! Is that our boys a firin'?"

A mustached man with his arm in a sling looked up at the approaching rig. "Sure am," he replied; "jus' blowin' 'em to bits!" A long smile spread across his face. Isaac could have reached out and touched the man. "Men jus' goin' up?"

"Ja, on our way."

"Well, da Lord be wich ya up der. I'm goin' back to Michigan, back home. Caught me some shrapnel here—" he pointed to his shoulder. "Our own guns, too."

"Our guns?" Henry was amazed.

"Yep. That there's a crazy place!" The soldier motioned toward the east with a nod of his head.

"Hear that, Ike?" Henry asked, poking Isaac with his elbow as the wagon passed the stranger. "We gonna get us some Rebs now, you best believe!" His eyes flashed as he grabbed the plug from his pocket.

The mules kept pulling, up and down the knobby river bluffs that girded the Mississippi. The sound of creaking wooden wheels punctuated the barrage of cannons that crept ever closer. Finally the wagon ascended a ridge overlooking a segment of the front.

"Damn! Will you look at that!" Henry spat tobacco juice forward and removed his cap, without taking his eyes from the scene before them.

Neither man spoke. Directly ahead lay a wide and steep bluff, the trees and underbrush scalped away. Dug into the hillside, all along the slope, were hundreds of tiny shacks, like caves. Some were roofed with dirt and mud, others with wood, still others with tree branches or brush. Men swarmed like insects, moving slowly, digging, walking, playing cards, some sleeping beneath the rough canopies. Everywhere spades and sand shovels were stabbed into the dirt, upright, like city gaslamps.

The mules kept pulling, following the wagons before them, plodding south and east until they finally reached a vacant bluff.

"Heeere!" Henry stopped the team. He saw the lieutenant approaching on horseback.

"This is it, boys. We'll be putting our guns up here," he said, pointing at the bluff with a drawn sword. "Now keep yer wits about ya—we're close to the Rebs. Tie up yer rig and leave it. Follow the others up the hill."

Henry did as he was told, and Isaac followed. A stream of drivers and guards abandoned their wagons, and, followed by more troops, moved through the gorge and up the embankment. The roar of guns increased as they ascended the hill and were issued their spades.

Another lieutenant stood high on the bank, breaking the company into groups and redirecting them. "And you six here! We need a hole this size—" He stepped off a good fifteen feet—" and about five deep here. And make it flat on the grade." He didn't wait for questions but pointed out the next six men with his sword and directed them to a parallel position.

The sun was hot and the digging difficult. The bluff was already stripped of trees and foliage, but thick roots were still implanted in the coarse soil. The air was thick and humid. In minutes, Isaac's shirt was soaked with perspiration from neck to waist, and his hands were scraped raw by the rough spade handle. Mosquitoes and other insects preyed on the diggers, and soon little red bumps dotted their arms and necks.

"How long you bin here, Ike?"

"What you mean?"

"I mean in this country."

Isaac stepped down the spade with both feet. The blade sliced through the hard dirt.

"Since '48," he said proudly. "We was some of the first to live in Wisconsin."

"No kidding? '48?" Henry stopped shoveling and leaned over the handle. "That long, huh?" A faint smile spread across his face.

"Ja, fifteen years by July."

"Why, Ike, you ain't even hardly a foreigner no more." He laughed outright, looking toward the other men in the pit. "I suppose you *tink* that doin' this'll make you an American?"

Isaac scooped out a spadeful of loose dirt. He had thought about such things. "Ja, Henry, I am an American. I fight here—for this country."

Henry laughed again. "Yep, well, maybe y'are, I guess. At least you don't wear them damn wooden shoes n'more!"

The other men laughed loudly at Zimmerman's humor.

Henry stopped digging again, leaned over his shovel once more, and poked at Isaac with his finger. "I tell ya, Dutchman, you're so good at this here diggin' that I think you could do the rest all by yerself. Course ya got yerself lotsa practice at this sorta thing, huh? Diggin' all them dikes and all." The men roared again. Isaac Te Kolste felt a strange fear, like a child in a parlor full of elders.

Zimmerman pushed his spade into the dirt. "I think I'm gonna take a looksee yonder, atop this here hill." He looked toward his friends. "Guys' comin' too?"

"But the lieutenant said to keep our heads down," one of the men replied.

"Ah, hell, he jus' wants us to do the dirty work. Ain't no Rebs around here. You think they'd jus' let us dig our guns in here so easy like?" He pulled his cap over his eyes to change character. "Shonuff, why don't y'all jus' put them big honeys right in this here hill. Hope y'all is comf'table. You Yankees sho' is sweet!" Zimmerman rolled his eyes. "Hell! C'mon, let's go!" He waved them all forward. No one responded.

"You guys scared or something?"

No reply.

Henry Zimmerman kicked at the dirt, jumped out of the half-dug trench, and looked back once more, his will weaker than the strength of a commitment he had already sworn.

Still, no one moved.

"Buncha damn chickens. Never seen the like," he muttered, stepping carefully up the steep embankment.

Soon he was near the ridge. He looked west, shading his eyes with his hat.

"Ain't nothin' up here, fellas, nothin' but another hill aheada us." He climbed even farther until he was at the crest of the bluff.

Isaac kept digging, jabbing and lifting at the root-infested soil, still thinking about wooden shoes, and what Zimmerman could have meant. He had stopped wearing them at least ten years ago, he told himself. The others watched Henry, faces upturned.

Isaac didn't see it happen. He never even heard a shot. Neither did the others, but they all saw Henry Zimmerman drop to his knees and crumple like burning paper. He fell backward, legs over his head, arms out, down the steep cliff. His body rolled over the hard ground, bouncing over stumps, down the bluff toward them until it thudded precisely into the pit they had been digging, and flopped like a feed sack at Isaac's feet. Zimmerman's arms were bent behind his back, under the weight of his body. Blood spurted from his mouth and surged from his matted hair. Isaac grabbed for his throat, feeling for pulse.

"He is dead." He looked up into the men's eyes.

"Should we call for help?" one asked.

"He is dead," Isaac said again.

Other soldiers had seen him fall. They rushed to the scene, curious and fearful. Again, suddenly, the lieutenant appeared.

"What is it?" he yelled, annoyed at the halt in the work.

"It's Zimmerman, sir," a soldier answered. "We think he's dead."

"Dammit!" he shouted. "I told you to be careful, didn't I?" The chestnut mare threw back its head and shook its mane, feet dancing. "Now keep your wooden heads down—and let that be a lesson to ya." He rode off as quickly as he had come, then stopped. "And get back to work. Get him outta there!"

Isaac stared at the horseman. The lieutenant turned sharply, sword in hand, and galloped off down the ridge.

In the inexorable din of cannon fire, time could be gauged only by the sun. Through long damp days and hot nights, the ceaseless thunder made work nerve-racking and sleep impossible. Like badgers, the twenty-seventh dug into the dirt. For days, Isaac's only weapon was his spade. First, the fortification for more artillery. Then, wide trenches for battle lines, so wide that the captain could ride through easily. Finally, holes for their own defense, and a level slab against the bluff so that they could lie flat beneath the protection of makeshift canopies. Mosquitoes swarmed in the camp, and little ant-like flies stung through the dirt and sweat, leaving pus-filled bites as large and red as chicken pox. Men dropped in the scorching heat during the day, and sickness and disease took others with each dawn.

But there was little fighting. Occasionally, the rebel artillery would fire a volley and send the men scampering for their mud huts, but the only real contact anyone had with the enemy was the nightly jokes swapped by pickets. For although the big guns never seemed to tire, the troops would relax under the cover of darkness. The lieutenant himself laughed at some of the nightly insults traded by daylight enemies.

And it was safe at night, safe enough for mud-soldiers to move behind their own lines freely. So Isaac, like many others, walked north and east one night to a bluff overlooking the city of Vicksburg and the wide Mississippi. He had heard that the sight was glorious, like thousands of Roman candles every night.

The bluff was steep and treacherous, but the blaze of artillery illumined the southern landscape with the orangered tint of a blazing campfire. Union troops lined the ridge, sitting, kneeling, or lying on the ground, hands back of their heads, watching the awesome display like children. Fires danced across the face of the city. Federal gunboats, rocked by the hard recoil of their mortars, sent long, dazzling streams high into the air, amid the slams of continual reports. There the missles would hang, as if suspended by the whim of some omnipotent warlock, fuses still sputtering; then they would drop, slowly at first, gathering speed and force as they bore straight toward the heart of the city. Finally, just inches above the skyline, they would burst into balls of fire, sending a thousand lethal barbs in all directions. Isaac watched it all, then turned away into what darkness he could find.

He made his way carefully down the bluff, past little groups of his comrades who laughed, played cards, or sang around the myriad campfires that spotted the hills. Past the tents of the wounded, where bright lanterns projected hunched silhouettes of doctors and nurses against the whited canvas. And music, strange music, from harmonicas and fiddles played through the camps. "Glory, glory hallelujah," from some men huddled beneath a paneled lean-to. And a woman, a nurse, leading that familiar song about "the rockets' red glare." Isaac had heard it before, in Wisconsin, and then in training in Illinois.

He stopped outside the small circle of light spread by a crackling fire. The men were wounded. One man had no hands; another's face was swaddled with wide, white linens. The woman's voice seemed to beg for participation—she sang high and shrill. Some men sang along, others nodded with the beat, some only sat quietly. And always, the deep bass drum of mortar and Parrott gun, out of cadence, belching the sharp smell of burned powder into the valleys where it hung like steel-blue mist.

Lufsana Ernijse hadn't understood when he told her he

would enlist. He had watched the reports closely, and when Jackson crossed the Potomoc, he knew that more men would be needed. The Americans in Holland township all spoke of the war, of slavery, and the glorious Union.

"Ik ben Amerikaan," he had told his oldest sister then.

She looked up momentarily, then returned to the book on the table.

"Begrijp je dat?" he asked.

"No," she answered quietly, without looking up. *"Neem dit toch mee!"* She handed him the Psalter, her way of saying goodbye.

He hadn't seen it for days, but he thought it was in his field bag. He hoped he hadn't lost it.

He crossed two more steep bluffs before he moved south again, then east, more cautiously, back to his regiment. The men were sitting around their fires. A few slept. Others played cards—"euchre," they called it, or "schops-kopf," another favorite. Lufsana would say it was all the *Duivels Prentenboek.* His mother would only cry.

Isaac sat quietly outside the circle of players, watching the game closely.

"Whose Jack?"

"Mine."

"Who led?"

"Schneider."

The cannons seemed like muffled drums from this distance. Isaac saw that the players were unaffected by the noise.

"More digging tomorrow?"

"What else?"

"I'm getting damned sick of it."

"Who isn't?"

"Good lead."

"Didn't join the army to be a gopher!"

"Make it?"

"Sure. Pay up."

Coins dropped and rolled over the stump table.

"All them negras around here too."

"What do you mean?"

"Whose deal?"

"Mine."

"Go back sometime. Hell, there's at least a thousand of 'em just doin' nothin', no two miles back." The soldier took off his cap and pointed toward the northeast. "And I'm doin' the damn diggin'!"

"Finally got myself a hand."

Isaac watched closely, looking at each darkened face. The fire threw long pointed shadows behind them into the darkness. He thought of Ma and Pa in the old country, Saturday night, preparing for the Sabbath.

His knees cracked when he got to his feet.

"Te Kolste?"

"Ja?"

"Can't sleep, Isaac?"

"Ah, Schneider, you dumb fool—"

The men broke out in raucous laughter at Schneider's poor play, their roaring nearly muffling the cannons.

Isaac walked up the incline to his own shelter. The thatched roof kept moonlight from spilling in. In the darkness he reached for his field bag, then felt for his sister's book. It was there. He felt it, small and thick. He pulled it from the bag and held it up in the dim light of the cave. He could barely make out the Dutch words. Then he lay back quietly on the blanket and felt the cool mud beneath him. He laid the book on his chest and looked up at the ceiling. Behind him, the barrage continued, the noise thudding into the thick mud walls.

Isaac Te Kolste opened his eyes slowly to the light of an almost quiet Sunday morning. The drone of artillery had dwindled into sporadic outbursts that rang through the valleys—like bells almost, he thought, like any Sunday morning. He turned and leaned on his elbow. The Psalter had slid off his chest into the mud formed by a light rain during the night. He grabbed the book quickly, wiping the sticky dirt off on his shirt. Mud stuck fast to its pages. He put it back into his bag.

He wasn't the first to awaken. He stepped out of the shelter and looked down and across the ridge. Campfires were lit all around and the troops were already eating their breakfasts. The men from his company were seated where he had left them the night before. He rubbed his eyes and walked down the bluff.

"Te Kolste, some breakfast?"

"Ja."

He reached for the hardtack, pulled some pork from the fire, and let the grease drip slowly over the bread, as he had seen the others do so often. The hard biscuit turned soft and edible in his hand. It tasted heavy, the oil clinging to his lips and face.

"Isaac, how about a game?"

He turned, surprised. He had never been invited to play before.

"But, I don't know—"

"Schopskopf?"

"I don't know . . ."

"Well, watcha play in Holland?"

Isaac took a big bite of the greasy hardtack and shook his head.

"Seven-up?" someone offered.

He hunched his shoulders, chewed quickly, and swallowed hard.

"I don't play with the cards. We don't—"

"Well, dammit, it's time you learn. C'mon!"

Isaac looked quickly at the others. They all watched him closely, smiling. *"Duivel,"* he heard his sister say again. He saw her look back down at the Psalter. His father was at church today, this morning, Sunday. All the Americans watched him now.

He nodded his head violently. "Ja, ja, but I know nothing."

"We all know that!" The men laughed in unison.

Isaac tried to laugh with them. The cards began spinning

his way from the dealer.

"Where is your money?"

"Money?" he answered.

"Hell, we can't play without money."

Isaac stood quickly. "Up there," he pointed. "I will bring it."

"Ja, ja, ja," the men giggled as he ran.

His heart thumped like the cannon as he ran up the bluff. He had never played with the Americans before. He grabbed the field bag quickly and emptied the contents on his blanket. He hadn't spent any money for weeks. Where was it? He brushed things out of the way indiscriminantly. The Psalter! Ja, of course. He flipped through the pages until he found the bills, grabbed them, tossed the book aside, and left the shelter he had dug for himself.

"I haf it!" he yelled.

The men roared their approval as Isaac ran down the hill to the fire.

"Sit here, Te Kolste."

"Deal 'em over, Schneider."

He sat, bending his long legs beneath him.

"We do no digging today?"

"Nope."

One soldier shuffled the deck. The cards whirred under his thumbs as if by magic.

"Captain was by before. Told us to take 'er easy. You know what that means!"

The men all nodded.

"Vat does it mean?"

"Means we gonna be movin' up later."

Isaac watched the cards slide slowly into place in front of him. He looked around at the other men and pulled himself closer into the circle.

"So, Ike, never played the game, eh?"

"No, never played with cards. Never." Isaac chuckled, laughing at himself.

By dinner the men were ready to quit. Isaac had lost

almost all his money after an hour, but slowly he was learning the game—"Sheepshead" they called it in English—and
soon he had won back nearly as much as he had lost. The
other men began treating him differently.

"Ah, Te Kolste, you pick 'em again?"

"I haf good cards."

"No kiddin'."

He enjoyed the game. It required quick thinking and stiff
concentration; he became so entranced with the strategy
that he lost consciousness of the barrage in the
background.

After dinner he returned to his lean-to, holding the
money carefully in his hand. He counted it slowly—almost
as much as he had taken from the book. He retrieved the
Psalter and put the bills between the pages, smiling, and
laid it carefully on his blanket. Suddenly he heard the cannons again and looked up as if they had just begun. Then
he looked back at the Psalter. He had forgotten, like them,
like all of them; he was like them.

There was Lufsana again, sitting before him, refusing to
look into his face. Church was over now. The wagon
pulled them slowly back along the road. They were nearly
home. He grabbed the book furiously, and threw it back in
the bag, pulling the cords tight. It thudded into the mud of
a dark corner.

He stepped out of his hut, the sun burning down on his
head, the artillery throbbing in his ears. He walked east,
blindly, past the men of his regiment, over the bluff and
through the company behind them. And he kept walking,
past troops that sat laughing around noon fires, past an old
house once occupied by real people, past bearded
lieutenants and portly generals on white horses, past the
wounded and the dead, until he stopped, raised both hands
to his head, and looked around, finally cleared from the
vile world of the sword. Somewhere it was the Sabbath, he
told himself; somewhere the cannons were bells.

So he began to run, eastward, moving farther and farther into the deep lowlands close to the river. But still he

heard the cannons, far off now, yet belching strong and deep, an earthshaking rumble that shook the trees and hills and rolled through him as if he were a cave. He stopped, breathless, and closed his eyes, remembering the scene from the bluff at night. He saw them again, closer, as if they were right here, and the men who fired them, charging the mortars, ramming down the loads.

He waved both arms violently, and screamed at them to stop, but they wouldn't listen. Then he saw the flash, here, miles away. And the missle flew slowly, so slowly through the sky. He could see it. It was something horrid, alive, strange, yet familiar. Something of himself. Of his sister. His family. Up, up it went, screaming like any missle, but louder, more horrid, far, far beyond human reach. He crouched near the earth, watching it rise in the air, sweat rolling from his cheeks. Then he saw it drop. Faster. Faster. Until it blew into a huge consuming flame, like any rocket. The explosion shook him. Destroyed, he dug his fingers into the earth. His face dropped into the dust of the road, and he lay still, whimpering like a child.

Minutes passed before he looked up, afraid, his eyes searching. There it was. A church. Another change. Small and white. Two short steeples. He rose to his knees cautiously, eyes jumping from bush to tree, forehead down, then ran toward the opened door. A thousand coal-black faces praying. One man knelt at the front, his head down on a chair, praying in song. The others were singing, slowly, plaintively, in long, groaning notes like the wails of the mourning. On and on they sang, different songs, but all the same, like a moaning wind through the pines. Droning, crying, higher and lower, but all the same, shrieking suddenly, spasmodically, as if death itself had come. He sat, fearful. His fingers trembled as he tried to rub the dirt from his hands. On and on the chanting. No joy—only the dirge of sorrow and pain. No triumph, no deliverance. As if each member took a turn at dying.

The pew groaned as he leaped to his feet. "Isn't all of dis for you?" he shouted.

Then they were quiet. Every white eye turned to him. No one moved.

"I tink dis is for you," he said, whispering, his eyes clouded by tears. His hands stretched toward the altar, then pulled at his own shirt, and gestured back in the direction he had come.

He ran down the road in the sunset. West, toward the front, back through the lines, past men digging new trenches, new homes, looking frantically for his own shelter.

His men saw him approach.

"Te Kolste," they yelled. "How 'bout a game?"

He didn't answer. He seemed not even to hear them, but ran instead to his cave, entered, and came out as quickly, holding a small, thick book.

They watched him climb the bluff, never looking back, disregarding their presence.

"Isaac!" they yelled, remembering Zimmerman.

But it was dark now. And Isaac Te Kolste soon faded into the darkness as he climbed steadily up toward the ridge.

The fire snapped, but it was barely audible above the cannons that rang through the hills surrounding Vicksburg.

"Whose deal?"

Sign of a Promise

The longer he prayed, the deeper his knees sank in the moat of muddy topsoil that circled the sod house. Undeflected by the usual prairie winds, the rain dropped from the gray sky like shot from a small-bore rifle, punching little craters in the mud of the path, craters that vanished when others exploded in the soggy earth. He had removed his wide-brimmed hat and was holding it tightly to his chest with his right hand as he bowed his head. Rain pounded into streaky hair that lay like flax on his head, then streamed down through weathered crevices in his temples and forehead, dripping, finally, from the tip of his nose and chin to his heavy overcoat, already saturated from three full days of rain.

He looked upward and turned to the west again to reassure himself of what he had seen. A layer of clear blue sky belted the horizon, tinted by the fire of the late afternoon sun, now dropping slowly from the cloud banks that still dominated the sky. Rain pelted his face, but he stared defiantly upward, the water running from the ends of his mustache, through the recesses of his cheeks, and into his gray sideburns.

To the east was the rainbow. It grew from two remote spots in the grassland, rising symmetrically toward a peak that was yet to appear. Its thick backdrop of rain clouds, suddenly curtained in purple by the sun, focused the colors, and made them burn almost mystically in the turbulent sky.

It wasn't the first time he had recalled Noah. Over a year ago he had left Wisconsin, taking his family in a "schooner," as the Americans had called it, bound for Minnesota. Several months later he and a few others had left Fillmore County for Northwest Iowa. Some of his friends seemed reluctant to give him their blessing. They watched silently as he loaded his wagon again, and they also saw his tired wife climb slowly up to take her place. There was some fear in the way they sang the Psalms then, but Antonie Vander Meer remembered the story of Noah and his neighbors—they had even mocked him, but Noah's faith was strong, the ark, the rain, even more of a test. Noah never questioned what the Lord had commanded him.

And then, the rainbow and the covenant. This was but three days, he told himself, three short days of rain. Noah had seen the heavens opened, the bowels of the earth erupt its inner waters, the entire world destroyed. Yet he had not questioned, he had not doubted. Antonie spat out the salty water that curled from his mustache into the corners of his mouth, rebuking himself for his little faith. "And one like me," he told himself, his head bowed.

A sudden downpour ladled more water over the land, as the storm poured out the last of its offering. He raised his left hand to his forehead, brushed back the wet shock of hair that fell into his face, then replaced the hat on his head. He held his hands up to his face, his callouses softened, it seemed, from too much rain, too little work. But they were clean except for the threads of black at the tip of each fingernail. And he was clean. Weeks of sweat and dirt had been washed away by the rain, transforming his spirit and body into readiness, into actual anticipation of what still remained to be done on the homestead. As the end of the day approached and the almost-forgotten sun spread its warming rays out across the sea of prairie grass, lighting the eastern sky with God's own promise, now Antonie Vander Meer was ready for tomorrow.

He rose and walked carefully toward the sod pile that marked the corner of his land. As he left the immediate area of the sod house, however, the heavy grasses made the path more firm under foot. To the left of the path lay a broad stretch of virgin soil, stripped of its mantle of flowers and grasses, already ravaged by the plow, and now left vulnerable to every whim of the Iowa weather—naked, rich and fertile. He saw there what he had feared to see—the scars of the late spring storm, jagged cracks running like bolts of lightning down the slope, but emptied now of the rain water that they had carried during the storm. His wife had walked every foot of that land, smoothing over the soil where the corn had been planted. Now the seeds were gone, he knew, washed from the earth as the chalky gray sweat lines had been washed from his temples, and carried by transient streams to some low spot on the land.

He didn't stop walking. He knew what he would find, but he needed to see it anyway. Telling Tryntje would be difficult enough; he knew he must be sure. When he arrived at the southern end of his field, when he saw the yellow seeds lying in clumps, he stopped, searching for the words to explain it to her. He prayed for wisdom and strength. He leaned over then, gathering the seeds into a pile with his clean hands. When he was through, he wiped the now-blackened palms against his trousers. He would return for the seed tomorrow. He stood and looked for a moment over the open prairie to the west and south before turning back to the sod house. When he reached the path to the house, the rainbow had grown to a completed arch.

Tryntje, too, had seen the belt of clear sky on the horizon, but unlike her husband, she didn't focus on its promise. She concentrated once again on the broad apron of wasteland that led to the sky, wide and barren, nearly unbroken by any sign of life. Occasionally a cottonwood, white and lifeless, rose awkwardly from the prairie bed, interrupting the endless monotony of the landscape. One such monument stood at the southwest corner of their own land; it projected against a background of rain clouds now, its uppermost branches barely distinguishable in the growing darkness. Tryntje saw the old cottonwood as a pioneer, too, for in its rash impulse to pull itself up from the dour grassland, it had weathered jagged scars and gashes that ran like stripes up and down its stubborn trunk. Finally, long ago, when no white man was yet foolish enough to settle here, one slashing blow had cured its temerity forever. Now only a shell remained, a corpse that somehow refused burial, a frame that seemed to mock the vanity of its own aborted dreams.

And the sky, spewing incessant rain, seemed to combine with the desert of grass to destroy whoever, whatever tried to exist here. The endless miles of prairie seemed to her a Godless expanse, and all the prayers she had learned as a child, no matter how loudly she could cry them to the heavens, could not bring her any closer to the God she had known in the old country. This land was so wide, so vast, so everlasting, that she felt her best prayers rise in futility, like the fingers of the cottonwood, to a God who had never minded this region of creation.

But she never spoke these things to her husband. Through all those days of dirt and mud she saw her children blackened by the Iowa soil, roughened by wind and sun, pushed prematurely into the experience of Adam's curse. Through the long hours she spent picking vermin from young bodies, she had said nothing to him—for he was her husband. And she knew his visions, his dreams.

She turned from the window and looked back to the family portrait that hung on the mud wall. It had been taken in Wisconsin. She had wanted it immediately after their arrival in America to send to her parents in Holland, for she knew their concern and felt that they would be reassured by the clean faces and the Sunday clothes of the children. They knew very little of America. Some of the stories they had heard were like those of the land of Caanan—a land most bountiful, full of opportunity. But others were fearful, accounts of drought, storms, savages, violence, strange and horrid stories of people who didn't know the Lord. The family picture had helped, she knew, for it showed them tidy and happy, wearing the smiles that reflected the hopes and jubilation of a life filled with new opportunities. She knew they would like it, for she liked it. This was the way she imagined things. There were four pretty little ones on the tintype; now there were only three. Toon had buried one in Minnesota. But soon there would be another, unless her signs were false. She ripped the very thought from her mind—this was no place, no time for a child.

The bolt rattled and the uneven door swung open slowly.

"Tryntje?" It was her husband. He was wet and cold, but his face widened into a comforting smile.

"Tryntje, did you see it? The sky—it is clearing! The rain will stop."

He set his hat on a nail that stuck from the wooden door frame, dropped his coat over another, and drew a wooden box away from the shipping crate they used as a table. He sat down and folded his hands before him, rocking comfortably back and forth, adjusting himself to the chair, still wearing the smile.

"That is good, Toon. The rain will stop now. Tomorrow a bright morning . . ."

"Ja, Tryntje, tomorrow we will begin again."

She smiled at him momentarily, then poured him a cup of coffee.

"We have not much coffee left, Toon. You must appreciate this."

"We run out already?"

"Ja, not long."

"Ach, do we drink so much?"

"We have much rain this week, and last—few days in the field. When you work so little, you spend more time here, ja?" Her attempted levity drew an understanding smile from her husband.

"We start again tomorrow, though." He looked at her and continued. "Tomorrow will be the first of many days of sun. Soon it will be summer."

She sat across the table, her cup next to his, and smiled.

"Tryntje," he reached for her hand, "we must start over tomorrow."

She didn't seem to understand. "Ja, tomorrow we start again—in the sun."

"Tomorrow we start over, *lieveling.*"

His smile faded as his eyes focused sharply on her. They seemed to reach for her, to try to hold her, to brace her from a fall.

"Wat zeg je nou?"

"The rain, Tryntje, it washed out the seed. The water ran through the ground, carrying the seed along to the bottom of the land." His arm snaked through the air, mimicking the movement. "We must plant again."

Her set smile faded in a moment with the collapse of her facade. She felt the mud between her fingers and saw the thick black dirt in her fingernails. And he felt it too. Fifteen years of marriage had brought them so close that no pretense was opaque enough to hide reality. She rose quickly from the table; he saw her trying to restrain her emotion.

"I think that it will be good," she said, taking the cups from the table, "but I do not want to tell the children."

He saw the sign of weariness in her eyes. She refused to receive his glance, not out of anger, but because she knew her eyes would speak too much. Instead, she made herself busy about the stove, preparing corn bread for tomorrow's meals.

"I know this is not good news, Tryntje, I am not happy myself, for I would do the work of oxen to keep you and the children from the land."

"Ach, Antonie, we can help again. It is part of our responsibility. The children are getting older. We all have strong backs—thick legs, we can do what we must . . . ."

"You are a good woman, *Moeder,*" he broke in, softly. His eyes followed the soft lines of her body as she worked, from her light shoulders through her waist. She was thinner since they had come to Iowa. He had seen her widen at the hips, bearing four children. But her legs were thin and weak. She was not made for this, he knew. Many had wanted her in Vroomshoop; he was blessed to have her for his wife. How it hurt him to see her plodding through the dirt, her back bent to the earth like a slave before its master, following their boy, Hendrick, as he dropped the seed into the furrows. Her hands were rough and blistered from the hoe, even today.

"Tryntje," he said.

"Ja." She still didn't face him.

"Someday I will give you what you deserve. The Lord will bless us. I know He will. He is faithful to those who love Him."

She grabbed another tightly-wound bundle of prairie grass and threw it into the stove, closing her eyes to everything. She had to tell about her signs, but she could not tell him now.

The sun, hidden throughout the day, dropped below the horizon, and the moon, like a replacement, poured its silver light over the wet grasses. Three Vander Meer children came in from their work, laughing. They, too, had seen the sun and the sky. They, too, knew the morning would be full of promise.

The sun gleamed like a hero the next morning. Bright and warm, it conjured little whiffs of steam from the broken ground of the Vander Meer homestead, and lofted them up into the atmosphere where they quickly disappeared. By noon the sun glared down on the prairie, drying the skin of the topsoil quickly, and turning the big chunks of upturned sod from shiny black to a coarse gray.

Antonie Vander Meer started working at noon. He harnessed his team to the plow, set the steel into the untouched earth, and spoke calmly to the horses. They responded grudgingly, but jerked forward, pulling the share through the grasses that had been chopped short earlier in the month. The ground ripped like cloth, and a black roll of sod slid cleanly up the share, then curled back and flopped to the stubbled grass, leaving the shiny-smooth loam exposed to the heavens.

Vander Meer loved this moment, for while he felt a certain reluctance to violate the land, to change it so drastically, he knew his task was significant. This rich earth, loose and clean, even smelled of life. It was to be his heritage, the beginning of a new life, a new land, for his family, for his people. To him this was not work, it was his call, for as his team jerked the share deeply through the earth, he saw here a farm and a neat white-frame house in the middle, circled by a grove of trees, cottonwoods and elms. This land, with the grace of the Lord, would bring him and others like him, good Hollanders, into that dream; it would bring his wife comfort, his children education, opportunity, happiness. And when the rows of corn would sweep like tight ropes across the broken ground, when regiments of golden tassles would float in the wind, this land itself would glorify his Lord.

All day Antonie Vander Meer worked in the field, alone. It was too wet to replant the corn, so Peter and Hendrick pulled the roots from the cut soil and gathered them into piles, while Maria, his daughter, wound some into tight bundles to replenish the supply for the stove. Tryntje stayed in the house, working constantly to clean up the mud from the storm, wash clothing, and prepare meals.

"Tomorrow," Antonie said after supper, "tomorrow we must seed again." The ground would be drier then, dry enough to use the harrow. The children sat silent. Only a week ago they had finally thought themselves finished; now they had to start again.

"How long will it be?" Peter asked.

"Three, maybe four days," his father answered. "I have broken more ground today, but what we have already done will not be hard to do again."

"Early then, Pa?"

"Ja, early."

Tryntje was up before the sun, getting things in order for

the long days ahead. Not even Maria was excused from the work; she would help her father, standing on the harrow at times to make it dig more deeply into the soil. Or, like yesterday, she could pull the grass roots out of the sod and gather them in piles. She would be kept busy, like the rest.

Tryntje turned down the lantern when the sun broke through the crude window cut into the "prairie logs" on the east wall. She sliced the pork into rations, planning the day's meals. Still she had seen no sign. She had given birth to four children, so she knew about these things, and as each day passed, she was more sure. She must tell her husband. The three children still slept soundly against the south wall of the cabin. Her husband had been up even before her that morning.

She leaned over the makeshift table, lifting the table cloth to select the eating utensils from inside of the box. Then she knew it. Her stomach seemed to jump and turn, but she swallowed hard as she stood again, erect. She held her sickness in. She put water on the stove for her husband, never stopping the preparations for the day.

Not long after breakfast the work began. It went slower than Vander Meer had hoped, for the moisture had not left the soil, and when the spikes of the harrow dug into the earth, thick clods formed quickly against the teeth, forcing Toon to stop and clean off the mud. Roots still lodged in the soil were as much of a problem; they jammed against the spikes, forcing the entire harrow to skid on the surface, doing no good at all. Hendrick helped his father then by scraping and cleaning the harrow, after his father, back and leg muscles straining, had lifted the implement and set it on end. When Antonie saw Hendrick's boots caked with mud, he realized that every member of his family carried this additional burden through the fields. He scarcely noticed his own feet.

The harrow smoothed over the rain-furrowed land. Because he was forced to work slowly, the entire planting operation was bogged down. Peter followed the harrow, digging little cones in the soil with a hoe. Then came Hendrick, swathed by a thick belt of seed corn rolled into his mother's old apron, dropping only three or four kernels into each of the openings. Finally, their mother, armed also with a hoe, tramped through the dirt, covering what had just been deposited in the soil. Maria flitted about, chirping like a red-winged blackbird, helping here and there, and constantly reminding her father of the strange stream of light smoke that rose daily in the southwest. Vander Meer told her he would investigate, and her curiosity diminished.

And so they worked, breaking off only at noon, as much to rest as to eat. As the day wore on, the sun dried the deeper earth, allowing the harrow to pulverize the flattened soil more efficiently. The brigade of Vander Meer husbandmen moved at a quicker pace.

Antonie never stopped, even for dinner. Tryntje gave him some pieces of corn bread and pork, but he continued to trudge behind the team of young horses, pulling out in front of the rest of the family. By supper his calf muscles were hard as melons, and his knees were weak, for the harrow moved easily over the dirt in the afternoon, forcing him to dig his heels into the soft earth to brake the pace of the team.

Tryntje could move no more by suppertime. She and Hendrick gave up their work for the day, while Antonie and Peter harnessed the team to the plow again and broke more prairie. By the time the sun set, a wide new swath of loam lay turned out of its centuries-old bed.

But Tryntje went to bed early. Her back was cramped by strain; it burned from her buttocks to her shoulders. Her hands were raw from the hoe handle. Even a week of callouses couldn't prevent the slivery wood from working through to the soft flesh underneath. The sun had turned her neck an angry red again. She had sipped her coffee slowly that night, wondering where she could draw strength from for the continuing assault.

She prayed, in spite of her hopelessness. She asked for a

blessing, expecting nothing, feeling that no one was there to listen, much less to give. The dead cottonwood, standing alone in the bleak expanse of grassland, seemed more real, more omnipotent than the God she once thought she knew. Surely He had forgotten them here.

And yet the work continued, for dawn signaled another day, then another, and another. The harder the family worked, she thought, the more fanatically her husband plowed, opening up more and more land to be planted. Each day she worried about her failing strength, and each day she saw her own children, subdued by their own exhaustion, sitting around the shipping crate like old people, their faces scraped and scoured by the fiery sun and the searing prairie winds. They should have been in school, she told herself. In Holland they would be clean and nicely dressed. At night they would learn their lessons: spelling, writing, music, history, poetry. They would read Huygens and Da Costa, and sleep well in soft beds built from wood, not sod and straw. She hated this land.

And each night her husband would return, tired and sore himself, wearing a hesitant smile that begged her to share his enthusiasm, while it offered his understanding and sympathy. They would lie together at night, close to their children, his heavy hand resting on her side as she faced away from him, too exhausted to sleep. They would lie in that position for hours, silent but awake, separated by a wall of fatigue and emotion, listening to the crackle of straw beneath the rustling bodies of their overtired children. In those agonizing hours, Tryntje would remember the thump of the hammer and the rip of the saw as the coffin-maker prepared the little box for her tiny daughter. They had lost her in Minnesota; the cause was still a mystery. And now, when she knew a new life was beginning to form within her, she wanted to cry out in anguish because this one would know only a vast, dismal ocean of grass.

"Tryntje," her husband said late one night. "Are you awake?"

"Ja, Toon."

"We have but a little left now. One, maybe two days."

"That is good," she said, remaining very still.

"We have done well."

"Ja, we have."

"We have more land planted than I thought." He wanted to act as hopeful as possible.

But there was no reply.

"If the Lord gives us a good year . . ."

"Toon— . . ." she interrupted.

"Ja?"

She said nothing. Maria turned in her sleep, breaking the deep silence. Then it was quiet again.

"Toon, I will have a child."

"Oh, *lieveling* . . ."

"Please, say nothing."

"But, Tryntje . . ."

"Please," she stopped him again.

Again, silence.

"Tryntje, the Lord . . ."

"Antonie, I know what you must say . . . Please?"

He said no more.

Late Friday afternoon Antonie Vander Meer worked alone, planting the seeds and covering them himself. He had little left to do, so he sent his family back to the sod house to finish the day away from field work. For the first time since they had started on Tuesday, he saw their faces brighten when they sensed the end coming. He sent Tryntje home first with Maria, then Hendrick and Peter. By tonight he would be done, but tomorrow he should work a garden for Tryntje, or mend the leaks in the thatched roof. The week had been good for him. The Lord had blessed him and his family with five clear, bright days of growing weather, enough warmth, certainly, to send young green shoots budding from the seeds. He removed his hat, dropped it over the handle of the hoe, then placed both hands over it, and gave thanks for God's goodness. He asked mercy for Tryntje, too, and strength for their children, all of them.

Then he looked up to the east and south, tracing the lines of his land by erecting the fences in his mind. Peter would help him, of course. Once the crop was growing well, they could start to fence in the farm—Peter would like that work. He followed the limits west, stopping at the big cottonwood, then moved back north toward the sod house. As his eyes swept over his little kingdom, he saw them—huge, billowing monsters rolling from the west, ready at any moment to swallow the sun behind a blanket of bluish-gray. The rain was coming again.

And somehow he had sensed it all day. He had seen the whiskery morning clouds evolve into harmless puffs in the early afternoon. He remembered the relief he felt when the sun was eclipsed. But he had not dared to acknowledge what would happen.

There was little doubt now. Cold air seemed to ride the back of the clouds, for when the sun finally disappeared behind the ominous bank, Vander Meer's sweat turned icy in the northern wind. All around, the prairie grass, blown in masses by the stiff, cold breezes, moved up and back, spasmodically, like the fur of a cat. It was obvious to him that he could not finish. He threw the hoe over his shoulder, and started walking back to the house, watching jagged branches of lightning play in the darkening sky, still far away.

By the time he arrived at the house, Tryntje had already lit the lamps. The three children were inside; Hendrick and Maria read quietly from two of the few books the family owned. Peter stared out of the window to the south, while Tryntje worked quietly over the stove. No one spoke.

"We have worked hard," he said, hanging up his hat. "The Lord will bless us."

Peter turned quickly; his youthful face was agitated by what he saw approaching. He sat down at the table, next to his father.

"The work is finished. Next week we can start to fence,

Peter, if we can get the supplies. The work will not be easy, but it will be good work. Soon our land will be marked to every corner." Antonie tried to distract his son, but the deep rumble of distant thunder was too easily heard and felt in the background.

Tryntje kept working. She didn't respond to her husband. The darkness swept into the house as the storm clouds approached the homestead. She turned up the lamps, and served coffee to Peter and Antonie.

"Sunday we will walk, Tryntje, all of us, to where Maria saw the smoke in the south. We must have neighbors there, eh, Peter?"

"I thought no one lived to the south, Pa?"

"Ja, so did I. But we will meet them on Sunday."

"Do you think they are Hollanders?"

"It seems too far from Orange City. Boschma said no one lived here when we took the land. We will see once on Sunday."

Peter looked up suddenly and ran to the window. Tryntje and Antonie heard it too, like a thousand little animals running together over the earth.

"The Lord will bless us," Antonie said again, quietly, to no one but himself.

Then the rains came.

Unlike the week before, the new storm was scattered and sporadic. The rain came in spurts, but water soaked through the bundles of prairie grass that lay like a mat on the roof. It slowly seeped through the ceiling, dripping finally onto the floor, turning Tryntje's home once more into a muddy den.

By Saturday night Hendrick and Maria had paged through every book, and all the coffee was gone. Other than the clatter of a frequent cloudburst, there was little noise within the thick mud walls. Peter and Antonie had gone out periodically to feed the animals in the lean-to behind the house, while Tryntje found plenty of work inside, mending and sewing.

All of this seemed another curse to Tryntje, but she uttered no words of complaint. The new life within her was the source of much anxiety, but it pushed her forward as well. When the soggy blankets and thick humidity provoked a chill, she would wrap a hot brick from the stove and put it next to her feet, or even put on more clothes—not for herself, for the baby. She watched herself closely, and in the process, the despair prompted by her environment settled into the recesses of her mind—still present, but for the moment subordinate to her instinct as a mother. This new attitude caused no change in her behavior, however, for her new concern dominated her activity with equal intensity; whatever strength was not expended on her children was absorbed by the infant suddenly visible before her.

Even Antonie saw nothing of the change. Her solemnity, her quietness, he felt to be the product of her covert distaste for the new land. And as the beating rain continued to blanket the land, he felt his faith begin to ebb in the stream of tribulations he suffered as father, husband, and believer.

"I can take no more," he silently told the Lord.

But the rain fell persistently for the next several hours. Antonie and Tryntje lay motionless on the bedding, hearing every drop while feeling the damp spring air invade and inhabit the sod house. Antonie stared into the darkness and groped for ways to accept the curse.

Then he rose silently, slipped across the muddied floor, grabbed his coat and hat from the nail at the door, and left the house. He ran over the slick earth as fast as he dared until he reached the field—the first field he had plowed, the one that sloped so slightly toward the bog. He cursed himself for his stupidity. He knew he should not have chosen this land first. It had already shed his first planting; now more rain threatened a repetition that could destroy the verdant farm he had envisioned and threaten his own belief in an omniscient God.

The rain continued; it smacked into his hat and ran

down around the brim where it dropped steadily, forming a kind of fringe. The land was already scarred by tiny rivulets beginning to connect with each other. Streams of water ate into the earth, carrying topsoil down toward the slough. In the face of the infinite black sky he felt powerless. He was driven back to his knees.

He realized but one frail hope. He threw off his coat, despite the cold, and rolled up his shirt sleeves as he stepped into the muck. He could barely distinguish the little mounds where seeds had been planted, but he tried to adjust his position to leave the seed undisturbed. He leaned over, buried his hand in the cold earth, and felt the wet mud strangle his fingers. He pulled his hand into a cup like a swimmer, dug out a scoop of mushy soil, and laid it to the left of the hole, taking a step forward. On and on he worked, back bent to the black topsoil. Soon a thin furrow crossed the slope, collecting the runoff as it moved slowly downward. For hours he reached and dug, until the field was ribboned by jagged lines. His fingers were caked with mud, and the heel of his palm and his wrists were gloved by thick dirt.

He stood, erect and strong, and surveyed his work. The rain continued to fall, but it ran harmlessly into the troughs he had cut.

Tryntje was awake when he returned, but Antonie laid his drenched body beside her, silently, his eyes open to the darkness, listening, like her, to the rain, waiting, praying, for it to end. All that mattered now was how long this would continue.

The grass roof, saturated again by more than a day of rain, continued to drip long after the storm had passed. Not until Antonie rose from the straw bed once more and stepped outside was he sure. It was over.

Even Tryntje sensed the relief and joy in the rhythmical throbbing of the Psalms that Sunday morning. The sun had appeared again, and when Antonie returned from an early walk, his face broadened by an authentic smile, she felt a twinge of the enthusiasm that her husband seemed almost always to possess. He told them of the fields—very little had washed away. So with another breakfast over, the sun drying the land again, and no threat of reseeding, the family found a relaxed and happy intimacy in their Sabbath worship. Antonie led even more songs than usual, prayed even longer, and read more lustily from the good stories of the Old Testament. Only the absence of a larger fellowship bounded his joy.

"We will start another sod house this summer," he told Peter after their worship had concluded.

"Another?"

"Ja, we must build a house of worship." He saw his family, clean and refreshed, in a good church building, singing the Psalms, listening to the dominie, worshiping with the greater family of God. And all around him would be other Dutch people who would follow the Vander Meers to this place, Christian people, who, like him, would thank their God for His blessings. Tryntje heard his words to Peter. She looked up at the family portrait, longing to share her husband's dream. And she smiled then, and poured her husband some of her home-brewed "prairie tea," made from some grasses she had collected.

After dinner the entire family stood beside the house, staring south, looking for the faint thread of smoke that Maria had pointed out to them on other days. But today there was no sign. Before them lay the slough grass, waving in a mellow southern breeze. It rolled like ocean swells, far, far into the south; but they saw no sign of other men.

"Maybe we stay home, Tryntje. I see nothing today," he told his wife. He himself had lost his directions in the tall grass several times; he was reluctant to take such chances with his whole family.

"No, Pa, I will show you."

He smiled at his pretty daughter. She was clean and neat. Of course, his wife had seen to that. No matter how muddy things became, no matter how wet, Tryntje always kept Maria clean and dry. She had already lost one daughter.

"Let's go, Pa. Let's go out past the sod-pile by the old cottonwood. We never been out there!" Peter was not to be denied.

"We will stay together. We promise, Pa!" Hendrick said his part. He looked into his mother's eyes and scampered toward the south, beckoning them all to follow. Antonie looked into his wife's eyes to get her permission. Her stiff, dry hair blew softly in the breeze.

"Can you, *Vrouw*?"

"Ja." She smiled.

"Very well. We go."

Once they were past the limits of their own claim, they felt like real adventurers, even though there was clearly nothing in the area besides the prairie grass. But at times the ground bottomed into soft sloughs and soggy marshes, and in order to find alternative routes, Antonie would make them all hold hands as they passed through grass that grew even higher than his head. Then they would scale a slight rise, and the grass would shorten. Suspicious blackbirds would scream out raspy warnings, and little bands of prairie pigeons would fly close to their heads, their wings thumping against their bellies like little drums. Hendrick said he saw a badger, but by the time the others looked, it was gone.

Still they pressed on to the south. Miles passed as they moved up the knolls and through the hollows. Then they saw it, suddenly, as they reached the crest of another hill— a real frame cabin, standing alone on a small incline. There was no fire just then, but even from a distance, beaten paths were visible, signs of life were there. The grass was chopped shorter around the house, and a wide strip of plowed land ran along the top of the knoll.

"I knew we would find it." Maria shouted, jumping happily and infecting the others with her enthusiasm.

"Maybe they will help us build the church, Pa." Peter had not forgotten his father's words.

They approached the cabin slowly but with great hope. The children seemed to want to hide behind their parents; even Peter walked behind his father, peeking around his wide shoulders.

Then the door of the cabin opened, and a woman backed out, closing the latch behind her. The Vander Meers stopped walking immediately, watching her. She turned, grasped the bottom of the wooden pail she was carrying, and dumped the contents on the stubble grass. As she finished, she glanced up and froze, confronted by this new and unexpected tribe.

"Hul-lo," Antonie stumbled over the little English he knew.

There was no reply. The middle-aged woman stood motionless, still holding the pail upside-down. She seemed entranced by Tryntje; at least she appeared to pay little attention to the rest of the family. Antonie looked at his wife; she, in turn, seemed transfixed by the woman who stared at her.

"Dina," Tryntje whispered.

"Dina?" she repeated, more loudly.

"Tryntje?" The woman's round face lengthened as she gasped in disbelief.

Both women drew their long skirts up from the ground and ran toward each other, then stopped at arm's length, incredulous, holding hands and studying each other closely, with obvious delight.

Antonie heard very little of their conversation, but when the women embraced warmly and kissed, he knew he had been blessed.

Tryntje turned back to her family, her lips in constant motion, her left arm still embracing the stranger. She waved her family forward with a girlish swoop of her right hand.

"This is Dina . . . my friend . . ." she said, her face as warm as the morning sun, "from Holland . . . the singing school."

The two women turned back into each other's arms,

while five children, one after another, exploded from the cabin and ran to their mother, keeping a steady eye on the Vander Meers. Then a tall, gaunt Hollander filled the door frame and looked suspiciously at the emotional reunion taking place before his home. When he saw the look on his wife's face, he glanced over to Antonie Vander Meer, who nodded and smiled.

As the sun inched closer to the horizon that night, Antonie and his family finally reached their southwest sodpile. Peter had gone ahead of the rest, and when they caught him, he was sitting on the marker, one hand holding the big sack of coffee, the other shading the bright sun from his eyes as he looked into the west. Tryntje held Maria's hand; Antonie walked arm and arm with her on the other side.

"Pa, look!" Peter pointed upward, and there, like fancy lace against the orange sky, a huge regiment of geese—three, four, five echelons—moved north in formation. The Vander Meers stopped for a moment, listening to the faint, discordant honking.

"Is it true what they say about the geese?" Peter asked.

"What is that?"

"The ones in front get tired," he said, pointing through the branches of the old cottonwood; "they slow down and drop to the rear. Then others lead. That way they can keep going."

They all watched the formation, perfect now in its distant perspective.

"A man in Minnesota told me so, Pa, but I haven't seen them change yet. Is it true?"

Antonie laughed as he watched the geese disappear into the heavens. He lifted his arm and circled Tryntje's shoulder.

Courting Dame Justice

"*Schiet op*, Klaas. *Opstaan.*" Griet Van Wechel jerked the quilt from her husband's chin and left him shivering like a long yellow bean in the wind.

"Ach, *Vrouw*—"

" 'Ach,' nothing! Soon the men will leave, and you will lie here whimpering like a puppy!" She grabbed the corners of the quilt and folded it quickly in her hands.

Klaas turned away from the glaring kerosene lamp, jerked his legs up to his stomach, and tucked his hands snugly into his lap.

"It is yet the middle of the night!"

"Ach, you are a *slaapsok!*" She laid the quilt over the foot of the featherbed and raised her hands to her hips. "Very well then, I will go." She cocked her head arrogantly.

"Griet, don't be so foolish, eh?"

"Foolish! Why foolish? We are Americans now, ja? We must think of our rights here!"

"Ach, rights, rights, . . . all this talk—" Klaas turned his head into his arms.

"Ja, our rights! You don't care, but the real men"—she leaned over the bed and pointed—"the ones with something between their legs *and* between their ears, the real men will go. They know we must hold our rights." She stood erect at the foot of the bed. "Ja, Klaas, I will go. You stay home and clean the house."

"Griet, you are so foolish—"

"Why foolish?"

"This is man's work. It is cold." He reached for the quilt.

She grabbed it away. "Well, it is man's work, eh? Then you must stay home for sure!" She walked around the foot of the bed and stood at the side. "And cold, you say? Ja, it is cold, and I have more on this body than you have on yours. Ja, I will go."

"Griet, surely no one will go. Calliope is more than twenty miles!" Klaas reached down and pulled the quilt back over his chest. "It is cold. Tomorrow maybe. It will be warm tomorrow."

"This is the day of the meeting. If they don't go today, who knows what will happen with those *schurken!* Greatrax and Betten are members. We voted them to be members. Those at Calliope are outlaws! The *men* will go, Klaas, I know it!"

Her husband turned and circled like a mother cat, winding himself into the quilt. Then he lay motionless, snorting softly in the warmth of his nest. Griet shook her head and walked to the door.

She looked through the window but saw no hint of dawn in the skies. But the moon, reflecting off the snow, lighted the cluster of dwellings they called Orange City. Here and there, flickering lanterns marked the movement of early risers. Griet Van Wechel looked back at her husband. Then she pulled on her thick coat, stepped into the frigid night air, and walked quickly to the lean-to where the animals were sheltered.

Since the water was frozen, she fed raw potatoes to the mules, then bridled them, her shortened breath rising like clouds in the still cold of the dug-out shelter. The leather was wood-stiff, and her fingers tightened into ten-penny nails. She worked quickly, but when she closed the door behind her, the cold had numbed her nose and cheeks. As she hurried for the house, she noted more lanterns over the face of the city. The men would go, she told herself.

She slammed the door against the cold, but Klaas never moved. She took out all her warmest wraps, then sat down for some pork and greased bread, which she swallowed with the help of hot coffee. When she reached for her wooden shoes, Klaas raised his head and peeked out from the covers.

"Grietje," he pleaded.

She pushed her toes in. She knew wooden shoes would be the warmest protection she could wear.

Klaas leaned up on one elbow, rubbing his eyes. Griet stood and rammed the shoes to the floor, over her feet and several layers of wool stockings.

"Griet, this is foolish! Now will you be a good wife and come back to our bed." He leaned back slowly. "I have a surprise for you here!"

She looked down at him. A leering smile snaked over his face. She stopped her preparations, and sat, momentarily, silent.

"Ja, *lieveling*, I will come, but you must wait yet a minute." She rose and walked over to the lanterns, her wooden shoes klomping on the floor. "It must be dark for us," she whispered.

Klaas chuckled beneath the quilt.

Griet Van Wechel grabbed a flour sack as she walked to the door. Then she stopped. "Klaas, can you wait once yet for your treat? I must bring in the ice."

"Ja, Grietje, but hurry!"

The door slipped quietly shut behind her. She jabbed bare fingers into the frozen snow, and gathered big crusty chunks. The bag filled slowly; she dropped it hard against the frozen path to pack the pieces. Finally it was full. Her fingers grew so numb she couldn't fasten the bag, so she carried it in open-ended, closing the door softly behind her.

"Oh, Klaas, it is so cold outside. Is it warm in your bed?" She spoke softly.

"Ja, Grietje, come and feel once, eh?"

She tiptoed to him in the darkness and dropped off her wooden shoes so he could hear them hit the floor. Then she gently pulled back the quilt, running her hands beneath his body.

"I am here, *lieveling*." Klaas reached out to his wife. She could just discern the outline of his head in the darkness.

She lifted the sack from the floor and laid it beneath the covers, making sure it didn't touch her Klaas.

"I'm here, *schat*," she whispered. "And what is this surprise?"

"Ahhh, Grietje . . . ."

Klaas Van Wechel finally found his wife bundled up aboard their wagon, listening, like so many others, to the final instructions.

"Greatrax and Betten were voted in—we voted them in the Board—and they *will* take their rightful seats. We will see to it!" Evert Vogelaar stood like a bear, his swooping arms swathed in thick black wraps. The men hooted their approval.

"And when we return, we *will* have our men on the Board, or *we* will have the county government! It will be done!" Griet pounded her mittened hands together. "Now you all know that we have tried to be fair. Twice we have asked them for what is rightfully ours. It is time now to run the money-changers from the temple!" Again, a resounding cheer.

"It is terrible cold today, and we have a long journey. Be sure you have enough clothing, ja? We don't want anyone to freeze. Does anybody need more blankets?"

The men questioned each other.

"*Vrouw* Scholten has yet more blankets. Is there anyone in need?"

Some raised their hands, and more quilts were passed around. The men nestled back in the prairie hay, pulling rugs or quilts or furs, whatever wraps they had around them.

Klaas jumped aboard the sleigh and nestled beside his wife, saying nothing.

"Here now, Klaas, sit closer." She grabbed his coat with her right hand and slung another quilt over both of them with her left. "You will be the warmest man in Calliope, eh?"

Vogelaar stood up on the seat again and surveyed the battalion of runners assembled in the darkness. "We are ready then?" The men trumpeted their approval; horses and mules pranced and fidgeted in the cold night air. "We will meet the men from up north farther down the trail to Calliope. Everyone ready? Very well, we will go!"

More than fifty sleighs funneled into an orderly caravan that streamed across the glistening prairie. Steel runners shrieked over the snow, but the frozen crust provided a more than adequate road bed. Westward they moved, over the slow persistence of hills and sloughs that gradually brightened as the overcast sky faded in the dawn of the winter sun.

"Griet!" Klaas yelled over the steady klomp of hooves, "where is that from?"

Griet had dropped the scarf that swaddled her face and taken a long deep snort from a brown bottle.

"Your drawer, *lieveling.*" She wiped her mouth with her sleeve, recapped the bottle, and shoved it back into her coat.

"*Dief!* You should at least offer a man a drink from his own bottle!" Klaas stamped his wooden shoes into the sleigh bed.

"You think you're a man, then?" She buttoned up her coat.

"Ja certainly!"

She looked closely at her husband, unbuttoned once more, and drew out the bottle.

Klaas leaned back and poured, then jerked forward, shut his eyes and shook his head like a mule. He gave the wife the bottle. Griet laughed slightly, pulling her scarf above her nose and mouth.

By the time several miles had passed, the sun had turned the prairie into a glaze of blinding white. Sun dogs hung like ghosts in the cloudless sky, but the sleigh train slid west, through frigid air that snapped at fingers and faces and penetrated layers of wool and fur. Finally, atop another roll in the prairie, Evert Vogelaar stood and pointed. There, at the appointed place, stood more sleighs, more teams, more men straddling the road to Calliope, waiting for their friends from the east.

Vogelaar barely slowed the procession. Amid shouts of approval from fellow Hollanders, the men from northern Sioux County filed in behind the train as if preordained, stretching the line even further. Warmed by a satisfying sense of righteousness, the men had a pervading feeling that this phalanx of saints was the called arm of the Lord. Had this been another season, one might have heard the throbbing bars of a Psalm from the ranks like an Indian war song, but today only puffs of steam blew from chapped lips.

When Vogelaar reached the summit of the hill that overlooked the Big Sioux and the quiet little town of Calliope, he pushed his team hard for the final descent, aiming directly at the log house at the middle of the town—the Sioux County Courthouse. Following their leader, the whole train moved faster and faster, until the long line of runners spread into a cascading front that outflanked the village limits, as it avalanched toward the river.

Sheriff Tom Dingman saw it from his office. One—two—three—ten—twenty—they kept coming, spreading into the valley, in a wave of scattered snow, until the leaders stood proudly outside his door, their horses trumpeting steam. Dingman strapped his pistol to his waist, pulled on his overcoat, and stepped into the morning air. Still they swarmed over the bluff, like grasshoppers, an endless stream of Hollanders from hamlets far to the north and east.

"Who's in charge here?" he bellowed.

The men looked from one to another, then pointed at Evert Vogelaar.

"You?"

"Ja."

"What is your business?'

Vogelaar stood again on his sleigh, turned, and waited for more men to pull up behind him.

Dingman looked over the assembly and put his hand to the gun in his holster. There were more than a hundred, he guessed, all bundled up like Yankton squaws.

"Well?" he shouted again. "What is your business?"

The Hollanders felt the strength of their numbers and gained courage quickly. "What is *your* business, *zwart-rok?*" someone yelled.

Dingman's eyebrows jutted forward in anger. "I am the law here! I answer to no one but the law! Now, what brings you to Calliope?"

Vogelaar stretched his hands out over his congregation, trying to settle their enthusiasm. Then he turned slowly, proudly, his mustache thickened into a frozen clump. "We are here, sir, to see our elected officials put into office. We come to this country for freedom, and when we find no freedom, we wonder about this law you speak of."

Dingman paced back and forth slowly over the wooden planks. "And what makes you think that you have no freedom?" He pulled at his lapels, pushing his badge out for all to see.

"You know, *huichelaar!*"

Vogelaar turned to his men like an offended father. "We must do this right." He looked toward Klaas Van Wechel. "We will have no more of that!"

Other residents of the village peered from behind shades and curtains, watching the commotion on the street.

Vogelaar stepped off the wagon and approached the sheriff. "We have heard that there are some who will not allow our elected supervisors to take their rightful places on the Board. We have come to see them installed, according to the law." He pointed at Dingman. "All we ask is to see this done. Then we will leave peacefully."

Dingman tipped his hat and put his hands on his waist. "I am the law. There will be no mobs in Calliope or in Sioux County for that matter—not as long as I wear this here badge! I will see to it. You wooden shoe Hollanders will just go back to your farms now, or I will have to take action here!"

"*You* will take action? *Opschepper!*" The crowd became more unruly, prompted by Dingman's swagger.

"Yes, I will take action." He drew his pistol. "I will not hesitate to use this!"

The Sheriff's draw was mirrored by similar movements on the sleighs. Some raised shotguns or rifles, others clubs or pitchforks.

Vogelaar spoke again. "Either we see them put in, or we will take the safe and seal and everything to Orange City!"

Dingman started to crouch as he read the obvious intention of the Hollanders. The pistol shook in his hand, but he swallowed hard and raised it menacingly higher. "You will have to kill me first!"

"Then so be it, Sheriff!" The men growled and raged in their sleighs. Some jumped from the runners and surged forward behind their leader.

Vogelaar shouted again. "Ho!" The farmers stopped momentarily. Evert Vogelaar stepped forward and faced the sheriff. Behind him stood a regiment of stubborn Hollanders, armed and angry.

Dingman cocked the pistol. Everything was still.

Then Vogelaar spoke. "Dingman, you know me, we fought at Antietam. Now you listen to me! Either we will see justice done here, or your body will sink in the river, full of the lead from our rifles!"

Tom Dingman scanned the crowd again. Some men were still pulling in, and far too many were already lined up before his office. He sputtered and growled like a tied hound, then offered his gun to Evert Vogelaar.

The men cheered.

"All right, men, now let's do this right! Some of you take the sheriff home. Stay there—don't let him back out. If he gets ornery, let him have some buckshot." Vogelaar stood in the doorway of the office and assumed full control. "Now, we must surround all the buildings—no one must escape. Some of you move around them right away and grab anyone who tries to get to the river. Rens, you and Van Zyl go to the courthouse, see if our men are there."

Squadrons swarmed through the snowy streets of Calliope, surrounding houses, knocking on doors, even inviting themselves in to get out of the cold. Klaas and Griet Van Wechel stood on the porch of a big house, jumping up and down to stamp the circulation back into their toes.

Vogelaar and two others went from one house to another, speaking to all the supervisors, trying vainly to make them accept the supervisors voted in by the Hollanders. Vogelaar had secured the services of one Mr. Pendelton, a judge from Sioux City, to observe the doings impartially. But try as they might, the men couldn't persuade the incumbents to relinquish their power. An hour or more passed before Pendleton himself turned to Vogelaar and said it was up to them to secure their own rights.

"One more," Vogelaar said. "Perhaps if we speak to Rudyard Stone, he will persuade the others."

Pendelton, Vogelaar, Rens, and Van Zyl walked down the street toward Stone's house and were met at the door by Griet Van Wechel.

"Is Stone in, Griet?" Vogelaar asked.

"Ja, and his *Vrouw.*"

The men knocked at the door. Klaas Van Wechel answered.

"What are you doing here, Klaas?"

"Trying to get warm."

"While your *Vrouw* is outside?"

"She is not cold."

Vogelaar muffled his laughter. "Is Stone here?"

"Ja, come in."

Stone met them immediately. He was round-faced, with bushy sideburns that crawled beneath his chin on either side. And he was red—burning with anger.

"Pendleton, what is this idiot doing in my house? And what do you want here?"

"Stone," Pendleton spoke, quietly, "we want you to

consider the election binding. You must install the rightful members of the Board."

Stone jumped like an old frog and waved his cane menacingly. "I will never give up my seat to these stupid Hollanders. They know nothing. They are not even Americans, Pendleton, not even Americans!" His heavy jowls shook with contempt. "No Hollanders will run this government as long as I have anything to do with it!"

Pendleton shrugged his shoulders. "Very well, then I cannot be responsible for what happens to you, Stone. You are an outlaw!"

"An outlaw!" Stone screamed. Blue veins pushed from his temples. "And what about this dunce who walks into my house and asks me for my liquor?"

"Stone, the Hollanders have their rights. When you deny them—"

Stone turned away and marched off, cracking his cane against the bannister and slamming the door to his porch.

"We will put him in jail, Klaas. Do not allow him to escape!"

Van Wechel nodded bravely. But in less than five minutes he was back in the cold. Stone had forced him out with a pistol.

Pendleton's notice gave the men license to fulfill their secondary objective. Sleighs were set next to the courthouse, and books and files were carried out and loaded. The men scoured the government office, leaving only the safe and whatever it held. It was huge and very heavy—too cumbersome, or so they thought, to haul all the way back to Orange City. "Find the key," someone said, so the hunt began.

Klaas and Griet stood watch by the front door of the Stone house, determined to keep the outlaw within. Suddenly the door opened, and a woman stepped out, closing the door lightly behind her.

"Morning, Mrs. Stone." Klaas bowed gracefully. He heard only a dainty giggle.

"Out for a walk this morning?" He tried to be polite.

"Yes, tee-hee!"

"It is cold here; are you warm enough?"

She didn't respond. Klaas watched her sway down the walk, stepping ever so carefully. He jumped off the porch quickly and raced to her side, offering her an arm. "Let me help you, ma'am. The ice is very slippery."

Griet watched her husband's gallantry, but noticed also the stubble of sideburn beneath the veiled hat. She walked over toward them as they marched handsomely down the street.

"Ja, Klaas, that is good of you, helping the lady."

Klaas turned back to his wife and nodded, frowning.

"She is a pretty one, too. Makes your *Vrouw* look like the mules."

"Now, Griet, you know that I must be a gentleman."

"Ja, ja of course." Griet walked behind them, mimicking their steps. *"Daar zou je mee naar bed willen, he!"*

"But Griet, though, you talk so *plaat.*"

She walked behind them slowly, then reached up and jerked the hat from Stone's bald head. Stone turned in a flash and scampered back up the porch and into the house, while Klaas stood paralyzed, his arm still bent graciously, and Griet laughed.

"Ach, *Vrouw, hou je mond!* And where is the bottle?"

Soon the street was filled with Hollanders once again, yelling and screaming in Dutch and English. Several pounded on Stone's door.

"The key for the safe!"

"Give us the key!"

"Where is it, Stone?"

Stone's wife appeared at the door and asked to see Vogelaar. She was allowed to pass through the mob easily, while the men kept screaming for Stone himself.

Vogelaar stood near the sleighs, watching the action, when Mrs. Stone approached.

"Mr. Vogelaar, Mr. Pendelton, please—I will give you

the key if you will allow us to go to South Dakota."

"I will not allow you to escape, ma'am."

Mrs. Stone glanced uneasily from face to face. "Very well then—the key—for our safety?"

"Do you have it?"

"Will you give us safety?"

Vogelaar nodded a quick reponse; he wished no one hurt.

The woman reached into her breast and pulled out a silver key.

But Van Wechel had recognized the coat immediately. He ran up to Vogelaar, just at the moment Evert had promised the woman her safety.

"Evert!" he yelled. "Evert, do not be deceived! It is Stone himself!" Van Wechel pointed at the woman. "He cannot fool me!"

The woman had already turned back to the house but Klaas was not to be mocked again.

"You try to fool us again?" he threatened, yelling in her ear.

Evert Vogelaar tried to stop him, but before he could lay his hands on Klaas, Van Wechel had a hold of her long skirt.

"Look at this, men! Stone thinks we are all blockheads. He tries to deceive us!" Klaas reached down and pulled up at the hem, raising the skirt above the woman's head.

"See!" he shouted, watching the crowd around him, "it is a man!"

Van Wechel was dead wrong.

The woman shrieked, pulled the skirt from his hand, and landed a stiff right to the side of Klaas's head. She dashed into the house, screaming about the barbarian Hollanders.

Griet laughed again as she pulled the bottle from her coat.

"Men! We have the key. Let's get into the safe!" Vogelaar led the stampede back to the courthouse where some still waited, standing guard on the booty already loaded in the sleighs.

Stone and his wife waited for the street to clear, then left aboard his own cutter, heading west over the river to South Dakota. By the time the men found out the key didn't fit, the Stones were half way to Eden and freedom.

"Now what, Evert?"

Vogelaar moved uncertainly, checking the huge safe. He knew the men wouldn't have everything unless they had its contents. He nudged the big black box with his thigh. It barely moved.

"We must have it," he said. "Can we lift it together?"

Six men surrounded it, and on Vogelaar's command, heaved it upward, then dropped it again.

"Ja! We will take the whole thing back with us!"

The men jumped and cheered.

"But first, we must have dinner. We can put the lunches over the stoves here."

Vogelaar's suggestion was happily received. The men scattered to their sleighs and took out lunches frozen hard as rocks. Someone pried open a barrel of smoked pork found in the courthouse. Its contents were eaten, cooked on pans borrowed from the townspeople. Dinner was a victory feast. The Hollanders laughed and joked like children, celebrating their accomplishments. Griet made coffee to warm them, and everyone had more than enough to eat.

Before they left, the men ran the Calliope tavern nearly out of its stock. Griet didn't have to push Klaas into stopping for another bottle.

Full and satisfied, the men boarded their sleighs for the long trip back across the county. Evert Vogelaar himself took the safe and led the procession back up and out of the Big Sioux valley.

The journey back was warmer than the way up, and when the men from the north steered their cutters homeward, away from the train, a volley of hoots and hollers heralded their mutual sense of victory. Sun dogs still shivered in the clear winter sky, but Dutch hearts were warmed by a new, exciting self-reliance, and a friendly snort or two.

By the time Klaas Van Wechel put up his mules, midnight had passed. He sang as he worked, lifting bridles and forking hay to the overworked animals.

When he stepped into the house, he yawned and looked around. He shoved wood into the stove, then ran back outside to fetch more. Griet met him at the door with a cup of hot coffee. He put down the logs near the stove and clutched the hot cup with his fingers.

Grietje spread the quilt over their bed.

"Well, *Vrouw,* you fought for your rights, ja?" He sipped at the coffee and yawned again, rubbing his eyes. "You feel better now?"

She didn't reply. She looked up at him, smiled, and blew out the only flickering lantern.

The Trapper

Smid jerked around, as if some eternal drums had unexpectedly stopped. He stared at the farm behind him, feeling for the gun with his right hand. No, he hadn't forgotten. He pulled the pistol from his coat pocket, hearing Klassen's echoes through the windstill morning.

"Don't shoot de *verrekte beesten*, Smid, use de fork. But if you must, just vonce, ja, ant in de head. An' be sure to go early. An' skin dem too yet vonce de zame day."

Evert Klassen commanded much more before he left his hired man alone. Sitting aboard the buggy, right hand on the reins, his left arm slicing the air, he seemed to be preaching as he left the yard, while his wife and five children, bundled against the damp, late fall air, sat still as sleeping birds behind him. But all Smid remembered now was the business about the trapline—use the stick, not the gun, stretch them tight, flesh them clean, and don't mar the pelts. As if he didn't know all that already. As if this was the first morning he had walked Evert Klassen's trapline.

Adriaen Smid replaced the pistol in his coat pocket and watched the thick column of smoke gush from the chimney of Klassen's homestead. Ten years ago, before Smid had come, the house had been constructed near the lean-to and dug-out that Klassen had built when he first settled in Eastern Sioux County. The house was strong and functional, sentried by sapling elms that pushed higher into the clear air of the flatland with each passing spring. It was a warm place. It was a good place. Adriaen Smid would have liked such a place himself, but it wasn't God's will.

He stood another moment, watching the quiet homestead, still thinking. Very little, for that matter, seemed to be God's will for him, if he dared to say it. "Go to Sioux County," he had read in the little fliers passed around in Pella. He had prayed about it—ja, he had prayed about it. Then he had silently walked away from the carriage-maker, just as he deserted the bakery in Eastern Wisconsin, looking, hoping, like all the rest, to catch a dream, to work hard and become successful, to have his own land, a farm, a wife, children, to be respected, an elder in a good church.

His overshoes had made dark tracks through the gauze of frost that stretched over the flat grazing land. The path ran straight as a tow-rope back to the barn he had left not long before. "Early, Smid," Klassen had said, so Smid dropped the pitchfork and picked up the forked stick, just as Evert himself would have done, when he could begin to make out the outlines of the house through the barn windows.

He turned back and marched on towards the river. There was no sun, but to the east the sky was colored with the promise of sunrise. He kept walking, moving north to where the Floyd snaked through the prairie grasses, cutting a gash into the land that made these acres undesirable to the first homesteaders. Within months of those early arrivals, any trees that had grown along the banks of the Floyd were stacked into woodpiles or notched and tiered into walls for some early cabin. Once trees were gone, no one wanted these acres, for frequent sloughs spotted the adjoining fields, making farming impossible—at least, so people said. But Evert Klassen had taken the bottom land. He was tough and bristly like a horsehide brush, and he made the land work for him. He was a deacon in the new church, and in less than ten years he could afford a hired hand.

When he reached the first bend, Adriaen got to his knees and slid carefully down the steep bank of the river where

Klassen set his first trap. For hundreds of years the river had gouged into the flatland, digging itself deeper and deeper into the rich black topsoil, creating sharp cliffs at the bends. Even though fall rains had swelled the flow of the river, the incline was so treacherous that Smid edged carefully northward on hands and feet, using his backside as a brake. He inched up closely to the first set, knowing that he wasn't to disturb the stand of wild oats that jutted out and up from the water's edge.

There was still no sun above the horizon, and although the sky continued to redden, Smid couldn't see the pan in the shallow water. He leaned over the set, grabbing a handful of brush to keep himself from falling into the quiet rush of the river, but there was no sign of the trap. Assuming it was unsprung, he grasped the brush to jerk himself back to the bank. Suddenly the weeds pulled out at the roots, and, anchor gone, Smid's right boot slid through the flaky ice at the edge and into the cold water. Fortunately, his foot caught on the trap stake, a heavy stick that just barely projected above the water, and in a moment, everything was quiet. He could feel the heavy cold pressing through his overshoe, while the flow moved easily around his foot, creating little eddies in the wake.

Then he felt it. His foot had come down on the chain that secured the trap to its anchor, and as he tried to regain his balance and lift himself back up the bank, he felt the chain jerking between his overshoe and the soggy river bed, then snap tight and pull, madly, making the stake jump like a bobber. He reached back up toward the bank and grabbed the big forked stick with his left hand, keeping his foot firmly in place. He knew he could control the frantic movement of the animal more easily if he kept his foot on the chain.

The fork plopped gently into the water as he started to poke in the current for the trapped animal. Then the chain snapped again, and he felt a powerful bite on the stick. The water splashed as the muskrat surfaced momentarily, leaving a chestnut trail of fur as its back arched toward the bottom again, slapping the water with its thick, naked tail. Smid poked through the darkened water with his stick, groping, touching, teasing the animal, but never quite finding the death grip.

He stopped, withdrew the stick, and waited for the muskrat to move. The gun would be so much easier. For a moment Adriaen saw himself here, poised, cat-like, holding, pointing Klassen's death stick. Adriaen Smid, the teacher, son of Hendrikus and Gesina, waiting here, now, for an animal whose fate was already drawn as tight as the trap chain. The river flowed quickly and gently past. Blood flushing through his cheeks, his insides turning, he held the stick inches above the water, collecting all of Evert Klassen's oaths to squelch the pain he refused to acknowledge.

Beady eyes surfaced suddenly, behind a mask of quill-like whiskers. Like a boy watching a stranger, Adriaen stared, his stick raised, hoping for the intervention of something far beyond himself, praying without words. The eyes were not suppliant but menacing, defiant, full of the rage for life. Adriaen plunged the stick into the water quickly, catching the animal's neck between the sharpened prongs before stabbing the points into the river bed. Only his arms held the muskrat down, but the animal jerked and pushed beneath the surface. Smid leaned more weight on the weapon, angered by the insolence of a creature so unwise in the face of its own obvious destiny. His whole body shook as the muskrat's powerful webbed feet kicked madly for freedom. Thick bubbles mushroomed to the surface, and little waves, pushed by the frenetic motion beneath the surface, slapped at the bank and pushed water up into the wild oats.

But it wouldn't die. The muskrat kicked and stamped and thrashed against the unrelenting prongs. Smid swore he felt the grate of sharp teeth on the wood again. He grew furious at such obstinate stupidity, and used the stick like a crutch for all his weight, breathing heavily in short, erratic gasps, as if he himself were engaged in mortal combat.

Then, slowly, the rabid humping abated. Convulsive jerks still roiled the water, but the bubbles rose smaller and less frequently. Smid leaned hard on the stick, his hands nearly numb. Water had begun to seep into his right boot. The river flowed on, smooth and undisturbed.

He leaned back slowly, still holding the stick in place, waiting for any sign of life beneath. Gradually he released pressure, gently pulling the fork upward. He could feel the suction of muck as the sharpened tips slipped from the river bed. The matted body of the muskrat surged to the surface and swung limp in the river, like a small, charred stump. Smid didn't change position. He removed his mitten from his right hand, grabbed the chain from the icy water, and lifted the animal and trap out of the current.

The rat was wet and ugly black. Still trembling, Adriaen shook the muskrat like a recalcitrant child, then stopped, shocked, when he saw what the dawn had thrown against the grass bank to his side. It was to him a vile image, the shadow of someone too steeped in the natural brutality of the wilderness to remember who he was, what he had been. And the rat, his prize, was changed from a hideous mockery of his own indecisiveness to a compelling vision of peaceful and final escape.

Gently, he leaned his weight on his right foot, flexed his knee and placed the trap on his lower thigh, holding the animal by a front foot with his left hand. He pressed on the steel spring with his right palm, and the big rat dropped, simply and cleanly, from the jaws of the trap. He lobbed the muskrat up on the bank and reset the trap with his hands against his thigh. He placed it back into the water, open and dangerous, in the middle of the wild oats, and pivoted away from the set, pulling his foot from the thick mud of the river bed as he climbed back to the bank.

He had done it right, but he knew the pistol would have been so much easier. This way there were no scars in the water-blackened fur, only a pink ring around its right foot where the muskrat tried to chew its way to freedom. Something buried too deep to be strong tugged at his lip when he saw the animal, river water coming from its mouth. But he turned away and looked back at Klassen's oat set, remembering the instructions clearly. He had done it well, at least. It was undisturbed. As good as Klassen himself. The clouds of muddied water had been carried away by the river that rushed along as if no one had been there.

Two hours later, Adriaen Smid trudged slowly back along the river bank. A radiant autumn sun had thawed the frosted prairie grass into soggy clumps, and the longer he walked, the colder his toes became. His black overcoat flopped open in the warm morning air; his hat was jammed carelessly in the left pocket. Aside from his feet, he was warm, hot almost, as much from the walk as from the heavy grain sack over his shoulder.

Klassen would be pleased. The burlap sack held eight dead muskrats, not an extraordinary catch, but none of them was marred by gunshot, for all had been caught in water sets and killed by the drowning stick. He hadn't used the gun once, although he could have. This morning, like so many others, he had seen the fox running across the open fields, its tail pointed into a burning stream as it ran.

"Shoot de *kippedief,*" Klassen would have said, for every time the farmer could, he tried. But Smid had stopped, momentarily, only to watch the slight but agile animal flow like the river itself across the stubbled prairie. Klassen would have sworn then, for sure. But Klassen was in Pella.

The burlap sack thumped against his back as he returned along the trapline. It was heavy with muskrats, bulky and thick like a clump of wet sod. So he had left Holland, against the wishes of his parents who saw their hopes vanish as he slung his few possessions over his shoulder and walked to the ship—one of many that arrived weekly at Amsterdam, only to leave again, full of ruddy-faced Hollanders. He hadn't much to take along, of course, since unlike many of his shipmates, he wasn't weighted down with the responsibilities of family. He was unmarried, free, able to resettle easily. It was then he wanted to leave, not years after when the move would be hard on a wife and children.

Slowly, thoughtfully, he walked back toward the farm. Long stalks of wild oats rose from the river bank, marking the first set again, and there before him lay the first, now last, of his catch, dead, yet warmed by the morning sun. The rat was dry now, its fur glossy and thick, sparkling with the brush of sunlight. The black, beady eyes, the violence of the attack, the frantic, slashing bites were erased from his memory when he saw the smooth fur, thick on the almost round body.

The shortened grass on the bank was wet and soggy, but the muskrat was dry and soft and so warm he wanted to hold it close to his cheek. He dropped the forked stick as if it were burning his hand, then stooped to his knees to pick up the animal, laying the burlap bag at his side. He could almost lose his fingers in the fur as he traced the sinewy muscles beneath. So warm, so soft. So peaceful now, the struggles long past. The river flowed on, just ten feet away, whispering, as he lifted the clump of fur to his knee. The sun warmed the air like an open fire.

He opened the bag with his left hand and carefully placed the animal in with the others, as if he might injure them. Rising slowly to his feet, he gathered up the burlap around the open end and laid the bag over his shoulder, holding it firmly at his chest with both hands. The forked stick lay in the prairie grass where he had thrown it; he turned back to the homestead.

That night, after the barn chores, he stropped the skinning knife until it was razor sharp. He spat on his left wrist, rubbed the tiny bubbles into his skin, and drew the blade slowly over the dampened area, once, twice, three times. Then he pointed the knife at the lantern on the wall and saw his own scraggly hair lining the blade. He licked his wrist and felt it smooth. The knife was sharp and ready.

Klassen had pounded twenty nails into a thick rafter of

the shed, hung long strands of twine from each, and tied the ends into slip knots. Nine muskrats were lined like a jury before Smid. All day they had turned and spun, suspended by the twine and changed, now, as if by magic, into lustrous balls of fur. Three legs hung limply downward from each body, while the fourth pointed straight to the ceiling, forcing the hind legs to open awkwardly to the skinner's knife. Klassen stored the thin, tongue-shaped boards against the wall beneath the nails, where they waited for the pelts like vultures, Smid thought, tantalized by drops of blood that formed, then fell from the nose of each upended carcass.

Surrounded by a tiered gallery of drying pelts that stood, cleaned and stretched, pointing up like tall church windows, Smid sat on an empty keg, one of several in Evert Klassen's tool shed, brushing the edge of the knife across his calloused palm. Once his hands had carried no such scars, once he had been a teacher, much removed from all of this, well-respected in the small town of Hellendoorn, an educated man, a leader. *Opa* had wanted him to be a dominie, and so had his parents, but he told them he had never felt the call like his friend Geert, who had seen a vision. But a teacher was good, his mother had said from behind a mask that hid her reluctance but not her disappointment. He told her that Dominie Brummelkamp had mentioned the calling of teacher as important service for the Kingdom. Gesina Smid just nodded, accepting her fate graciously.

For almost two years he had lived in Arnhem, attending Dominie Brummelkamp's church regularly, as he studied the teaching profession at Kweekschool. Then he had returned to Hellendoorne, where he had taught at the Franse School for three years, three long years. He was respected by some for his work. But not by his students. And when he left, no one asked him to reconsider; they seemed to acknowledge by their silence that it was best for all. In fact, no one saw him leave the tiny apartment in the village; no one spoke to him as he left town; no one kissed him on the lips when he boarded the vessel in the harbor.

Now he was on the prairie of this new country, and as he carved into the crusty skin of his palms, he saw Evert Klassen standing here, stripping the pelts from cold, red carcasses. Klassen was quick but careful, and he demanded the same from his hired man. His knife often gashed the flesh of the muskrats, and his hands would turn scarlet in the blood that flowed over his thick fingers. But rarely did he cut the treasured pelt.

"Smid!" he would spit right now, "*schiet toch op!*"

Adriaen's mind echoed with Klassen's command, even though the farmer was more than half a state away. He reached for the strop again and ran the blade up and back, making a patterned swish-swop over the smoothed leather, until the nearly blackened blade was ready. Then he rose from the keg and walked toward the catch.

Muskrats were easy prey to the skinner's knife, he mused, as he sliced little circles around each of the back feet. He jabbed the tip of the blade beneath the open skin, toward the tail, pulling back the loosened pelt from the carcass as the blade seemed to melt the thin membrane. His fingers held the dank flesh on the thigh as he cut down deeper toward the rat's vitals. Another slice around the tail, and a loose flap of skin dropped away from the meat.

When he had finished the other leg, he grabbed the flap of loosened pelt on both sides of the carcass and pulled down, trying to strip the carcass in one motion. Often he had seen Klassen do it, saving time, for sometimes the pelt could be jerked clean from the smooth back and underside. He pulled again, the left foot stretched with the tension, the twine tightening with a screech around the suspended foot. He gave up, pulling the skin back toward him gently with his thumb and forefinger, and drawing the blade lightly through the thin fat that held the fur to the rat's carcass. Down, down, quickly and deftly, the fur peeled away easily from the midsection, urged by the sharp blade. The redolence of musk, heavy and cloying, lay in the air like an unseen mist.

Nightly repetition had long ago faded Smid's reluctance to skin animals. The only tension he had felt this fall resulted from Klassen's persistent competition. Although it was never mentioned, Evert's lust for a match would create an awkward quietness in the shed and an unspoken game of skill and speed that Klassen invariably won with a barely muffled laugh. But tonight he was alone; he would make no mistakes.

When his knife finally reached the rat's shoulders, the pelt hung like a skirt from the carcass. Smid poked a finger through the membrane at the forearm of the rat's front paw, holding the unskinned foot and pelt in his right hand, and the meat of the shoulder with his left. The pelt ripped off like paper, leaving only a gloved paw on the carcass. The other paw stripped just as easily, and the carcass hung, nearly naked, only the head draped by the discolored skin of the loosened pelt.

Adriaen drew the knife carefully around the back of the skull, and the skin lifted cleanly from two greyish lobes. He swung the carcass and continued skinning around the muskrat's neck in short, swift jerks. Suddenly blood, purple as the skin of a ripe plum, flowed down and over his left hand where he clenched the wet pelt. He pulled the loose skin, hoping to finish quickly and avoid matting the fur with spilled blood. He wheeled the carcass around again and attacked the skull, cutting and carving at the eye. He sliced quickly, but it wasn't there. He pulled down hard on the pelt, and fur oozed out from a gash he mistakenly laid in the skin, a slice that opened ever wider with the incessant tugging, until, as if by fate, he sat, stunned, the wet, scarred pelt draped over his bloodied hand. And Evert Klassen never marred the pelts. Adriaen Smid trembled.

In little more than two hours, nine pink-red carcasses swung slowly in the dim light of the lantern, and nine prime pelts stretched tight over the drying boards. Adriaen Smid wiped the blood and flesh from the blade, swept up the fatty lumps from the floor, and tried to clean the dried blood from his hands and wrists.

Klassen returned two days later as the sun rose over the Iowa prairie. It was crisp that morning; a cold winter wind blew some light snow out of the northwest: the seasons had begun to change. Klassen bellowed for Smid the moment his rig entered the yard, but when he got no response, he sent his family to the house carrying their own bags. He leaped from the wagon and ran to the barn, incensed at the tardiness of his hired man. He jerked the iron latch and swung open the barn door, letting it fly from his hands. The barn shook as the door hit the wall with a violent slap.

"Smid!" he yelled again. But there was no reply.

He broke out of the barn, slamming the door behind him, and nearly ran to the shed. It was empty, except for nine purpled corpses suspended, still as death, from the rafter, and nine matching silhouettes etched against the wall by the flickering lantern.

He rushed back out, yelling as though his fury could compel obedience, but Smid was nowhere on the homestead.

He found him near the river, lying on his side with his feet planted in the wild oats on the bank. He seemed to blend into the grass, for his hair was sugared by the frost, and his face and clothes were layered with a thin, white crust of early winter snow. There was no sign of movement around him.

Klassen's gun lay at his side, and there was a hole the size of a pea in his right temple.

Evert Klassen picked up his pistol and swept off the frost and snow. He straightened up and stepped back to the river bank. The forked stick stood upright in the middle of the wild oats, messing the yellow shafts. The trap was sprung, its upright jaws harmless in the mud just beyond the flow of the river.

The Snowstorm

There was no sun on that early March morning, but even so, the day held the promise of warmth, and that itself was a relief from the long Iowa winter. A southern breeze spread comfort over the prairie, melted what snow still remained, and loosened the grassland turf from the grip of the winter frost. The ground around the schoolhouse, well marked by children's footprints, had begun to soften the day before; and when the night failed to bring its ritual frost, it continued to thaw, until by morning, the topsoil warmed into a slippery lake of mud above the deeply frozen earth beneath. The children splashed through it along the furrowed paths they daily took to school, and by the time they arrived, their shoes and boots were layered with a gummy coat of soil.

Miss Katharine Baarman knew the warm weather would make the outdoors even more inviting to the children, but her better judgment insisted she call them in early from their playground games. The schoolhouse suffered badly enough through the early spring, and if she allowed them to romp in the mud all morning, the wooden floor would be turned into a desert of dried mud. Besides, the county superintendent hadn't been through these parts in months; it would be her luck to see him open the door today and look over a barnyard.

So she called them early that morning, interrupting a precarious game of "pom-pom-pullaway" about five minutes before they would have even begun to expect to hear her. But some were actually happy. Nick Oldersma looked almost relieved when she rang the bell; he smiled broadly from the goal nearest the building, then tiptoed like a ballerina, trying in vain to avoid the splattering mud. Most of the girls, wanting no part of the dirt at all, had come in immediately upon their arrival. They peeked out the door from behind the teacher and beckoned to their classmates, as if to share in the authority of their young instructor.

"It's too early, Miss Baarman!" a familiar voice, deep and rough, shouted from across the playground.

"Ach, that John Mulder," one of the girls said. "He has already pushed some little ones in the mud today."

"It ain't time yet!"

About five or six boys, half his size, crowded around him, following his leadership and enjoying the rebellion. John Mulder was old, probably sixteen, and unlike other boys his age who stayed on the farm and worked with their fathers, John remained in school.

"Baarman," he yelled, his confidence bolstered by the numbers around him, "we ain't comin' in yet, hear?"

"John Mulder, you and the boys come now. You listen to me!"

His underlings were wavering in the face of her authority; they looked at their general, then to their teacher at the door of the schoolhouse.

"John Mulder, you come in—now!"

The teacher turned quickly into the face of Mary Boersma and gave her a mild reprimand with her eyes. She didn't need any help from eleven-year-olds.

Three little boys lit out like scared chickens, running as fast as possible across the slick ground, and flew into the school. Dirk Ver Gowe and Henry Baker remained with John Mulder. Like miniature ruffians, they pulled their rabbit-skin hats low over their eyes, pushed their mittened hands firmly into their pockets, and rocked their weight from foot to foot.

"*Ach, verdomd.*" The rebel finally conceded and lumbered toward the door. He mumbled something to the boys about their teacher, and his troopers' hands jerked up to their faces to cover their snickers.

"That John Mulder. If his papa wasn't so rich. . ."

"Now, Mary, you just remember that John is here to learn too, just like you." She had turned back into the doorway where several students were cleaning their shoes before entering the room.

"But he don't care nothing—"

"Doesn't."

". . .doesn't care nothing—"

"Anything."

". . .doesn't care anything about. . ."—she had almost forgotten her original statement—"about learnin', ma'am. You know that's true."

"You girls take your seats now, and I'll be right in." She deliberately sidestepped the comment, then turned back to the door to follow the movements of the mutineers. As Katharine Baarman looked out over the prairie and saw the last of the students enter the schoolhouse, her eyes were drawn to the sky, thick, this morning, with bluish-gray clouds that rolled past her like locomotive steam on a cold day. They were right above her, close, so close that their movement was almost frightening. She didn't understand it fully, but she felt a strange warning, nonetheless, simply to be aware of things.

"I *know* it's too early," Mulder snarled, pouting dog-like at the entrance.

"It is, John," she said, "but the younger children mustn't get themselves full of mud."

He raised his head at the distinction, glared arrogantly at the two boys at his side, walked in and took his seat at the rear of the class, leaving big clumps of wet mud on the floor with every step.

Dirk and Henry longed to emulate their hero, but they capitulated instead to this teacher-mother before them, scraped most of the muck from their shoes, and took their seats directly in front of Mulder, nearer the front of the room.

She looked once more over the bleak and endless

prairies and into the rampaging clouds above her. Then Katharine Baarman entered the room, moving past the straight rows of children to the wide oak desk at the front of the room. The children rose quietly as she entered, their hands folded before them; they watched their teacher and awaited the morning prayer.

Her lip trembled slightly, so she bit it quickly as she looked over twenty heads, twenty shaggy-haired children who stared at her expectantly, probing for her authority. Oddly hesitant to begin even the "Our Father," she fumbled with a wisp of hair that had fallen from the tightly-wound bun at the back of her neck. She stared down at Edgar, the youngest, then back to John, who waited as usual, hands boldly placed behind his head. Then, she prayed.

Shortly after the Bible lesson, John Mulder rose and paraded out of the schoolhouse. He hadn't asked, but then, he never did. Although other children had to request use of the little auxiliary building in the corner of the playground, John had special freedoms in this regard, freedoms which he simply took. And few days went by that he didn't exercise them, always staying outside longer than anyone else would have dared, then walking leisurely back into the room as if he had done nothing wrong. His actions always secured the respect of the younger boys and, for the most part, the disapproval of the girls, who felt that his behavior showed disrespect to their own beloved schoolmarm.

Whenever he left, the atmosphere within the school changed. Henry turned around completely in his chair, for he now found it unnecessary to watch John's antics, or to perform himself. Miss Baarman's rule was unquestioned during John's absence. The children even smiled more readily, it seemed, and responded more freely in recitation.

Four small children skipped to the front of the room, happy to share with the others their slate work in arith-

metic. Miss Baarman sat behind her desk and rotated her
chair toward the side wall to be able to watch both the
class and the students at the chalkboard. All the children
were busy, some with their slates, others watching their
friends and checking their work. As she glanced from the
class to the board, her eye was caught by a window to the
west, the square shack in the corner of the schoolyard, and
John Mulder who was walking, ever so slowly, toward his
destination. He stopped for a moment. His hair flew back
roughly from beneath his cap as he looked into the sky.
The wind had changed. It blew more powerfully now. She
could see it. John Mulder pulled the collar of his woolen
shirt more closely about his neck, stepped up his pace
toward the toilet, and looked down at the ground at his
feet.

Mary Boersma was the first to finish her work at the
board. She walked past the window, taking the teacher's
attention with her, and bringing her back to her feet before
the class. Katharine walked down the aisle, checking the
work of the students busy with their slates. She saw Dirk
busily completing his arithmetic. He looked back to her,
then to his slate. Without thinking, he moved closer to the
big black stove in the middle of the room, sliding quite unconsciously across the floor on his chair.

"Are there any mistakes?" she asked finally when all the
students had returned to their seats.

Two or three hands shot into the air as the last of the
boys sat down.

"Nick?"

A small-boned boy, hair neatly brushed, rose from his
seat and took a thousand tiny steps to the front of the
room.

"Mary has two errors," he announced. There was no
arrogance in his tone, simply a matter of right and wrong.

"$19 = 4 \times 4 + 3$," he stated, erasing Mary's final seven, "and
$19 = 3 \times 6 + 1$, not 4." He glanced almost shyly at the class, his
bright blue eyes gleaming despite his slightly lowered
forehead.

"Very good, Nick. You may sit down. Does anyone else notice any errors?"

More hands were raised this time, and in the battle for the teacher's attention, some students leaned forward and upward from their chairs, adding a muffled grunt to their gestures.

Miss Baarman called on a quiet pupil to correct the work, and a little ten-year-old girl got up from her seat and stepped to the front of the room.

The outside door opened just then, and John Mulder walked back in, being careful to shut the door quietly behind him. All heads turned to observe his entrance, and the room turned suddenly silent. Mulder pushed his fingers through his windblown hair, removed his heavy coat, and then sat down without making any further appeals for attention. Katharine Baarman deliberately turned away from his entrance, refusing to acknowledge his usual obvious disregard of her authority. She hoped that her own efforts to reconcentrate attention on schoolwork would lead others to follow her example. It never worked; everyone watched John Mulder.

But the children were mystified, surprised to see their hero—or villain—so soon, for there were times when his exit would mean an absence of close to an hour. But he had come back very quickly this time and then taken his seat quietly. He had pinched no one, nor said a word. The arithmetic lesson went on smoothly.

Outside, the wind was growing in strength. It seemed to find every hole and crack in the schoolhouse, turning the roof itself into a chorus of tea kettles. The three windows on either side of the building rattled as if they were afraid, and cold toes bumped drum-taps on the hardwood floor, as the children tried to restore circulation to their feet. To most of the students, however, the changes in wind and temperature were insignificant, for they kept up their work, leaning cheerfully or laboriously over their slates.

"John, you take number 51, please. Henry, 52. Dirk, 53. Margaret, 54." The arithmetic lesson continued; the older children's turn had arrived and the younger students worked on other assignments or watched their hallowed superiors.

John Mulder strutted toward the front, down the center aisle. He feigned tripping on one of the little pile of bricks around the old box-stove in the middle of the schoolhouse, and fell on the floor, arms and legs splaying out in a wild spasm, to the amusement of all the other children. Miss Baarman, typically, scolded him for his clumsiness, then looked away to the left side of the room and spoke to a student, while John rose very slowly and stood, just for a moment, beside the stove.

He had correctly calculated her reaction, for when she turned away from him, he dropped a marble as big as a crow's egg into a crevice of the old stove. Katharine's attempt to divert attention was a failure, however, and while she spoke to ears, not eyes, almost every student in the school observed John's plan. Only the youngest didn't foresee what would happen.

Admirably composed, John Mulder arrived at the chalkboard and proceeded to divide 4,360 by 3, 4, 5, 6, 7, 8, and 9. His answers were usually correct, and today's were no exception. The students were more impressed by his other calculations. A dark blue marble rested comfortably in the stove, slowly absorbing the intense heat.

Quite unaware of the plot, Katharine looked once more through the shivering windows as her students completed their arithmetic. The thick, low clouds of the morning were gone now, absorbed into a gray, uneven sky, almost purple, moving slowly from the northwest.

Tiny flecks of snow were already noticeable in the air; they bounced like dust off the windows at her elbow, coming like spies to plan the attack of the storm which loomed behind. She stared at the Iowa countryside and into the ominous clouds. Whatever smile had appeared before on her face was nearly erased by the realization of her fears. Two boys and a girl worked at the board. Sixteen other students seemed absorbed in their work on the greasy, well-carved benches before them. Only John Mulder was preoccupied. She saw him looking out the window to the west, already finished with his assignment, but intent on different thoughts, probably not unlike her own.

By dinnertime, the snow was falling faster. The boys were gobbling down their buttered bread, anticipating a game of "dare-gool" in the snow. But Miss Baarman refused to let them eat their whole lunch, and while they were disturbed by her unusual proclamation, the fact that all were similarly treated seemed to make them forget the deprivation. The older girls noted the darkening weather too, and while generally despising the rough games of the boys anyway, they chose to stay inside and do some tatting or just talk among themselves or with their teacher.

Since school terms usually ran only through the winter months, the snow itself was no immediate cause of concern to the children. Once a week, at least, the snow would brush off the windows, or accumulate in little drifts on the glass and cover the whole playground. The students much preferred the snow to the chilling cold of early winter when even the boys felt reluctant to leave their schoolhouse sanctuary.

"When will school be over, ma'am?" one of the girls asked as wood cracked in the stove, making some of the timid children jump in their seats.

"End of this month, Mary. Very likely."

"Well, I for one am not anxious the teeniest bit." Mary looked quickly at the other girls for approval. Most consented readily, acknowledging their love of school. She glanced up at her teacher who sat at her desk, gazing through the east windows.

"Miss Baarman!" There was a hint of scolding in Mary's tone, and the preoccupied teacher turned abruptly, apologetic.

"I'm sorry. I'm worried about the boys getting dirty." Her response was an unsettled lie, but it convinced her audience.

"Don't worry about them, ma'am. They'll take care of themselves. I was sayin' that I'm not anxious for school to get out this year."

"Oh, really, why not?"

"Well, we really like to come to school, you see. 'Sides, we only got to work at home."

"Oh, and this isn't work I suppose?" she carried on the conversation, hardly attending.

"Ja, this is work, but it just ain't the same."

"Isn't."

"Just isn't the same." The girls worked on their tatting; some were busy with schoolwork, as the conversation idled on.

"You mean you enjoy schoolwork more than housework, Mary?"

"Yes'm." The girls chuckled at the ridiculous question and nodded to each other.

Nick Oldersma opened the door slowly, and peeked into the room. The girls turned quickly, feeling that it was too early for the boys to come in, and knowing that they never reentered of their own volition.

"Nick, come in. Is something wrong?"

"No, ma'am."

"Well, is there anything we can do for you?" Katharine continued to question the little boy whose blue and gray clothes, brown-visored hat, and wool mittens made him look like a miniature man.

"Not really, ma'am. It's just that, well, we were wonderin' if maybe you need some wood from out back."

The bin in the back was full, or at least full enough for the afternoon.

"No, Nick. I think we'll get along just fine on what we have." She looked quizzically at the serious little fellow, for the interruption was extremely unusual.

Nick swung the door shut behind him, happy, it appeared, to be leaving.

"Nick." She tried to stop him, then, but he was gone.

The girls continued their work, taking bites now and

then from the doughnuts that a few had brought for dinner.
Katharine walked to the window and watched Nick Oldersma race across the ground that had been slick as ice this
morning. He ran toward the boys who were playing some
schoolyard game, and as they saw him appear, they stopped
their competition and trooped around him. John Mulder
towered over the rest. It was apparent that Nick would
report to him. As the brown hat shook in a negative,
Mulder scratched his chin, brought two hands into the air
as if to say, "Who cares?" and waved the boys back to
their game.

Mary Boersma watched her teacher turn away from the
window, stop for a moment, and then gaze into the air as if
she saw something miles away. Katharine Baarman
walked slowly back to her desk as the girls continued their
chatter.

Not long after, the boys came in together. Once more
the door opened, this time quickly, as all twelve rushed in.
They hadn't been called, but this time there was no way to
ignore their obvious motivation.

"Now that's a storm, ma'am!" Henry was adamant.

"The wind is really strong."

"We're gonna get a ton, sure."

"This here's a real bad one."

A volley of high-pitched voices brought emotion into
the room. Behind them, snow flew through the doorway
thick and heavy as sawdust. The girls jumped to their feet
and ran to the windows, blurting out bluejay warnings
and little shrieks of excitement. They looked into the
shroud of snow that seemed to overwhelm the frontier
schoolhouse, swallowing it in a cloud of gray. And yet it
was thrilling; the little children jumped and hurrahed at the
advent of the storm. Only Katharine sensed that their very
lives were subject to this late winter storm and to the God
who controlled it. Eyes fully opened now, hands on the
shoulders of a little child, she silently breathed a prayer for
the Lord's care, knowing that twenty young lives were
dependent on her wisdom and strength.

"Should we go home, Miss Baarman?"

She smiled as calmly as she could and messed the fine, blond hair of Nick Oldersma.

"Let me go outside for a minute. We'll see."

The children continued to celebrate the storm, running, shouting, holding hands, and dancing about as if it were the last day of the school year. Through the middle of the room she walked, passing each row. John Mulder sat in his chair at the back, looking intently at his teacher. She passed his seat. They said nothing.

There was nothing she could do and she knew it. When she got to the door, she opened it quickly and stepped out into the full violence of the blizzard. She could hardly see the outline of the shack or the pump. Big heavy snowflakes stung her skin with their force. Now out of earshot of her excited students, she spoke from deep within, "Help me, my Lord."

Already blanketed with a thick, wet layer of snow, she stepped back into the room. Dirk looked up into her troubled blue eyes. Her face and hair were outlined by a layer of melting snow that left big drops on her cheeks.

"Well, let's go on with school," she said, moving resolutely to the front of the room. Only she felt the hollowness of her confidence.

"Are we going home?" Nick asked again, obviously worried.

"No, I don't think that this will last too long. In an hour it will probably be all over. Then we can dismiss at the regular time."

The children plodded grudgingly toward their seats, groaning aloud and muttering little inaudible complaints. Haltingly, the afternoon session began. Miss Baarman suddenly realized how dark it was, and asked John Mulder to light the lanterns and a few candles. He was, all at once, very considerate and efficient; he made none of his usual comments, nor did he even attempt to get the attention of the class.

Just as Miss Baarman concluded the Bible story, John

Mulder finished his task. It was then that Katharine saw the nearly empty bin at the back of the room and linked it with Nick Oldersma's mysterious noonhour appearance. She asked John to come to the front of the room again, then turned to three other older boys, while holding John's arm.

"This morning," she said, "it was obvious that you three didn't know your lessons in multiplication."

All eyes were directed toward their teacher. This was a change from her usual manner, a significant departure from the ritualized school day.

"So, this afternoon I'm going to ask you to do something to practice. Each of you three, with John, who knew his lesson, will go to the woodpile and get several logs. Then, when you return, John will count the stack while you put a multiplication problem on the board to explain to us what the correct total should be. . . ."

The boys stood and left their rows, prancing like show horses. They wrestled on their jackets and caps and were gone. John warned them not to wander away from the side of the building in the blinding snow; then he led them to the spot where the cut wood was piled.

Meanwhile, penmanship and spelling had begun inside, and once more departing from the routine, Katharine wrote new words on the board, rather than taking them from their books. "Snow," "drift," "storm," "flake," for the younger children, "moisture," "crystallize," even "precipitate," for the older children.

Outside, the wind continued to roar and the snow seemed almost to pound against the windows. If the room had been brighter, they could have seen the snow that was pushed by the wind into the roof. It was melting now and falling in little drops to the floor or onto the heads, shoulders, or arms of the pupils.

Only a short time had passed before the boys returned, arms loaded with logs.

"Henry, come up front and write it out."

"Yes'm."

Henry peeled his coat off as if it were burning and marched to the front of the room.

"We took—"

"Brought."

"Um, we *brought* in twelve logs, ma'am."

"Write that on the board." He wrote "12". "Now tell us how you came to that conclusion, Henry, or better yet, show us."

"We took in—"

"Brought in."

"We brought in four logs each, ma'am." He turned to the board again, chalk in hand, and wrote "3x4" leading up to the "12" that he had already put there. He turned in triumph and faced the class.

"Very good. Now, John, you count them."

The class was quiet. Henry stood at the front of the room, rocking confidently from his toes to his heels.

"There's 17, Miss Baarman."

"How did that happen, Henry?"

He shoved his hands into his overall pockets, and his forehead dropped as he looked down at the floor.

"Dirk? Peter?"

His friends were equally speechless.

"I brought in five, ma'am." John broke the silence.

"Very well then, boys, your punishment is to go back and do it again." She spoke through a howl of derision from the other children.

Henry bounded back to the rear of the classroom and slapped on his cap again. Peter and Dirk were already dressing when he got there. Even John smiled momentarily at their antics, while casting an eye on the teacher. But she didn't see him, and she wasn't laughing. In a moment she was back behind her desk, looking busily through her books.

A half hour later the little bin at the rear of the room was standing in the melted snow of more than thirty new logs. Not only was the box full, but on both sides straight piles of logs were neatly stacked. The class was quiet and unusually interested in what was going on. The older children knew the readers nearly by heart, having read from them for several years. Nonetheless, even they appeared interested in "The Battle of Waterloo" and the old favorite, "Prisoner of Debt," as read and recited by their classmates. Katharine felt their close attention and used it to advantage, going beyond the normal time allotted to the subject as long as the interest remained high.

She called on Dirk, whom most respected as the best reader in school; she had him read "Regulus Before the Carthaginians," a favorite of his. Henry turned in his chair and looked back at John, as Dirk moved to the front of the room.

"The marble," he urged in a whisper.

"What?" John looked puzzled.

"The marble," he repeated, forming the sounds with his lips.

"Oh, yeah." John shut the book he had been reading, and looked toward the front of the room. He sat up in his chair as Dirk began to speak, spotted the big marble in the crack of the stove, and then looked back at his teacher. Thick strands of brown hair dropped loosely on her neck, framing the smile that had spread across her face as she listened to the little orator. The marble was certainly hot by now. As the temperature had dropped that morning, more and more wood had been fed into the stove. Miss Baarman looked almost childlike, resting her chin between her hands as she listened to the recitation.

"John!"

He looked back at Henry.

"John, are you gonna do it?" Henry's head dropped quickly as his shoulders heaved upward, and he brought a hand to his mouth to cover a convulsive laugh, anticipating John's trick.

"Ja," he said, "of course I'll do it!"

The class broke into applause as Dirk finished his oration. There was even a whistle or two left unreprimanded by the teacher. Dirk bounded back to his seat, still elevated by the emotion of the speech he had delivered.

"John, do you have anything for us?"

Outside, the daylight had almost disappeared behind the mantle of darkness; only scattered lamps lit the interior of the room, sending shadows dancing on the walls and over the students. But John could still see every student in the room and feel the anticipation in their eyes.

"Ja," he said finally. "I have one to read."

Well-worn chairs squeaked as they turned again towards the front, each student now doubly interested in what would happen, for while they enjoyed John's deep, manly voice, they also remembered the marble.

He turned abruptly when he got to the front of the room, opened the book he was holding to the story he had chosen, and looked out over his audience. He had their full attention.

"Go on, John," Katharine prompted.

He looked back at her quickly, and saw the smile lighting her thin, youthful face, but her eyes looked deeply into his in the few seconds they shared. He fumbled through the book once more.

" 'General Putnam,' " he stammered, " 'General Putnam' is the story I will read."

A satisfied murmur moved from table to table as the students recognized the selection.

"There once lived in Connecticut. . ." he began, and as he continued, his low voice rolled evenly through the story of Israel Putnam and the wolf in the cave.

" 'The wolf was very angry,' " he read. " 'She growled in a way that would have frightened most men. But Putnam was not afraid.' " The children moved comfortably in their seats at his assurance. They smiled appreciatively at each other, then refocused their attention on John Mulder and General Putnam.

John fell deeply into the story. After he had read about the Indians tying Putnam to the stake and piling dry sticks around him, he read " 'But Putnam did not show any signs of fear' " with conviction, with a kind of majesty almost, as if he were the General himself. The students sat numb as he read the last line: " 'In a few minutes both he and his men were out of danger.' " They all leaned back in their chairs and let out a relieved sigh; then they applauded.

John looked just like Dirk as he came from the front of the room. His head was high, his shoulders back squarely, as he soaked in the admiration of the other pupils. When he was passing the stove, he pulled out a bookmark from his reader, and with his left hand, dropped it on the bricks around the stove, his back to the teacher. Then he took his seat.

The readings continued, for Katharine felt the enthusiasm of the students still hadn't waned. One of the younger girls was next, and when she had completed her recitation, there was a cry for the teacher to read.

"Miss Baarman, how about you?"

She realized that as long as the storm raged outside their plastered walls, keeping the children calm was her greatest concern. If Mary or Nick or little Edgar came to understand their danger, the children might panic and become hysterical. So she rose and selected a book from the shelf behind her, as if she had prepared for the request.

"I thought it might be fun today to read 'Snowbound' again."

From all corners of the room a chorus of young voices gave eager assent.

"I know we read it about a month ago, but with the snow falling so beautifully outside our windows right now, I just thought we might enjoy the poem again."

"Read it, Miss Baarman."

"Yes, read it!"

"Goody."

If any were not interested in hearing the poem again, they said nothing. Teacher wasn't always willing to read to them.

"Very well then." She began slowly, repeating the familiar words with precise control and tempered enthusiasm. Dirk especially loved this poem; he sat forward in his chair, crossing his arms on the table, resting his head on his wrist. His eyes were alive with the excitement of the storm in the poem, for he sensed a oneness with Whittier's portrait, as all around him the swirling winds whipped across the Iowa prairie. And yet it was only his imagination that visualized those favorite lines:

> The gray day darkened into night,
> A night made hoary with swarm
> And whirl-dance of the blinding storm,

for he never paused to look out the window, and neither did anyone else. Whittier's words and the teacher's reading wove a spell for vivid imaginations.

All, of course, were not equally enchanted. Henry enjoyed the poem, but he was still plagued by the matter of the marble. Half facing the front, half listening to the teacher, he would frequently jerk his head to the rear to stay in touch with John Mulder's actions, watching closely for any hint of movement toward the stove. John knew that he was being watched, and he understood that what was expected of him would certainly make his teacher's job more difficult. He watched her pour herself into her reading as he felt the rage of the storm outside. She read so fluently and intensely that one might think she had composed the lines herself.

John raised his hand to his face and covered his eyes for a moment, then dropped his hand a bit and chewed at the cotton sleeve of his shirt. He rested his forehead in his hand, closed his eyes again and listened to the reading and the background from outside the school walls.

> Shut in from all the world without,
> We sat the clean-winged hearth about,
> Content to let the north wind roar
> In baffled rage at pane and door.
> While the red logs before us beat
> The frost-line back with tropic heat.

The long poem continued. He saw the children dreaming as they watched her and listened to each syllable. His mind raced to the end of the poem, to the line, "a week had passed," and he felt, for a moment, the anticlimactic reaction as the poem would end and the children would return to the reality of the blizzard. As he felt them fall, he realized her plan and knew that it had worked to perfection. They were soaring through their own imaginations, up so high that all the world was with them. But he realized that their flight was in danger. Something was needed to keep them from a disastrous fall. He had, he realized, only a few minutes to plan his aid—something to keep them from seeing beyond the schoolhouse windows.

"After the poem, Baker." He kicked the younger classmate with the point of his shoe as he spoke, and the little idolator broke immediately into a barely stifled laugh.

On the teacher read, taking the youthful minds with her.

And melt not in an acid sect

The Christian pearl of charity!

That was his cue. He grunted like a pig as he raised his hand to get her attention.

"So days went on: a week had—"

Her head jerked upward as she was jarred out of the poem. Her eyes stabbed into John's.

"What do you want?"

"Miss Baarman." The whole class turned in their chairs. His voice was cocked with politeness and mock respect.

"I dropped my bookmark by the stove. May I retrieve it, please?"

Her face burned with anger at the clever rudeness of the interruption. She wanted to say, "No, wait till I've finished!" but she heard herself saying, "Yes, and hurry, please!" She reopened the book and scanned the lines to find her place. Most of the class turned with her, eagerly awaiting the end of the poem, but others, less mesmerized by her reading, became suddenly aware of another drama unfolding.

As she resumed reading John rose quietly from his seat and stepped swiftly to the bricks around the stove. As he approached, he drew out the handkerchief he carried in his rear pocket. Kneeling down near the red-hot stove, he picked up the bookmark with his left hand, raised the handkerchief to his nose with his right, closed both nostrils with his fingers and pushed air between his lip and teeth, creating a strange rumbling whirr that only faintly resembled nose-blowing. Some children giggled impulsively, while others heard only the words of the end of Whittier's "Snowbound." Removing the handkerchief from his nose, he snatched up the hot marble with the cloth, and exaggerated a tiptoe back to his chair.

Henry had seen everything. As John passed him, he raised his left forefinger to his lips to warn Baker to control his stubborn laughter. John sat back in his seat, holding the marble gingerly in the cloth, waiting for the last few lines. If she were to hear it, he would have to roll it forward while she was still reading.

> Sit with me by the homestead hearth,
> And stretch the hands of memory forth
> To warm them at the wood-fire's blaze!

That was the end, he remembered it well, having heard it at least once every school year. He quickly peeled back the cloth from the marble, feeling its intense heat through several layers of handkerchief. Leaning alongside his table, he rolled the marble straight up the center aisle.

It was no small marble. And as it rolled innocently across the hardwood floor, it produced a resonant hum that drew confused stares from students on both sides. It wasn't far to the front of the room, but to John Mulder it seemed that a week had passed before the hot marble struck like a stone against the baseboard at the front of the room just as Miss Baarman completed the poem.

She glanced momentarily at the marble as she closed the book, then faced the class with a benedictory smile. It broke quickly, however, as she looked into the faces that were tense with anticipation. Her eyes narrowed as she searched from face to face in an effort to locate the reason for their reaction, and, without any thought of a possible relationship, she moved unhesitatingly to pick up the marble that had stopped, finally, perhaps a foot back from the wall. Then she reached out for the marble. As if connected like puppets to her every movement, the students pushed themselves up on the tables before them to get a better look.

She couldn't have held the marble for more than a fraction of a second; in fact, Henry said later that he thought she had never even picked it up. Almost everyone else disagreed, for they were sure that they had heard it bang off the wooden floor when she dropped it. Whatever did happen, it was a severe shock to a teacher who was convinced that if they were to survive the storm, she, at least, would have to keep her wits about her.

She shrieked and flapped her hand above her head, making her limp fingers fly as if to shake off the burn. Then she jammed her thumb and forefinger into her mouth and closed her eyes—all of this without raising herself from her haunches. There was no laughter, only a horrified silence. Even Henry couldn't smile when it was done. He cowered in the face of her anguished question.

"Why? Why *now?*"

No one dared move. Their teacher's obvious pain sickened all of them.

"I'm just trying . . . trying . . . I'm . . ." She knew that she must say no more or she would be leaving herself defenseless. Instead, she realized her only hope for maintaining control of herself and the situation was discipline and punishment.

"John Mulder, you stand up!"

John Mulder rose to his feet slowly, playing his usual role with an odd reluctance and a sadness that was entirely new to him.

No one had ever seen her like this before. Her hands shook with anger. She put them on her hips, attempting to control her fury.

"John." Her voice was controlled, but there was nothing in her demeanor to suggest that she was as calm as she wanted to appear. "John Mulder, I have no proof that you did this. It could have been anyone, I presume." Her voice was pitched high, but she spoke very slowly.

"I have no reason, really, to pick you out from all the others, but something tells me that it was you. And for that reason," she paused, swallowed, and continued, "for that reason, I'm going to tell you what I think of this."

She moved back behind her desk, deliberately, it seemed, to allow some time to pass. She knew she must try to divorce her emotion from her punishment. She placed both hands on the desk in front of her and raised her eyes to John Mulder who stood at the back of the room.

"John, someday when you get older, I hope that you will feel what I feel right now. Oh, not the burns on these fingers—they will heal, but the hurt that you've given me here." She pointed to her heart. As she spoke, she gathered her strength in steady breaths of air; the pain itself seemed to clear her head.

"Someday when you want to explain something you love to your children, when you want them to share something that you enjoy, when you do something special to make them enjoy themselves, and they despise it and reject you, just think about that marble," she pointed to the floor, "and remember me, too."

The class was petrified by the confrontation. No one moved. No shoes tapped the floor or scraped against others' chairs. Only the wind moaned and howled through the square schoolhouse, slapping heavy snow against windows that were already opaque.

"Remember me, because once when I tried to be . . ." she hesitated, "to be good, to be strong, to be . . . to be of help, you hurt me. You hurt me very badly."

Outside, the storm had grown into a massive attack. John Mulder stubbornly fought the tears that threatened his facade of rebellion. He accepted her anger and suffered for his act. He could not have guessed that she would be hurt so deeply. But the children were bound by the emotion, and in the midst of his anguish he was strengthened by the success of his own heartless act.

"Well, John, do you have anything to say?"

He raised a hand to his head, combed through his hair with his fingers, and looked down at the floor. It must continue.

"No, ma'am," he said, and sat down.

Still there was no movement, and again the sound of the storm broke into the silence. Katharine jerked up quickly, as if she had been slapped, and glanced at the windows to the west.

"We must go on," she said.

No one really asked about the end of the school day. The children seemed to sense that going home was to be determined not by the clock, but by the storm itself. She had done her best to keep their minds off the storm, working and laughing, smiling and helping in a way she never would or could have done otherwise. She knew that her strength was not her own. She had, for instance, collected some snowflakes on a frozen log, brought them inside, the door almost tearing from her grasp, and showed them to the little children with the help of a pocket magnifying glass. They were enchanted by the beautiful designs and struck by her analogy of the beauty of God's love for each of them. Then, she had them spell "s-n-o-w-f-l-a-k-e" correctly before they were permitted to leave the cold corner of the schoolhouse and return to the circle of heat around the stove.

By late afternoon, most of the children huddled close to the stove. The porous walls of the schoolhouse admitted far too many icy drafts, which, in turn, defied the radiant heat of the old black stove, making its effects imperceptible beyond fifteen feet. The cold increased the foot-tapping and led, eventually, to the end of the formal school day, for when coupled with squeaking chairs and tables, the noise within the room almost obliterated the sounds of the blizzard. Katharine knew that something would have to change.

As the lanterns seemed to grow stronger in the failing light of day, she drew the children in a circle about the stove and had them begin singing. Not just the old standard Psalms and hymns, but she let them sing away on any song they desired, some American songs, some old Dutch favorites. When interest began to diminish, she started them on the Christmas carols. The carols filled another half hour.

"Miss Baarman, I'm hungry."

It was not the first request for whatever was left of their noon dinners, and she knew it wouldn't be the last.

"Let's just see if we can wait awhile yet, Edgar. It's not quite time for supper."

It was another lie, of course, but she knew that the little food left had to stay outside of young stomachs until at least tomorrow morning.

When voices trailed away into hoarseness, and all interest in singing was gone, she felled her last tree. She asked the boys to gather all the chairs and stack them together at the back of the room. Ever since the marble incident all her requests had been honored in a moment. And among the most ready responders was John Mulder. He took four chairs himself now, while directing the younger lads in the placement of theirs. He still didn't smile; he was, at most, restrained.

"Now listen very closely," she said, gathering them around her once again. "I'm going to let you do something very naughty for a while, but I want to be sure to explain it first." She spoke with a bright smile to the little faces. They glanced almost guiltily at each other, smiling and smirking in anticipation.

"You may arrange the tables any way you like and play games inside the schoolhouse. But please be careful that no one gets hurt or nothing gets broken."

Whoops of happy laughter echoed through the room, and, almost without thinking, most of the students turned to John Mulder for leadership. He was caught off guard for a second, but realized quickly that she had actually given him leadership and responsibility, this time consciously and willfully. He responded by laying down the rules and giving instructions.

First they arranged the old tables like a big grass snake meandering in a circular pattern throughout the room. At the end of the line, they laid their coats like a big pillow on the hardwood floor. Each child ran as fast as he could down the crooked runway and jumped like a diver into the cushion of coats at the end. Only John himself and a few of the younger girls did not participate. John stayed at the end of the line, fluffing up the coats when they got matted and nursing a sore knee or skinned hand when a child needed that attention.

Then it was "leap frog" over the desks, and an improvised kind of "tag," and a restricted variation of "pom-pom-pullaway." In two hours the windows were thoroughly steamed from the strenuous activity, and, one by one, as the younger children began to tire, they walked slowly over to their teacher's side. But the games continued. Nick Oldersma fell on the floor and was kicked, accidentally, by Dirk. A trickle of blood fell from a thickening lower lip, and when John's admonition to be a man didn't seem to help, he brought the wounded one to Katharine who was sitting in the midst of three or four children.

"Nick's hurt, Miss Baarman," he said.

She looked at him and smiled. John turned quickly, then returned to the other children. In a few minutes, Nick Oldersma was giggling at his classmates' antics, the comforting arm of his teacher draped lightly over his shoulders.

Things went very well for Katharine Baarman. One by one the children tired, took a seat by her side, or sat quietly, watching the play of the others. Soon all were exhausted, and John himself turned the tables on edge and made a circle around the old stove, a trick he learned, he said, from some prairie birds. The coats were laid on the floor in the circle, and in a short time, little Edgar and several others were off to sleep, far away from the schoolhouse and the blizzard.

Katharine sat with her back against one of the tables, resting comfortably now, with only the older children still awake. The worst of her job, for tonight anyway, was over. The youngest children, those who would have felt most fear at being away from their own families and homes, were already fast asleep. They lay on her lap, propped against her side, leaning against her breast, all asleep in the warmth of the inner circle.

It was probably an hour or two more before the rest were sleeping. They had all told some of their favorite stories—of Indians, of the big ships, of the old country—then, slowly, they too began to drop off to sleep to the sound of the wind. Katharine looked over the twenty children lying peacefully before her, all bundled together like cattle in the fields, sharing each other's warmth. Her own eyes, weary with the burdens she had carried for too many hours, grew heavy and misty. Her back against a table, she fell asleep, the blizzard gales howling like wolves outside the square schoolhouse.

There was a sound, or at least she remembered telling herself she heard one, half asleep in what must have been the middle of the night. Her mind focused drowsily for a moment, and she knew that she heard someone or something walking slowly over the wooden floor. Looking quickly about, she felt her heart thudding in her chest as she numbered the children hurriedly. The footsteps halted. She looked up at a figure encased in ice and snow. It was John Mulder. His head was covered by his hat and a scarf was wound about his neck. In his arms were a dozen snow-covered logs.

"Had to go, ma'am," he whispered faintly. "Thought I'd get us some logs once too."

She made no reply as he laid the logs quietly on the floor, took off his hat and scarf, and, after putting several more dry logs in the stove, lay back in the place he had been earlier. The stove cracked and snapped and pushed out more heat into the little circle.

"John, thank you," she whispered.

"Don't mention it," he said, turning over on his shoulder.

There was no dawn the next morning. The darkness of the night carried on a slow but futile struggle with the light, until, at last, the lanterns faded in the face of a gray morning. Katharine awoke first, having never really slept soundly. Even her dreams were plagued by half-formulated plans of what should be done the next day.

The immediate problem, she knew, would be a decision about the food: should she allow them to eat what remained of their lunches, or should she try again to have them put it off until at least the afternoon? The key to the decision rested in the weather, of course, for if the storm gave no promise of breaking, then it was imperative that she hoard the little food that still remained. The windows were of no help in her dilemma, however, since they were thickly coated on both sides.

She saw a movement where John was lying.

"John," she said, still trying to be as quiet as possible.

"Yes?" It was obvious from his quick response that he hadn't been awakened by her questioning.

"Would you do me a favor, please?"

"Ja."

"Go outside and check the weather. But bundle up well."

"Ja."

He rose without further comment, pulled his cap down as far as he could over his ears, wrapped his knit scarf about his neck, and walked softly toward the door. The wind burst through the doorway, bringing in a sheet of snow. She was sure that she could guess his report.

"I don't know, ma'am," he said a minute later as he stood before her. "It's still snowing hard, but not as hard as yesterday, or last night even."

"Do you think it's letting up?"

"I don't know, ma'am. I'm just a kid, you know. But I

think it is."

"Goed zo," she mumbled to herself unconsciously, then looked up to see a reserved smile part his lips. He sat back where he had slept the night before, pulled his jacket over Nick Oldersma, and lay back, closing his eyes again.

In an hour all the children were awake and devouring what food remained. Those who had extra shared with those who had none—after they were prompted by their teacher. The chairs were set back behind the rearranged tables, and, as if nothing at all had happened, another school day began with a morning prayer. She had no trouble this morning; she thanked God for their protection, asked Him to bless each of their families and their cattle, and asked forgiveness for their sins. John opened his eyes—he saw her warm and bright and happy, standing over twenty peaceful children.

Just as the little children were finishing their math, the door opened suddenly and two frosted men stumbled into the schoolhouse. They were white from head to foot, and even their hats were heavy with snow that fell to the floor in chunks as they stomped their feet and clapped their mittens together.

"Miss Baarman," one said, taking off his wet cap and overcoat, "we've brought some food."

Katharine Baarman ran over to Edgar, picked him up from his chair, and hugged him as if he were her own child.

The children looked amazed at the sudden and strange entrance, and seemed equally surprised at their teacher's response. They recognized the men shortly, as Mary Boersma tumbled into her father's arms, and after following their teacher's instructions and example, they crowded around to share in the food.

Miss Baarman sat back in her own chair for a moment, relieved and thankful to see them eating and joking with each other. Then she circled about the room, and saw John Mulder sitting at his table in the back of the room, eating a huge ham sandwich. He looked at her, then at the festive scene in the middle of the room where the men were handing out apples and cookies.

She stopped.

"I'm sorry," he said quietly.

She smiled, broadly now. A great burden was taken from her.

"Thank you, John, for your help," she said, and continued walking toward the intruders.

The Mocker

To be perfectly honest, Egbert Kok didn't like the idea at all. Even though he was the appointed spokesman, he had no more desire to speak to Aartje Korsman than he had to clean out his hog yard. And while he recognized that the full authority of the church—and the authority of the village—was now vested in him, it didn't help to firm his resolve. His bony fingers shook so badly that he could barely form a fist to knock on her door. And when he did knock, finally, his knuckles hurt so much he had to shake out the sting. With a wiry smile, Aartje let him right in, and set him down on a wicker chair in her front room. But he was most uncomfortable.

"And your nephew, Dirck?" he asked meekly. Aartje's dog flashed pointed incisors his way.

"Ja, fine, Egbert." She sat straight and proud in the high-backed rocker near the stove. A roll of wrinkly flesh curled over the starched collar of her dress and formed a base for her spherical head, giving her the appearance of a sculpture. Kok thought she resembled the dominie's bust of Kuyper, the one that stood on his desk. But beneath those shoulders was a huge body, covered by a black dress as big as a Civil War tent. She filled her favorite chair so completely, only the two points of the pressback were visible.

"He is a tall boy already," Kok continued, peeking up over the top of his rimless spectacles, blinking timidly.

"Ja, he grows fast now." She rocked very slowly, trying to calm her leering dog.

"And your daughter's family, in Platte?"

"Ja, I see them not so often anymore, but she has four little ones already." Her Dutch face was broadened by cheeks as round and red as apples.

"Four?" he acted surprised.

"Ja, little Eduard come last summer. I took the train to see him."

"The Lord blesses her and her husband, surely."

"All healthy, Egbert."

Kok pursed his lips and nodded a slow assent. His fingers combed through his curly beard. A prickly silence grew between them like a summer thistle.

He moved his lean backside across the wicker seat, and the chair squeaked. "Ja, Aartje, we must be careful eh? *Je moet nooit over een andermans kinderen praten totdat je je eige schapen op't droge hebt.*"

"Ja, it is hard to raise the children today," she said, muffling a little amusement.

Egbert thought he had found the opening, so he chugged along. "Ja, that is true. In our day things were not like this. The children, they understood what was right, what was wrong. And the church was strong then, Aartje, when you and I were children." He readjusted himself again as he spoke, preparing himself for the attack; one of his sharp elbows dropped awkwardly off the arm of the chair. But he continued, gesturing like the dominie with his left hand, always shifting about on the chair.

"But today is different. Today the children want this, want that—they want to forget Law, the Commandments." He raised both hands, palms uplifted, as if awaiting a blessing. "They don't even want to go to church always on Sunday!"

"I tell my daughter this, too." She continued her even rocking. "In the old days there was more respect, ja? The children never questioned my Frederic."

"Ah, your husband, Aartje, that was a good man."

"His soul is with the Lord, I am certain."

Kok stopped momentarily. He pulled his ragged beard to a point. He knew he had missed his first opportunity.

"Ja, ja, ja," he blurted out as an obligatory afterthought,

"Frederic was a good man. The promises of our Lord are coming to him for sure." He kept moving, inspecting his knuckles. "Did you ever think, Aartje, about what he must see now? All the glory of heaven—all the questions we must wrestle with here below answered clearly for him. It must be glorious, ja?"

She stopped for a moment; her left hand moved over the fern table to the left of her chair and rested on the big *Staten Bijbel* that lay there. "Someday I will see him again."

"Surely, surely."

Then there was silence, profound silence—only the clunky ticking of the big wall clock she had brought from Holland.

And so it continued—Aartje Korsman moving slowly, the big chair rocking back and forth, back and forth beneath her, groaning musically, and Egbert Kok, blinking constantly, the wicker chair crackling like an open fire as he tried in vain to make himself comfortable. The dog grumbled now and then to further punctuate the silence.

It was Kok, finally, who spoke again under the compulsion of duty.

"There is good weather this summer."

"Ja."

"The farm is green and full of life. We have good water, and the sun shines warm on the corn."

"Ja." She nodded. No hint of a smile appeared between her bulky jowls.

"We will have a good harvest, too, the Lord willing. He has blessed us here in Iowa, ja?"

"Ja, He has, Egbert."

Kok took his hat off the table where he had set it when he entered, and flattened the brim between his thumb and forefinger, his eyes following the motions of his hands. Aartje Korsman kept rocking.

Then she stopped, rapped her cane lightly on the floor, and looked at her guest.

"What brings you here, Egbert?" She looked directly at

the little man, her eyes consuming whatever courage he thought he had gathered.

He coughed twice, three times.

"Wablief?"

"I say, why do you come this night to my house?"

"Oh, why do I come here?" He looked back, his face tightened by a hollow smile.

"Ja?"

"Well, . . ." he coughed again, covering his mouth with his hand, "I must come here to . . ."

"Ja, speak up . . ."

"I must come here . . . ah, from the church, *Vrouw* Korsman." His pleasantries died quickly. He tried to muster a Jeremiah by sitting straight in the chair and staring back at his hostess. She started rocking slightly faster.

"But, *mijn man*, I come to church every Sunday."

"Ja, Aartje," he raised his left hand and pointed a bony index finger in the air, "we know that you come faithfully to the church. That we are happy for." He slid himself around once again, and leaned forward, pushing his glasses up from the tip of his nose. "But we are not so happy about this business, Aartje."

"My business? What is wrong here?"

"It is the liquor, woman." He sat back then, silent.

"The liquor?" She sat forward, and the chair creaked to a sudden halt.

"Ja, the liquor. It is a mocker; it leads our people to hell, woman!" His timidity faded as his mission began to materialize, strengthening his passion. But Aartje was no milksop.

"No one, Egbert Kok, no one drinks too much in my place! If you know one man, you tell me, and he will not return. No fathers spend their nights in my place. No wives ever come here to pull out their drunken husbands. Never!" Her cane thumped the wooden floor at every word.

"Ja, Aartje, we know . . ."

"If you know, then why do you come here?"

"We must purge our town of evil, woman, we must . . ."

"You call me 'evil woman,' Egbert?" The cane banged the floor again. Kok felt the vibrations under his feet.

"You know that I come to the church—every Lord's Day. I read my Bible every day, Kok, every day. You will not call me 'evil woman.'"

"It is not *you*, *Vrouw* Korsman," he said, pointing a trembling finger again, "not you, but your liquor. It is of the devil! It makes men sick and foolish. It keeps them from their families, their farms, their duties to God and their fellow man."

"Not in my place, you *heilig boontje*! Not in my place!"

"Woman, keep a civil tongue."

"No one gets drunk in my place. I will not allow it. And, what about your own farm, Egbert Kok? It could stand a little cleaning up, ja? You spend too much time yourself on the street—yah-tah-tah, yah-tah-tah—all day about the last days and crazy things!"

"Those things are not crazy, and my farm is no concern of yours." His skinny face scrunched up like a prune.

"Do not the Scriptures say that a little wine is good for the stomach? eh?" She dared him to contradict her.

"Aartje, even the devil can use the Scriptures . . ."

"So, you *fijne*, now you say I am the devil . . ."

"Listen," he stood suddenly, trying to assume command. The rocking chair whimpered as she quickened her pace. "I do not call you Satan, Aartje Korsman. I know you, I know your family, your husband. I am not foolish. I do not even like to be here. But I must say what I must say, and you must listen to the admonition of the Scriptures and of the church!"

He straightened his top coat, tugged at his tie, and sat back on the wicker chair as if he had forgotten what came next. She continued, rocking quickly and steadily, saying nothing, her lips pinched tight, her eyes smoldering with fury.

"Our young men become drunk often." He tried to start slowly and steadily now, his chin raised, his gray kinky beard pointing at the woman. "Some say that the boys even take our young women and drink—in the country, ja? And at night, in their wagons . . . why, the Lord Himself only knows what sins have already been committed because of the *zondige* liquor." Egbert gestured with both hands again. He was thoroughly aroused, his eyes blinking as if he were in a dust storm.

"Why, the young boys swear and fight, they say, right in the taverns. Then, when they are blinded by drink, they fall asleep in their wagons, and their horses carry them home, poor creatures of God. And it is the liquor to blame, Aartje, the liquor!" He threw his hat to the floor in a grand gesture of frustrated indignation.

The rocker was moving so quickly that it inched ever closer to Egbert Kok. Aartje's legs were spread wide beneath the full skirt, and her thick wrists pressed the arms of the chair. Her knuckles turned white, and her shoulders shook.

They stared at each other for what seemed weeks. Then Kok forged onward.

"Aartje Korsman, the good Christian people of this town send me here to tell you—either pay the new tax or we close the business. This we tell all the other tavern owners, too." He sat erect once more.

"The tax, the tax, the tax," she said. "It is not fair! That you know. My place is not a saloon; you and the Christian people know that! Let the saloons pay the new tax." Her huge arms flailed the air. "Run *them* from the town! But not me. I run a good business."

"I say what I must," Egbert squeaked.

"Then, I say what *I* must . . . you *huichelaar*. No one will stop my business. You and your 'good Christian people' can all go to the devil!" The dog leaped up, bristling and growling.

"*Vrouw* Korsman, I. . ."

"You hear what I say, Egbert Kok, you hear my answer. You come in here, to *my* house, about *my* business, wiggling and grunting like a dog in heat, telling me, a good

Christian widow, that I am the devil . . . you Pharisee, now I tell you . . ." Her cane cracked against the floor, and she stood, her hulking frame looming over Egbert Kok like a thunderous hailstorm.

"I tell you what, you get out my house . . . now! You get, this moment, or the Lord Himself restrain me, I will crack your empty head with this stick!" It was already raised like a cobra.

"Aartje, I have the church . . ." he tried to screech over the barking dog.

"You take the church, the good people, the town, you get out, *now!*" She took one step, another . . .

Egbert stooped to retrieve his hat from the floor, then ran like a frightened squirrel out the front door, screaming out fragments of Bible verses in a jumble of Dutch and English, Aartje's dog yelping at his heels.

"She is a stubborn woman, Johan," Egbert reported to Dominie Vander Byl and Constable Brink the next morning. They had gathered in the dominie's study to hear Kok's report.

"She won't pay, Egbert?"

"No, she won't pay, Dominie. She threatened to crack my head with her stick."

"Ach, what now!" Brink's frustration was apparent; he leaned forward on the chair, his elbows resting on his knees.

"We must be fair here, ja? *Vrouw* Korsman must be handled like the other owners. It is just." The dominie sat in a captain's chair at the head of the rectangular oak table, his lips puckering almost involuntarily.

"But, Dominie, she speaks the truth," Kok continued. "The stories we hear, the complaints, they come from the other taverns. She is right. None drink too much there. And there are no vile pictures on her walls."

"But when we tax the others for alcohol, we must tax her. She, too, sells whiskey, Egbert. It is the law."

Egbert Kok looked down at the table and traced its grain

with his finger. He had walked back home the night before—almost three miles to the farm. It had been quiet in the country, and after the first half hour, after the trembling had disappeared and his humiliation had passed, the whole situation came back to him again. By the time he had reached the farm, he was prepared to tell his wife that the men were wrong and Aartje was in the right.

"But I must close her down, Dominie?" Constable Brink was tired of the whole affair.

"Ja, she must be closed." The dominie's lips pursed.

"And then?"

"What do you mean, 'and then'?"

"Well, Dominie, what if she still don't pay her tax? She is bullheaded, you know."

The dominie sat motionless. He inhaled and exhaled as if to cleanse his lungs.

"Well, then, we must arrest her!" It was obviously the only decision.

"Arrest Aartje, Korsman?" croaked the constable, sliding up to the table.

"Arrest her?" echoed Egbert Kok.

"Ja, arrest her!" the dominie nodded.

"Put her in jail?"

"Ja, Constable. You must lock her in the jail."

"Oh, Dominie," he whined, "the people will not like this. They know Aartje is a good woman. Ach, they will think me a beast. She is a widow, you know, with only one daughter, in Platte. And I must put her in jail?" He seemed ready to cry. "Oh, Dominie . . ."

"Ja, Brink . . ."

"But, Dominie," Kok rose to the constable's defense, "what will the people say? They know she works like a man; she is kind and shows charity to strangers. My wife tells me *Vrouw* Korsman has given many free meals to the poor Americans, even to some of our own. What will the people say?"

The dominie never blinked.

"It is just. We have already closed two saloons; another

will close this month. We are doing the Lord's work, purging the village of the devil's charms. If Aartje's tavern is closed, we will be rid of the evil of liquor, the town will be clean, and the Lord will be pleased!" He brought his fist down lightly on the table and broke into a triumphant smile.

"Oh, Dominie, how can I arrest a widow-lady? How can I put a good woman in my jail? Why, my wife cleans it, and she yet thinks it is *vies.*"

"It must be done, Brink. It must be done."

The dominie's righteous chin jutted proudly.

Brink stared at the floor, rubbing his forehead.

Kok blinked as if wounded, then rose and stumbled out the door.

Constable Brink took his work very seriously, and that was not always easy. The next morning, when he and a quickly recruited deputy took the wagon to Aartje Korsman's inn, he couldn't decide whether to laugh at the decisions made for him, or cry at his peculiar fate, so he just winced painfully all morning long.

"But why the wagon, Constable?" the deputy asked, trying to pin on his badge as they bumped along the dirt path.

"The ways of the Lord are sometimes strange," Brink replied without turning to his comrade.

Deputy Verhage looked puzzled. "What has the Lord to do with this?"

"The dominie says we do the Lord's work, Jan." Brink held the reins loosely as the horse plodded along. "He says we must purify the village, get rid of the whiskey."

"The Lord?"

"No, the dominie."

"But why arrest Aartje Korsman? And why *me* here? And why the wagon? I still do not understand."

"She will not pay the tax; she refuses. Last night she threatened Elder Kok with her cane. We must arrest her this morning if she still refuses to pay."

"Ah, Brink . . . I don't know why you need me then. I have work to do." He spat tobacco juice into the dust of the street.

"Aartje Korsman is a big woman, ja?"

Jan Verhage broke into a fit of laughter; the seat of the wagon jiggled with his guffaws. "She is a big woman, man? What do you say? She will fight with two men? Ha! Come now, Johan, you have more sense than that."

Brink was silent and serious.

When he stopped chuckling, Verhage inhaled deeply, and leaned back, shaking his head.

"*Verdorie*, Brink, what will the people say about us? Two big men wrestle a woman to the ground and take her to the jail? And this woman—Aartje Korsman?"

The horse's hoofs clopped along the dry roadbed.

"Ach . . . ach, *gekheid!* Why could you not ask someone else for this business? The people will laugh about this for weeks!"

"Ja, Verhage, that is true," Brink mumbled, resigned to his fate.

There was little movement in town that morning. The constable had planned the arrest early so they would make no spectacle. When they turned the corner to Korsman's inn, both were relieved to see nothing moving on the street.

"Ach, Brink, though . . . now I know about the wagon." His laugh was sharpened by the sudden realization. "We will carry her to jail like an old cow! Throw her in the back here, eh? Ach, *dat gaat te ver.*"

Brink pulled on the reins gently, stopping the horse before the inn. Verhage jumped first from the rig.

"I don't like it, Johan. It is foolish and stupid," he said, spitting out the remnants of the chew.

Brink descended after him and walked to the door of the apartment, badgered all the way by his reluctant deputy.

"But what will people say," Verhage whispered, drawing near the door. "She is a good woman, you know that. And her husband—well-respected, God rest his soul. Now you tie her like a criminal and haul her off like crow-bait. *Ben je gek?*" He kept haggling the constable, like a sparrow teasing a hawk.

Johan Brink stopped as he reached the door. He turned like an angry father. "Verhage, *hou je mond!* This is no good for me either. I do not like it, you hear? But the law—it is the law, ja? All businesses that serve liquor must pay the tax. Aartje Korsman's inn serves liquor. Aartje Korsman must pay the tax, ja? It is fair, it is just. If she won't pay, her business must close and she goes to jail. It is that simple, ja? It is the law."

He turned sharply and knocked—once, twice, three times. A dog barked within. But there was no reply.

"She may be working at the inn?" he asked the deputy.

"No, Catharine Heebink is there now. She opens in the morning."

"You know?" he shot back.

"Ja, Brink . . . I, ah . . . I know . . . ja, that is what people say, eh?"

"Verhage! You go in her place, too?"

The deputy looked at his boots, removed his hat, smoothed back his hair, and put the hat back on his head. "Ja, I was there . . . what? Once, twice, not often," he looked away, "not often, no."

"Ach, Jan . . . I think, 'Jan Verhage, no, he would not enter the tavern, no'—so I ask you this morning. Now what must I do?" He raised his left hand to his head and scratched his temple. "Well, here we are. We must do what we must. It would be more stupid to leave now."

He rapped again, but still there was no answer.

Verhage pulled at Brink's coat. "She is gone, eh? We come back later."

"No, she is here, I think, but she will not come to the door."

Once more he rapped. Bang, bang, bang—with the heel of his fist—bang, bang, bang. Still there was no reply.

"How do you know, Brink? She is not an evil woman? She would not hide. Let's go!"

"Her dog is not barking, you *stommeling*. She must be in."

Brink was not to be defeated. He opened the door to the apartment, turned to his deputy, and waved him in. Then he walked through the open doorway. There sat Aartje Korsman, rocking steadily, holding the ugly, snarling dog in her lap. Brink was dumbstruck; Verhage peeked from behind his shoulder like a guilty child. They stood cramped in the open doorway.

"Close the door, *je bent niet in de kerk geboren.*"

Brink stepped into the house and pulled his deputy with him. He removed his hat and shut the door.

"Take off your hat, you *lompe boer,*" he commanded Verhage, slapping him across the chest with the back of his hand.

"Mrs. Korsman . . ."

"I know why you come," she said. "You must collect the tax, I know."

"Mrs. Korsman, we come—"

"Am I not right?"

"Mrs. Korsman—"

"Well, I will not pay. It is unjust, Johan Brink. You know that. My place is no saloon. Ja, you, Jan Verhage, you know. You drink yourself here."

Verhage looked down.

"Mrs. Korsman, we come here as representatives of the law—"

"The law! You mean the tax is a fair law—*verrek!*"

"Mrs. Korsman, we must do what we must. Now, will you pay your tax?" Brink straightened himself, desperately summoning all the authority he could muster.

"Brink, be you deaf?" She rocked slowly; her dog kept growling.

"Mrs. Korsman, you must pay your tax . . . or suffer the penalty."

"The penalty? What is this —'penalty'?"

"You must go to jail, and we must close your business."

She pulled her dog more tightly into her arms to quiet

him.

She squinted at him. "To jail?"

"Yes, Aartje, it is the law."

The dog laid his heavy head on her forearm, and rumbled as she scratched around his ear.

"And how long?"

"Thirty days."

"Thirty days?"

"Ja, thirty days."

She rocked slowly now, looking down at her dog. She leaned over and brushed her cheek across its head.

"Then I must."

"Aartje? You will pay?"

"If it is the law, it is the law. I will go to the jail, for I will not pay the tax."

"Ach, Mrs. Korsman—" the deputy interrupted.

"Be quiet, Verhage," Brink snapped. "Let me speak. Now, Mrs. Korsman, we don't want to put you in jail—"

"And I don't want to go."

"But we must be just. The dominie says we have already thrown two saloons out, and now we must be just with you."

"Dominie Vander Byl says so?"

"Ja, Dominie Vander Byl says so."

"Dominie Vander Byl is right then; I will pay my fine by going to jail. He is the dominie."

Verhage pulled at the constable's jacket again. "Brink, this is—"

"Jan, be still!"

Aartje Korsman was obviously stunned by what would happen, but she was firm. She sat very still on her rocker; her dog licked her hand.

"But Johan, I cannot go without my dog."

"Ach, Aartje, we cannot take care of a dog in the jail."

"I cannot go without him. Who will care for him?"

"No. We will not have such an animal."

"Please, Johan?"

"We cannot have the dog."

"Very well then, you must carry me to jail."

"Oh, Aartje, you . . ."

"The dog must go too."

"But you must live with it. What will we do if the dog must . . ." he searched for the proper words.

"Why, you must let him out."

"Let him out? We cannot open your door . . ."

"You *idioot!* You think I will escape? Ach, Johan Brink, you are dumb." No one spoke for a moment. "Well," she said, leaning back in her rocker, "I will sit here and you can tie me . . ."

"Ja, ja, ja," he consented, "the dog comes, too."

"And my Bible, Constable?"

"And your Bible."

"Must I go now?"

"Ja, Aartje, we go now."

"Then I must get things ready. Catharine will take care of this place."

She put the dog on the floor, rose slowly from the chair, and plodded out of the room, her massive body swaying like a huge black bell.

"We will wait."

"Thank the Lord, she will not fight, Brink. What would we do?"

Brink was equally relieved. He laughed for the first time that morning. "Ja, that would not be easy."

"But what about the dog. What if he . . . messes the floor? Ha! Brink, will you clean it?" Verhage slapped the constable's shoulder playfully.

"Ach, the dog is trained, ja? Don't be so foolish."

When she returned, her hair was pulled neatly into a bun at the back of her head and her woolen shawl draped loosely about her shoulders. She had washed, and she looked ready for church.

"Brink," she spoke from the hallway to her kitchen, "what will I sleep on?"

"Why, on the bed."

"What bed?"

"The bed in the jail."

"You have a good bed?"

"Ah, it is—"

"Very well then, my bed goes too."

"Aartje, please!"

"I will not sleep on wood, Johan. Here, you and Verhage take the bed."

"Aartje . . ."

"Brink," Verhage grimaced as he whispered, "she will not fit."

"Ja, ja, ja, ja, we take the bed, Aartje."

Not long after, Constable Brink and Special Deputy Jan Verhage sat meekly on the seat of the wagon, their eyes focused straight down the road as if they expected imminent danger. Behind them in the wagon, Aartje Korsman sat like a queen on her own huge brass bed. The dog looked scared even though it sat in her lap, and her right hand kept her Bible from bouncing off the rig.

By the time they arrived at the jail, they had developed into something like a parade. Many villagers noted their passage. Little children ran along behind, laughing and joking.

"Every night the people complain to me, Dominie. She is a woman, a widow. And we keep her in the jail like a thief or murderer. Women call me *"rotzak"*; men laugh at me when I walk on the street. They yell, 'Brink, *hoe gaat het met je, dikzak?*' "

Constable Brink looked beaten as he slouched in his chair. Egbert Kok just shook his head, blinking often, the tip of his beard curling out from his chest as he stared at the floor.

"They are not happy the saloons are gone then?" the dominie asked.

"Ach, ja, of course. But Aartje is no saloon-keeper. They know that. She never had tables, or gaming, and no filthy pictures. This they know!"

The dominie puffed away on his cigar, sending billowing

clouds into the motionless air of the study.

"She has been there how long?"

"Fifteen days."

"Then she has only fifteen left to go, Constable?" He poked a finger into his right ear and shook it as if to bring his ear to life.

"Dominie, you do not understand . . ."

Kok tried to help. "He is right. We must do something. Even my wife will not speak to me." Kok didn't dare look the dominie in the eye, but he knew what he must say. "There are but a few who feel that we do things right. Most think we are just stubborn."

"But our stubbornness is for the cause of justice. That is not wrong, Elder Kok. You know that. We cannot serve two masters here, ja?"

The men were silent.

"Tell me, Constable, what does the woman do all day long?"

"She reads, Dominie."

"Reads? Reads what?"

"The Scriptures."

"The Scriptures?"

"Ja, the Scriptures."

"Well, . . ." He sat back slowly and inhaled the cigar. Little specks of ash floated down like snowflakes and landed softly on the lapels of his black suit.

"Maybe we should do something for this widow?" The smoke leaked out slowly as he spoke.

"Ja, Dominie."

"Well, what can be done?"

Brink sat speechless. Egbert Kok slumped in his chair and rubbed his blinking eyes. The pale blue smoke lay thick as a quilt in the air.

It was Dominie Vander Byl himself who walked to Brink's jail the next morning to call on the recalcitrant innkeeper. Kok and Brink agreed that if anyone was to convince Aartje Korsman of the wickedness of her ways, it could only be the servant of the Lord himself.

Vander Byl shut the door behind him and looked up at Brink who was sitting in his chair behind the desk, sorting through a gallery of "wanted" posters. The constable rose without speaking and nodded to the dominie, asking him to follow. They walked down the short hallway to the only prison cell in town. Brink pointed to the door and unlocked the cell.

"Dominie Vander Byl to see you, Aartje." He didn't bother looking in at his prisoner; he simply announced her guest.

"Ja, Aartje, how goes it?" The dominie wasted no time. As he stepped into the room, he confronted Aartje, sitting on her bed, the big Bible opened on her lap. Her toothy dog sat at her side looking up at him, panting slowly.

The dominie jumped forward when the door slammed shut behind him.

"I am fine, Dominie." She looked up gently, a thin smile parting her lips.

"You have no sickness?"

"No, I am fine."

"The food, it is good?"

"Ja, *Vrouw* Brink makes good meals for me. I think I will get fat here."

"That is good." He did not laugh.

Aartje Korsman didn't move from her position on the bed. She rolled her eyes back to the Scriptures and pretended to be reading.

"It is warm enough, too, for you here?"

"Ja, it is warm."

The dominie nodded. He shifted his weight from foot to foot and held his hat in his right hand.

"You read the Scriptures, Aartje?"

"Ja, Dominie."

"That is good."

She nodded without raising her head.

"What do you read?"

"I have read the Gospels now, and some of the letters of

the apostles."

"Good. Good. You have much time to study the Word now. Not all of us have that blessing. Perhaps we should sit here too, eh?" He realized too late his joke was in bad taste, and he tried to cover his indiscretion with a cough.

She made no reply.

"Your dog is here, and this is your bed too. The dog keeps you good company?"

"Ja, he has been with me since Frederic passed on."

"Do you have visitors?"

"Ja, Dominie. Many of my friends visit and talk."

"Good. You have many friends. Some visit you, but there are others in the village that love you, too." He was getting more serious now, preparing the way for the offer. "The people are very sorry that you must be in jail, and all because of that vile liquor."

She looked down still, moving her head back and forth as if she were reading. Then she removed her glasses, wiped them on her dress, and sighed deeply. The dominie understood.

"Aartje Korsman, you know I am your friend. Your husband was my friend, too. You are a good woman. You do many things for other people—as the Lord Himself has commanded us. It is as a friend that I come, ja? I must tell you that I advise you to give in. The laws have changed, and you cannot hold out against the law. If you promise me that you will quit selling liquor, then I will call Constable Brink and we will go home at once. We will not close the inn, but you must not sell liquor. You can go back to work today. Will you promise?"

He heard only a few sniffles and a light cough. She raised her left hand and rubbed her eyes, then rested her forehead in her hand. Three wet spots had formed on the pages of the old Dutch Bible. Her dog raised his head to his mistress.

"I will promise, Dominie."

Dominie Vander Byl stood immediately and moved to Aartje's side, cautious of the dog, but willing to thank the woman with a touch on the shoulder.

"Aartje, it is good. It is good. Ja, it is good." He reached down, but pulled back when the dog snarled. "I will call the constable now." He yelled down the short corridor, and Brink responded as if he had overheard the entire conversation.

"Brink, Aartje will be going home now. She will sell no more whiskey."

Brink smiled for the first time in fifteen days, then slipped the skeleton key into the door and opened it in one motion.

"She may go now, Dominie?"

"Ja, she may. Aartje, you may go."

"But what of my bed, and my Bible? My dog?"

Dominie Vander Byl pursed his lips and looked toward Brink. "Why, Constable Brink will help you."

Aartje Korsman looked up as if seeing a vision; a haunting smile spread slowly across her face when she caught Brink in her stare. "It would be good," she fawned on the dominie, "to go back again once all together."

Brink's smile dropped like a sledge. "But, Aartje, surely . . ."

"Ja, Constable, why not like I was taken here?"

Brink choked. "Dominie," he turned, "you will not make me?"

"But Brink, we must do all to help the repentant."

"But Dominie . . ."

"Brink, you must help her now in any way she desires."

Brink looked back at Aartje. She sat comfortably. The dog seemed to purr.

"It is the middle of the morning, Aartje. Many people are doing business now." She knew he was pleading.

"But it was such a good ride, Brink, so nice on the bed."

Dominie Vander Byl nodded graciously.

Brink leaned up against the iron bars.

The dog closed his eyes, and slept.

Homeward

GOING BACK

When we came back
no one had lived here
    since '45—
           and you looked
    like a woman out of time,
      broken, used,
       gone past your prime.
  I knew you had been waiting.

You'd been too long
with the sun and rain
and those infernal prairie winds—
    scarred where they'd beat you
    but still smiling—
  how much of a lover
  could you expect the wind to be?

  You're tired of the talk
  that has run about you—
    some have forgotten you
    years ago and some can
    never forget what you
    used to be—

You'll finally die
burdened by memories
and relics of the dead and gone.

You'll creak and collapse
in a gentle way—
in slow decay,
    as a woman going down
    caressed by her lover—

still smiling at the wind.

        —Bonnie Kuipers

    Almost unconsciously, Albertus De Kruyf flicked the ashes from the bowl and dropped the pipe, still warm, into the breast pocket of his coat, while his eyes held fast to the mountain range and the grace of the majestic Yellowstone meandering vein-like down the musculature of the Rockies. For nearly two hundred miles his perception was owned by the view from his window, for ever since Livingston, the Northern Pacific had courted the wily Yellowstone, crossing it once, twice before Billings, but contented thereafter, it seemed, to follow the river's leading through a backdrop of snow caps and jagged cliffs. Downward, slowly, elegantly, the train slid, leveling here and there for a grassy prairie, or, while the river waited politely, rising momentarily to follow the sloping hills west of Custer. De Kruyf rested in his bench, one arm propped beneath his chin as he beheld the view, and juxtaposed it with the devil's offer to Christ in the wilderness. Israel was barren, a desert, he remembered, but had Christ been offered this—he scolded himself for such mockery. Besides, he told himself, this land was unproductive . . . .

    Then there was blackness. The lamps burned faintly in the Pullman, but the rapid and unexpected switch from sunlight to tunnel darkness rendered only blindness. The coach lurched as De Kruyf squinted into the dark, waiting for his eyes to adjust. Then he felt a thudding jolt on his bench, and groped with his left hand, neck craned, trying to catch some glimpse of the sudden intruder.

"Excuse me, sir. Been working for this railroad for close to ten years. Been up this way three, maybe four times before, but I—so dumb couldn't remember the tunnel. Shoulda chosen another time to visit the convenience. Shoulda remembered the tunnel is what I shoulda done."

De Kruyf grunted lightly, shook his head and snapped back his hand from the back of the bench, folding his arms together in a fluid motion which he hoped would convey some sense of ease.

"Tunnels are something, eh? Them Irishmen bully their way through mountains, zif they were made a nothin'."

De Kruyf's eyes adjusted slowly to the glimmering wall lamps, and gradually the dim light evoked an image quite unfamiliar. The man who presently shared his bench was dressed in a brown striped suit, buttoned tightly through the chest over a matching vest and a white shirt with a turned up collar that pointed simultaneously into two bushy black sideburns. His right arm draped over the bench, and in his left hand he held a brown derby. A thick black mustache fanned over his lip and straightened into his sideburns, forming a kind of cow-catcher over a thin pointy face.

"It's no wonder the Union was first. Ever been to Nebraska? Nothin' but flat land. Layin' track's easy as cuttin' butter. Just roll along." His right hand pushed snake-like toward the front of the car. "Don't cost as much either. You imagine how much blastin' them Irishmen had to do through this area? Why sometimes they couldn't lay no more than a few feet a day. Darn mountains look pretty, but they make for tough roadbed. Where you from?"

De Kruyf adjusted his weight to better face the visitor. "My home is in South Dakota now."

"Dakota? Yeah, then you know. The Northern had to deal with winters, too—you know about the winters on these northern plains, I'm sure—and Indians. I'll tell you, Dodge never knew how easy it was to the south. Why we just passed Custer; go south 'bout fifty miles and you could still see the blood a the general, I'm sure. Them Sioux are a rough bunch. Don't get the message easy. Cost Villard a fortune to get 'em moved safe outta the way—darn near broke the company." The derby jumped into a gesture with each sentence.

"Say, the name is Stevenson, George Stevenson. Been working out of Seattle. And yours?" He held his hat in his left hand and offered a thin right hand, cleaned to lily white, palm upward.

"Albertus De Kruyf." De Kruyf's hand nearly swallowed the visitor's, but Stevenson's shake was tight and energetic.

"De Kruyf? Hollander, eh? Immigrant?"

"Ja."

"Ahmmm, heh." George Stevenson nodded. "Going back to get some family or so?"

Stevenson's eyes were dark, set far back in his head, and when he squinted, his thick, black eyebrows nearly hid them. His nose pointed downward, straight and rigid as a roofline, and his nostrils were well hidden in the underbrush beneath.

De Kruyf folded his arms again and crossed his legs. "No, I have been to Washington to look at land there. I am thinking of moving maybe."

"To Washington? Seattle?" Stevenson raised the black mantle above his eyes, forming two separate brows.

"No, north. Whitby Island . . . Lynden."

"Never been there. Got to be beautiful country though, I'm sure. All of it is up there. Got it all over South Dakota, that's sure. Ever notice that none of the companies push through there? No sir, Union took Nebraska, Northern takes North Dakota, even Hill chose North. Yessir, that's some country you got there. Can be downright inhospitable. Gonna be moving quick?"

De Kruyf found Stevenson engaging and warm. The natural antipathy he felt toward Americans faded easily in the company of such a man. He, too, rested an arm over the bench.

"I don't know. I must yet decide if we will move."

"Not movin'? Why in God's name not?"

The train emerged from the tunnel as quickly as it had entered. Sunlight splashed into the Pullman, dousing the lamps in its wake. Instinctively, Stevenson visored his eyes with his hands.

"Ah, that's better," he said, turning slightly away from the window. "Beautiful country this. Like to have me a cabin here someplace. Do some fishing and hunting. Right there maybe." He pointed out the window with his right hand. "Right there on the old Yellowstone."

De Kruyf looked once more from his window. It was beautiful. "A cabin?" he asked.

"You know, some place to go for a time. Just rest. Don't have no worries, no cares. Just fish . . . you know." Stevenson's smile pushed his whiskers back to his ears. He shook his head as the Pullman rocked steadily down the tracks.

"Mr. Stevenson—"

"Call me George."

"—are you working now for the railroad?"

Stevenson sat back again, fingered his mustache, and tightened his lips. "No, sir. Don't work for the railroad anymore. Don't like what's goin' on, you see. Decided to get myself out. Got a family someplace in Minnesota, I think. Thought I'd check up." He stared into the air.

"Your job, what was wrong?" De Kruyf had read about the scandals. He had seen the giant paintings of America when they had all lived in the old country. People from all over Europe had been cheated. He knew many who had come to this country with nothing but a picture from a lantern slide in their minds, thinking themselves somehow heirs to the riches of the new paradise.

"Double-dealin'. Railroads do some lyin', friend, some lotta lyin'. Jus' couldn't live with it no more, no sir, couldn't do it, you know, 'cause one day all them lies are gonna fall in like a big circus tent, and everybody that's under that tent—especially the little guys like me—is gonna be in big trouble. No sir, I couldn't take them lies no more. 'Sides, didn't see no kind of advancement in front of me—just no future at all. And if a man can't be movin' up in life, I mean, well, that's somethin'. Then when I just know the whole darn business is gonna be fallin' in, why, that was it—you know what I'm sayin'? I just decided to take what I could get an' clear outta the place." Stevenson turned back to face his new companion. "You know what I mean, friend, I mean a man's gotta take what he can get, you know."

De Kruyf said nothing.

"Why sure you know. Otherwise you wouldn't be lookin' for no land in Washington for you and yours."

Albertus De Kruyf smiled at the man and nodded politely. Stevenson, accepting the response, settled back on the bench, then slid forward suddenly.

"Well, seems to me I was on the way to the convenience. 'Sides, I been stealin' your attention from the Yellowstone. Been on this trip myself, what—three, four times now— getsa bit old, you know." He pointed to the window.

"You're welcome to stay, Mr. Stevenson."

"Call me George."

"I enjoyed your company."

"Well, thank you. I'll stop again."

Albertus watched his friend march to the end of the car. He reached for the tour guide and located the position of the train. Next stop would be Miles City, at the confluence of the Yellowstone and the Tongue.

Just outside of Bismarck, Albertus De Kruyf decided to work his way through the train, since he had somewhat less than several hours before catching the Union southbound out of Jamestown. He checked his baggage beneath the bench and walked back uneasily toward the retiring room. A news butcher approached him with an English paper, but De Kruyf, more to rid himself of the nuisance than anything else, bought an additional supply of tobacco before opening the red oak door to the next car. The air was cool and moist beneath a canopy of clouds that shrouded the sun since the train's descent from the mountains. Yet he felt almost joyous, for he knew that moisture would be thankfully received by the people here; he hoped it would also reach his own people in Douglas County. Furthermore, the tension of living with so many strange Americans could be at least momentarily forgotten in the isolation of the decks between cars. No one saw him smile broadly here; no one saw him raise his hand upward, pulling out the stiffness that had worn into his arms and legs. There was something in him that wanted to shout, to scream like a child, to release the fatigue of doing nothing but sitting through the interminable expanse of the American West. He stood straight momentarily, observing the heavy, gray clouds of spring rolling through the sky, unpropelled by any locomotive monster. He was nearing his home.

There was some uneasiness in that knowledge, however, for he had been sent to Washington as a representative of the colony. Albertus De Kruyf, no one else, had been able to see the beauty there. No one else had tasted of the bounty, had felt the moisture deep within the dark earth, had envisioned a new town, a transported colony flourishing in verdant new surroundings. But now no one else could make the decision. This barren land, this flat, lifeless land, or the new land. This land of frequent fires, this land where grasshoppers came in waves, the land of drouth, of violent, brutal winters—this land, or the promise of a vision only he had seen.

He stepped into the adjoining car, closed the door softly behind him, and walked in. The car, like his own, was a Pullman. People sat comfortably on upholstered benches, reading, talking, some even playing cards, while others, sprawled in rather unsightly postures, tried to catch more sleep. The next three cars were all Pullmans, well-provided with the ingenious, collapsible, well-padded upper berths, most of which were pulled up and out of the way during the day, held snugly to the ceiling by chains, while the passengers lounged beneath, separated, perhaps, by the hinged table which stood between the two facing seats. Pullmans seemed, to him, a taste of the promise of America.

With the next car, however, he was much more familiar, even though it stood empty. Although the passage was marked by no additional obstructions, De Kruyf knew immediately that a change was imminent, for the picture differed drastically. The same stove sentried the door, but in the place of upholstered seats and collapsible bedding, clean but hard wooden cubicles stood, boxed atop each other. The immigrant car was not new to him, for he and his family had made passage to South Dakota with such accommodations, packed like animals into cattle cars.

And it all came back to him, as if it were but yesterday. Here, old women had sat as if in a trance, their grayed hair swathed by triangular scarves. Children ran and played where they could find an opening, chattering and squealing in German, Swedish, or Irish. Men had sat here soberly, smoking pipes or cigars. Some sipped from clear, unlabeled bottles. The air hung heavy with the odor of uncleanliness, the stench of stale smoke, the pungency of open liquor. The vision, the smells, the noise still haunted here, even though the immigrant car was empty now, and only the clickity-clack of the rails chanted through lifeless walls.

He passed through slowly, as if it were a graveyard, and came to the next, this one alive with Chinese whose monotone staccatos almost hurt his ears. Some smiled as he passed; most failed to acknowledge his presence. Thick square-shouldered Russians filled the next car, then more Orientals. But one idea drew them all together on this pilgrimage, one vision compelled them all, and De Kruyf understood so painfully the sweetness of the illusion, for he too had slept on such a hard bench as these, hoping for something which existed only in his mind, but pained by a gnawing realization, growing with each passing mile, that somehow reality wouldn't, or more pathetically, couldn't fulfill the vision. But he was different now, he told himself, for this time he had seen the land, tasted its crops, and smelled its richness. He passed back through the immigrant crowds, walking like an American in a land of Babel, face forward, chin lifted in a vain display of acquired self-assurance, the human desire to empathize subordinated to the knowledge that his car was the Pullman.

When he left the last immigrant car, he drew the door softly shut behind him, as if he might wake the occupants from a satisfying sleep. The cold spring air woke him to the realization that he was learning something, that the Lord was committing something to his understanding, if only he could discover what it was. He paused for an unspoken prayer, then passed back into the Pullman, shutting the red oak door and turning directly into the face of George Stevenson.

"Hey, you're the Hollander." Stevenson pointed up and into De Kruyf's face, then offered the right hand again, palm upward. His drawn face broadened into a smile, and his black eyes shown like onyx as De Kruyf shook the hand once more.

"Ja, George." De Kruyf's own face lit with the exuberance that Stevenson seemed to emit.

"Back by the Zulus, eh? Know someone back there?"

De Kruyf's limited English vocabulary didn't include such a word, and his face illustrated his ignorance.

"Zulus—immigrant cars. Always call them Zulus. Don't rightly know why. Just everybody does. Zulus. That's what they call 'em. Come to think of it, it's kinda crazy, isn't it? No real reason for it. Like I say, just that everybody says it in the business. Zulus they call 'em. Anyway, some of your people there?"

"No, no," De Kruyf shook his head lightly, still smiling, unbuttoning his coat. "I wanted to see once yet the whole train. My family will want to know everything. They may, too, travel like this someday."

"That's right, you from this area, aren't you? S'pose you'll be leavin' the company soon, then?"

"Jamestown."

"Jamestown! No sir, don't have long no more." Stevenson pulled at his sideburns, thinking. Then he moved toward De Kruyf, causing him instinctively to lean backward slightly. "Listen," he whispered, grabbing De Kruyf by one lapel, "ever been in a ritz?"

De Kruyf looked puzzled again.

"You know—the show car, the private Pullman?" He released him, quickly, easily. "Well, course you haven't. Aren't allowed. Well, let me tell you, Dutchman, you haven't seen it all till you've seen that. You come with me, I'll get you in. The family won't believe this. C'mon." Stevenson snickered and giggled like a little girl as he led De Kruyf through the Pullmans, finally bringing him to a stop when they were close to whatever was ahead.

"Now, you let me do the talkin' here. You just speak your own language if I say anything at all to you, understand? I can handle these darkies. Just got to know how to speak to 'em." Stevenson reached into his pockets for his gloves and pulled them tightly over his fingers. They left the Pullman and stood on the deck.

"Well, here we go!" Stevenson opened the door quickly and rushed in, pulling De Kruyf along by the sleeve. In a moment the Negro porter, dressed in a neatly pressed black suit, stood before them, and a huge black hand put an immediate halt to the venture.

"Ahm sorry, sah. Y'all can't be in heah."

Stevenson had anticipated the encounter and began with parry and thrust. "Oh, I'm sorry, my friend, for barging in so unexpected, but the name is Stevens, Theodore Stevens, and I'm with the company. Work out of Seattle. Special Accounts."

The Negro towered over Stevenson, but the little man countered his own physical inferiority with ostentation that vaulted far above the lowly spirit of the porter. He never once glanced into the Negro's eyes, but calmly and assuredly jerked off his gloves, one finger at a time, eyes downward as he spoke.

"Here's the story, my dear man. This gentleman behind

me is a very rich Hollander, interested in taking some of his friends and associates on an excursion to the coast." He took a quick half-turn back. "Now, granted, he may not look like our rich friends from New York, but then, well, this is the way his people normally dress. Surely you can understand that." He turned back, eyes still lowered to his hands. "He desires, of course, the private accommodations, you see, and it is my responsibility to show him these accommodations for his personal perusal. Now, will you please remove yourself from—" he waved his hand as if at a fly "—from here?"

"Ahm sorry, sah, but ah ain' allowed to admit no one to this heah cah while the train is runnin'."

"Please, sir," Stevenson raised his eyes to the ceiling and inhaled deeply. "I'll have no more of this insubordination. Master Villard himself is a personal friend. Fortunately, my friend here can speak no English or he may already have decided to go with Union Pacific. Now, as calmly as possible, move to one side, please. This will take but a moment."

The Negro placed himself strategically. There was no crossing his path.

"Do you have a cahd, suh, or a lettah or somethin'?"

Stevenson looked to the side as he exhaled deeply, pushing the air through partially closed lips. "Now listen, boy, and you listen good, y'hear? This here Hollander is a rich bird, you hearin' me? If the Northern loses his money 'cause of you, some other poor darkie will be wearin' that sweet black tuxedy there, and you'll be back in the cotton—I'll see to it personally. Are you getting my message clearly?"

For the first time, Stevenson's black eyes stared in the Negro's, causing them to flicker slightly. The porter inhaled slowly, then his eyes dropped to the floor. "Yes, suh," he said, moving slightly.

"Well, thank you, son. What's your name?"

"Washington, suh, Elijah."

"Elijah Washington, eh? Well, I'll remember. You can be

assured that Mr. Villard himself will hear of your good work, for I'm proud of the way you stood up to me. After all, we can't be havin' trash waltzing through here as if it were a museum. Villard will know, Washington, be assured, he'll know." Stevenson patted the Negro on the shoulder lightly and easily. "We'll just be standin' back here for a minute or so."

Elijah Washington walked to the front of the car, leaving the visitors to their freedom.

"Well, how's this?" Stevenson's hand swept through the air in the grand gesture of a master magician. De Kruyf was stunned. Not even in Europe had he ever seen anything so lavish. The ceiling was rich, hand-carved walnut, festooned with what seemed gold embroidery. Stained glass windows ran along the canopy, surrounding a flamboyant chandelier. Velvet curtains framed the huge side windows, and matching upholstery, complete with dangling fringe, dressed a showroom of rockers and straight chairs on a shimmering oriental rug. Spacious mirrors adorned the walls that separated the compartments, giving the whole interior even more elegance and at least the appearance of extra space. It was a palace on iron wheels. He imagined himself sitting here, pipe filled with imported tobacco, his wife clean, content, happily watching her fair-skinned grandchildren play on the colorful carpet.

"What does it cost?" he asked, astounded.

"To build—who knows? Couple thousand? Couple hundred thousand? To rent? Fifty a day, I think."

"Fifty?" De Kruyf was incredulous. "Who can spend so much money?"

Stevenson seemed to purr as he shaped his mustache with his fingers and pursed his lips. "Goodly number, my friend. Car like this is always booked. There's a lot a rich folks in this land, you know. That's what I been tellin' you all the time. There's lots of 'em what already got theirs. The rest of us just gotta take it when we can get it, you know. This here's a great land. Who knows, move yerselves up to Washington—coupla years you might be here."

Albertus De Kruyf never saw George Stevenson again. He left the Pullman and the Northern Pacific as he planned at Jamestown, but searched for the dark-haired American, hoping to give some kind of farewell. But Stevenson hadn't appeared, and when De Kruyf had boarded the older Union Pacific for the long ride to Armour, he felt almost guilty that he hadn't been able to end the relationship as he would have liked.

Once off the major east-west line, he saw all quality dwindle. The cars were dark and cramped, old and worn; the rails were poorly laid and bumpy, and the train had to grind to complete stops in clapboard towns like Sydney, Millarton, Nortonville, Edgeley, and Monango in North Dakota, and Winship, Frederic, Barnard, Westport, and Gage in South Dakota, railroad towns slapped together at the whim of some businessman in some city far removed from the Dakota flatland, towns that lived only on the blackened breath of the steam locomotive, towns that stood on the naked land like rows of boxes, unsheltered from the whimsical, pestilent wind that had, with the passing of the buffalo, become sultan of the desert plains, ruling with a seasonal caress of hail or dust or snow.

But this was his land. Even the prairie grass grew thin on the long, undulating hills. It was so like the ocean, he thought, remembering the joyous arrival in the new country. But he recalled, too, how some of his own group, seduced by the scurrilous land agents, had departed and broken their promise of homesteading on Dakota land. He was their leader. His plans were always Dakota. Even in the old country. The remainder had come with him to Harrison, to Overijsel, to Friesland and Nieveen, to towns built with their own hands.

But the land was dry. Drouth in '85, crop failure in '86, hail-out in '87, average years in '88 and '89, nothing again in '90, a good year in '91, '92 and '93 were slow, nothing at all this season. Too many years of drouth, of bugs, of too little yield. Some settlers had left, others suffered badly. He watched from his window as the Union Pacific rolled on over the Dakota grassland, brown and lifeless in the early spring. He had seen Washington now, tasted its produce. Weeks he had spent there, touching the land, pricing the land, trying to envision his own Dakota colony transplanted. Here, outside his window, stunted gray stalks barely stood upon the crusted face of the prairie, retarded and beaten by weather that seemed anathema to man and beast. Not even trees could grow in Douglas County, some had said before leaving.

But there was more, he knew. The trains were part of it, the immigrant faces, the velvet chairs, George Stevenson. The Lord had laid before him another vision of sorts, but like a man blinded by the sun, he could but dimly see the meaning behind it all.

This was his Dakota, the land of his dreams since leaving Holland, the land of horror since his arrival.

Two nights later, Albertus De Kruyf had supper with his children, and afterwards, while the women worked in the kitchen, he walked in his son's fields, his own grandson on his arm. He kicked at the soil and found it loose and dry. He saw his son's footsteps raise tufts of dust, even in the spring. He stopped a moment, cupped his hand in the soil, then poured the earth slowly from his palm. It ran in fine grains.

"Not so good today, Father," his son said, watching him. "But we are learning. There's more livestock this year—more cattle, more hogs, less reliance on crops. The Hollanders don't learn quick, but they learn. But look at this." He pointed at tiny fragile shoots poking through the dusty topsoil.

De Kruyf reached down and dug beneath the plant. He scooped up a clump of earth and searched through the dirt for the seedling. There was a root there. He broke the earth around it and saw it, soft and weak.

His grandson laid a hand over his shoulder. Albertus De Kruyf took the boy in his arms and rubbed the dirt from his hands, remembering so clearly a very clean, upturned palm. He stood, lifted the boy with a mock groan, and started walking back to his son's frame house, the child laughing over his grandfather's shoulder.

The Paths of Righteousness

Johnny Ver Steeg was dead.

Roelof Vrielink, the dominie, felt sweat run from his forehead and into his brows as he sat, elbows on his knees, back bent over the reins he held in his hands. His gold-rimmed spectacles kept slipping down his nose as the wagon bumped over the road, so he removed them and slipped them into the pocket of his black wool coat. A gray film had risen on the mare's buttocks as she plodded along.

Johnny Ver Steeg was dead. Now the dominie must tell the loved ones. His work oppressed him like his heavy coat, for many times in the middle of his sermons he had seen Johnny, always alone at the end of the last bench, staring at Janna Korten. Willem Korten had promised Johnny his only daughter, if Johnny could meet the financial requirements.

Through a year of hard farm work Johnny had worn that look every Sabbath; and Janna, as eager as he, would sit with the women, straining to hear the Word over the whispers of her own desire. Johnny had always watched her as she rose to sing the Psalms. He observed the way she clasped her fingers around her leather Psalter and how she straightened her long skirt behind her before she sat. But Janna could never return his attention, for her eyes were righteously fixed on the preacher.

Roelof Vrielink had seen it all from the pulpit, and he had known about them long before Johnny Ver Steeg's dying words, for he too had once been so human. Long ago, it seemed to him, long ago in Wisconsin. His own Cornelia had been but seventeen when she died, and no one, not even he really knew for sure, for she had told him only two weeks before that she was late. But then diptheria had run like a mad dog through Alto, taking Cornelia and several others from his church.

He knew about Johnny and his Janna, but now the thick black coat lay heavily on his shoulders. The Lord had spared him disgrace by robbing him of his lover—his own new life by Cornelia's death. But never could he comprehend the exchange, nor could he ever fully accept the benefits, for he always felt cheated somehow—cheated by death itself, cheated out of the guilt which was rightfully his. Cornelia's death for his reputation, for all he was today—the dominie in Chandler. The Lord worked so strangely.

Cornelia had died, like the others, separated by quarantine.

And it was then that he had decided to finish his schooling, go to Michigan, and study for the ministry. All of Alto had been so proud.

And now Johnny Ver Steeg was dead. Gored by a bull this very afternoon on the farm where he had labored like Jacob to meet Willem Korten's demand.

And Janna Korten was pregnant, alone, unmarried. The father of her child was dead. Roelof saw it again, somehow, dimly—first death, then life, and all of it without understanding. Something within him wanted to point that preacher's finger skyward, to tighten a fist and shake it. He saw it all, but he knew so little. He wanted to blame someone, something for such play with mere, fallible men and women.

Johnny Ver Steeg was dead. The horse stamped patiently through the valley, her muscular thighs snapping with each step. It wouldn't be long now. Just a few more miles to Willem Korten's. Roelof had not thought about what he would say. He carried too much news.

The buggy squeaked along, moving deeper into the valley southwest of Chandler. The hills held back the prairie winds, and the heat grew more intense, drawing sweat from Vrielink's body as if he were haying. Beneath the coat, his shirt clung to his skin.

The farm was clean and orderly. Despite its location, Willem Korten had drained the sloughs, like his father before him, turning the bottom acres into fertile cropland. There was a barn behind the frame house, and a chicken coop, and footings were already laid for another building. Korten was a prosperous man. He had made himself what he was.

The house was not new, but it was kept in excellent repair. Three quartered windows faced the path to the front, and white siding ran vertically in the old style, like barn slats. Four unfinished beams held up a perfectly horizontal porch roof. Long cold winters and hot summers had grayed the shingles, but not one was out of pattern. The steps to the porch were sturdy and scrubbed, and the traditional mat lay before a front door that seemed uncharacteristically weathered.

Roelof climbed from the wagon. He had been here before. Like some others, Willem Korten had been vocal in his criticism of the dominie. Once, in the middle of a sermon, he had pulled his wife and daughter to their feet and stomped out of church.

"You must talk to the offended brother," Isaac Brethhower had told him at the next consistory meeting. So he had come here before, a year ago, and had been reprimanded for not preaching doctrine.

He straightened his coat and shirt and knocked at Willem's door. They must have heard or seen him coming, for in a moment Janna met him and asked him in.

"Is your father at home, Janna?" he asked.

"Ja, he is just in from the field. But come in, Dominie. You're just in time for supper."

"No, no, I cannot stay." He held up a hand to decline the invitation. "But your father, can he come? I must speak to him."

"Ja, sure, I will—"

"Ja, Dominie, what can we do for you?"

Willem Korten stepped from the kitchen like an old bear. His face was square, dominated by a nose that seemed wider than it should have been. His cheeks were full and red from the spring sun; they pushed his eyes into slits that seemed always to be probing.

Roelof walked to the center of the room to meet him and offer his hand. Korten raised his left as was his custom. His right hand was nearly gone, a gray flannel sock covering the angled stump that remained. Roelof had never seen that hand. Few had.

Gertrude Korten came out of the kitchen after her husband, wiping her hands on a towel. She too was heavy, but beneath the dust cap and the ring of silver hair that circled her round face were the dark, deep-set eyes of her daughter. She nodded politely, then sat on a wooden rocker by the stove in the far corner of the room.

"Nice to see you, Mrs. Korten," Roelof had managed a momentary smile, "but my visit is not easy this time."

"Sit, Dominie. Now what trouble?" Willem sank slowly into the padded captain's chair and offered his guest the wicker seat near the door.

"Janna, what I must say is not easy." Roelof saw the girl's eyes widen in anticipation. Her face was drawn and tight. He knew what she expected. "But it is your . . ." he struggled and turned fully to her, "It is your . . . it is something which you will feel even more than us." He stopped again, poised at the edge. "That is not to say that we all don't feel this too, but . . ."

"Ach, Dominie, tell us, eh?" Willem fidgeted, glancing from his daughter to his guest.

"Janna—Willem and Gertrude—Johnny Ver Steeg is dead." He stopped, then continued. "Today. This afternoon."

Gertrude rose immediately from her chair and ran to her daughter who sat, stunned, gazing at the preacher.

"But how, Dominie?" Even Willem looked shocked.

"At the Haverkamps. On the farm there."

Korten shook his head. "He was a good boy, Johnny. He

would make a good son." He looked up, nodding. "He was a good worker, Haverkamp said."

"Janna, cry once, come now, just cry." Gertrude tried to pull her daughter close, but she sat motionless, her eyes filled by the glaze of tears.

"Ach, Dominie, are you sure? Haverkamp said he was a smart fellow."

"He died in my presence, Willem. He wanted to see Janna before he died." Roelof saw the tears begin. He stopped once more.

In the silence, Willem spoke, incredulous. "How Dominie, tell us?"

Roelof looked toward the girl. Her mother held her in her arms. Janna cried without restraint.

"Well, perhaps when your daughter—"

"Ach, Dominie, you are such a lamb. Tell me now."

"Haverkamp's bull," he said slowly, uneasily.

"But Johnny Ver Steeg was smart. Haverkamp said he was a good worker. How could it happen?"

Janna looked up from her mother's embrace. Gertrude looked sharply toward her husband. Janna's troubled breathing was the only sound in the room.

Roelof hesitated, then inhaled deeply.

"They say that Haverkamp had been breeding his cows. Johnny jumped into—he went to the bull too quick, ja? The bull was excited yet. They say the bull moved fast. Very fast." Roelof pulled nervously at his beard. "The bull caught him with a horn and threw him to the dirt. When Johnny tried to get up, the bull gored him here—" he pointed to his chest.

Janna began crying again; her mother held her in her arms.

"He was dead then?" Willem continued to urge.

"No, he lived—he lived for nearly an hour."

"Haverkamp get him to the doctor?"

"He brought him in the wagon to town. Doc Saathof sent for me. He knew Johnny would die."

Willem Korten leaned back in his chair, put his chin in

his left hand and stared vacantly at the braided rug on the floor of the frontroom. He glanced at his daughter, who wept heavily.

Roelof breathed deeply again.

"Janna, he is with the Lord, ja? You will see him again someday—he was a fine young man."

She looked again at the dominie, eyes full of tears, tore herself away from her mother's arms, and ran from the room. She slammed the door behind her.

"Ja, Dominie, he was a good boy. He would have made for her a good husband. He was a good worker."

Gertrude sat in her daughter's chair. Like Janna, she cried. No one spoke. The warm southern breeze slapped the curtains against the window frames.

"I must go to her," Gertrude said suddenly and stood up.

"No, mama," Willem interrupted. "Let her cry by herself. She must be left alone."

She sat again.

"Roelof, we will bury him here, ja? He was to be my son."

"I don't know. His parents must be consulted."

"Ja, do they know yet?"

"I sent a wire to Corsica before coming here."

"Good."

"They probably know now." He took his watch from his coat pocket and checked the time.

Willem sat forward again. "They are good people. Ja, the Ver Steegs are good people. He was from good parents. I wanted him to be my son, you know."

Roelof remembered the strange arrangement. It was Willem's idea to bring Johnny Ver Steeg back to Chandler. He knew the Ver Steegs well—they had lived in Minnesota before moving to the Dakotas. Korten had thought he could choose a suitable husband for his only daughter, and his plan had worked—worked very well indeed.

"It is hot today, Reverend. Would you like some milk or coffee?" Gertrude's offer was obligatory.

"No, Gertrude, I cannot stay." Roelof loosened the coat

from his shoulders. His shirt was soaked by perspiration. "But there is more I must say." He looked down and rubbed his forehead with his left hand.

"What else?"

"Johnny had no will, but before he died he said that all that he earned at Haverkamp's should be given to Janna."

"He was a good boy, Dominie. Ja, he was a good boy." Willem rubbed his maimed right hand with his left. The coarse sock jerked above his wrist and a pinkish scar jutted from beneath the gray veil.

Roelof's nervousness had not disappeared. What remained to be said would be no easier.

"Willem, I must tell you the rest. You will know soon, but there is one more thing."

"Go on, Dominie."

Gertrude watched him closely. She appeared mystified that further revelations could be as difficult. Willem sat upright in the captain's chair.

"Janna is to have a child—Johnny said so when he died. He wanted to be married before . . . but he died." Willem sat stonefaced.

Gertrude was sobbing. Willem looked up as if suddenly awake, and glanced at his wife.

"She is *in verwachting*, *Vrouw*," he mumbled almost inaudibly. "But how? We kept them apart. That was my agreement."

"I don't know, Willem," she said without looking up.

"Gertrude, how could this happen? We kept them apart."

His wife wiped her eyes with the dish towel she still held and made no attempt to answer.

"She is *in verwachting*!" He turned back to Roelof, shaking his head in disbelief. "Now what, Dominie? How could Janna do this? Behind our backs, Gertrude? And now what, Dominie? A bastard grandson?"

Roelof Vrielink felt sweat trickle down his cheek. He wiped it off with his hand.

"Gertrude, get your daughter." Willem brushed the perspiration off his bald head with the sock on his right hand. "Get your daughter."

His wife arose from the chair, looked at the dominie as she wiped her tears, then left the room.

"Ach, Dominie, now you see, eh?" he pointed a finger in the air. "Now you see why you must preach on sin." He paused and shook his head again. "But how could this happen? I told him, 'Johnny,' I said, 'you may have my daughter, Janna, but you must prove you will be a good husband.' She is my only daughter, Dominie." Korten couldn't seem to sit still.

"Ach, ja," he continued, "he proved it all right." A sarcastic laugh punctuated the silence. "He proved he could be a father, ja. Ja, he proved it. Ach, Dominie, can't these kids—ach, what's wrong with them, eh? Can't they keep it—ach, can't they keep it in *de broek*?"

Roelof felt little relief since telling everything. The sweat continued to run down his temples. "Willem, Janna has just lost her—" he searched for the right word—"her child's father. You must have patience now. Don't hurt her anymore."

"She is *my* daughter, Roelof Vrielink, flesh of my flesh. I will speak to her as her own father." He paused, wiping his eyes with his fingers. "But she must confess, Dominie, she must confess her sin to the church!"

"Willem, there is time for that later. There is no need—"

"She has sinned, Dominie, she must confess. Johnny has sinned too, but he is dead." He looked up suddenly, as if in sharp, unexpected pain.

"Ach, Dominie, you told my daughter—I heard you, too—you said Johnny Ver Steeg was in heaven. Either you lied to her or you are a heretic. Which is it, eh?" His finger pointed again. "That boy did not confess to the church, did he?"

Roelof remembered those few minutes at the doctor's office. He had held Johnny's hand as the young man bled to death. Johnny had told them all to love his Janna, to be good to her and their baby. Doc Saathof had worked with all his speed and skill. But Johnny Ver Steeg died.

"No, he did not confess before the church. He had no chance!"

"But one must ask to be forgiven, surely they teach that in the seminary. You lie, Dominie. Johnny Ver Steeg is not in heaven now!"

Gertrude Korten appeared, holding her daughter by the arm, one hand on her shoulder. Janna's eyes said that she had heard her father's words. Her mother helped her into her chair, then slid another next to her and sat.

"Janna," Willem looked rigid, "how are you?"

"How should I be, Papa?" She bit her fingers and blinked her swollen eyes.

"Well, we are sad . . . ja, sad, and we are . . ."

"Mama says you know about the baby. I would have told you, Papa. I swear. I knew I would have to tell you, this week, maybe next week. I couldn't hide it much longer."

"But how, Janna, how did it happen?"

"It just happened, Papa—how can I tell you?" She wiped her eyes with her fingers.

"Janna—"

"But, Papa, my husband—"

"He was not your husband!"

"—my husband is dead. The father of this child within me. Please, Papa?"

Willem Korten was blind. His eyes glanced from object to object—the walls, the ceiling, the floor. His stockinged hand rubbed his head continually, front to back, front to back.

"Janna," he blurted, "was it just once?"

"Papa, what does it matter?"

Her mother held her.

"Matter! You must confess, you know."

"Papa—"

"Your sins must be confessed."

"Willem, there will be time—"

"Vrielink, be quiet. This is *my* daughter!"

Janna turned her face into her mother's arms. Roelof wanted to deliver her from this house, from this man, take her away quickly.

"When you confess you can be forgiven, Janna." He leaned back, rubbing the sock over the thin line of sweat on his upper lip. "You knew that when you laid with him too, eh? You should have thought of that then."

Gertrude's eyes pleaded with her husband, but he wouldn't see their supplication.

"Where? *Where* did this happen? In some buggy? In the fields?" He looked down quickly; his eyes squinted as if he were about to break down himself. "It must have been dirty, ja?" It was an afterthought, but it was audible; everybody heard it.

Janna jerked herself away from her mother's arms, raised herself in her chair, and straightened her shoulders.

"Maybe you were at fault, Papa."

"Janna, watch how you speak to your father," her mother cautioned, holding Janna's arm. Janna jerked it away.

"Maybe it was your fault. You kept promising, promising, promising. 'A little more yet, Johnny,' you would tell him—'I want you to be comfortable, Johnny,'—'Just a few more weeks yet, Johnny.'"

Willem Korten burned. "How dare you blame *me* for your sin. Were you thinking of me when you laid together, eh? Were you thinking of your unjust father when you sweat together?"

"Willem—"

"Be quiet, Mama, this is my own daughter," he snapped. "We must hear these things." He looked back to his daughter, "Ja, Papa is to blame. But I am not *in verwachting*, *you* are. And you are not married!" He pointed continually with his sock.

"Papa, you lied to Johnny. You know it. You kept saying—'in October,' then 'January,' then 'March,'—Johnny didn't know what to believe anymore. He *loved* me, Papa. I loved him! Can't you understand?"

"Do I understand, girl—do I understand *love?*" He stood, towering over his daughter. "I wanted the best for my daughter because I loved her. Was that wrong? Was it a sin, Dominie?" He swung to his left, "You tell me—was it a sin to want her to marry and start a family without having to suffer?"

"Willem, I think—" Roelof knew that he couldn't begin to pacify this man with words.

"How can that be wrong? To have some things we didn't have to make her life a little easier—that's all I wanted. And then—and then—you and Johnny Ver Steeg decide you can't wait. You let your desire—your damned lust—lead you into sin!"

Janna sat defiantly, but the stream of tears continued. Then, suddenly, she stood and faced her father.

"Papa, I will go."

"Ach, ja, you're a child, and now a mother too. Where will you go, eh? Don't be so foolish!"

"You are ashamed of me—I can live here no longer."

"Sit down, you child. You can go nowhere. You have wronged us, Janna Korten. You should be on your knees begging forgiveness. Your sin will be known to everyone in Chandler. The daughter of Willem and Gertrude Korten!" His arm swept the air. "You should beg to stay in this house!"

Vrielink's thick black coat lay like lead on his shoulders. He wanted to speak in Janna's defense, but he couldn't. The sweat bubbled out of his chest as he sat silent, agonized.

Willem Korten stood numbly as his only daughter walked past him, opened the front door, and left the house.

"That unrepentant whore!" Korten lunged around the chair and ran to the porch. His daughter was already near the gate.

"Willem, don't let her go—" Mrs. Korten pleaded.

"You will come back! And when you do, you crawl, ja? You will beg us for forgiveness!" He screamed it out, but she continued walking down the path and never looked back. He rocked on his heels and jerked his suspenders with his good hand. He stared, furious and unbelieving.

Roelof Vrielink rose then from his chair. His clothes were damp and cold against his skin. He went to Gertrude, laid one hand on her shoulder and nodded reassuringly. He walked past Willem Korten, saying nothing, and he left the house.

Nor did Korten say anything to his dominie when he left. Roelof heard the door kick shut behind him as he unfastened the reins of the buggy.

In a few minutes he had caught up with Janna Korten. She would not look at him as she walked rapidly along the road.

"Come with me, Janna." He looked into her face as he spoke, awed by the force of her resolution.

"I will never go back to that house, Dominie. Not ever! I swear I will not return to my father's house." Her eyes were puffed, her cheeks stained with her tears, but her determination hardened her. Finally she stopped walking and allowed herself to be helped up into the buggy.

Vrielink's mare worked hard to pull them up out of the valley. Roelof Vrielink held the reins with his left hand, the girl with his right arm.

Several miles passed before another word was spoken between them, but his mind was spinning with options for the girl. He knew he couldn't take her to the parsonage—people would never stand for that, his being unmarried—so he tried to think of someone in the church who could help her. He thought of several good people, respectable people who would accept Janna into their homes. But finally it was Mina Van Zee.

As the mare pulled them along toward town, he was split between what he felt and what he knew. There would be few complaints if he brought her to the Brethhowers—she would be treated very well. Yet he felt that only Mina was really capable.

So he bypassed Chandler deliberately, just as the sun

seemed to rest on a flatboat cloud above the horizon. Yes. Roelof decided that it would be Mina Van Zee.

"Is he there, Dominie?"

The question broke the stillness.

"You mean with God?"

"Ja."

He glanced at her. The full gray dress and flowered smock couldn't hide the age of Janna Korten. Her hair was drawn back and pulled into a bun, but a day of work had loosened curls that fell freely over her ears. Her face was streaked where tears had washed through the housedust, but beneath, her youthful skin was smooth. And her eyes, reddened by sorrow, still seemed to hold the glow of a young lover. Roelof repeated her question to himself and realized that Janna was in some ways only a young girl.

"Ja, he was a good boy, and he would have been a good father."

"But," she hesitated, never looking up, "I heard my father—"

"Your father was very upset, Janna. He didn't know what he was saying all the time."

"But he said that Johnny didn't ask you for forgiveness, Dominie. He said that Johnny didn't confess . . . our . . . sin."

Roelof tightened his arm around her, steadying her.

"Johnny doesn't need us to forgive him—what good would that be to him now? You and I know that Johnny was a good man. We both know too that all of us have sinned. Johnny, too, was a sinner, but all of us can be forgiven—not by each other, that's not important—but by the Father." He tried to speak convincingly.

"But surely people will say—"

"People will say, people will talk, ja, and people will sin that way, too. Johnny's peace is not here in Chandler," he pointed toward the town, "it is far from here. Don't worry about him. God's own Son died that Johnny could live, and you and I. We still must seek our salvation, Janna. Johnny is already with the Father."

Roelof tried to stop himself from shaking. It hurt him to speak so reassuringly, for he too felt the sharp bite of doubt, now and long before the death of Johnny Ver Steeg. It was all too close, for he had seen it all before. He had lived through countless scenes like that at the Korten's, imagined scenes but nonetheless real, haunting scenes so vivid they plagued him like an eternal curse. And all he knew was that only time would reveal what their God would deal to Janna Korten, to her father, and even to himself, again, this time. He wanted to be so sure, to be strong now like a dominie, like one who saw it all and understood.

The wagon climbed the knoll that overlooked Chandler as the sun finally dropped beneath the horizon, and the little houses in the village lit their own lanterns, turning the hillside town into a little galaxy.

"Where are we going?" Janna asked finally.

"To a friend."

"Who?"

"Someone I know will help you."

"Do I know her?"

"Maybe. It is Mina Van Zee."

Janna looked directly at the dominie for the first time since their ride had begun. There was stiffness in her surprise, almost an admonition, but she said nothing.

"Mina is a good woman. She will take good care of you."

The road was dark, but Roelof knew the way. Mina Van Zee lived alone on a farm six miles east of Chandler. In the dark it looked like any other—a square, gray cabin, with the yellow glow of lanterns gleaming through the windows.

As their wagon approached, a horse whinnied from behind the house, and the sound of moving animals came from the old barn just beside the house. Janna looked into the darkness almost inquisitively. Roelof knew that she was questioning her preacher, but he was sure that Mina Van Zee would show her the compassion she needed. He stopped the mare in front of the house, climbed down from the wagon, and tied the reins to the porch.

He didn't have to knock. Mina was already out of the house when he looked up.

"Dominie?" she said with some reserve, holding up a lantern.

"Ja, Mina. I come to ask a favor." He turned and beckoned to Janna who still sat in the wagon.

"What is it?" she asked, tossing back the long yellow hair that had already been brushed for the night.

"May we come in?"

"Of course. I'm sorry for being so ill-mannered. I am not used to company so late."

Roelof helped Janna off the wagon and led her up the porch stairs and into the house. There was no formal front-room here, for the house had been built long before anyone in these parts was able to afford such a luxury. The furniture was old and in poor repair; cushions were torn and several spokes were missing from most of the chairs that surrounded the small square table in the middle of the room. A long chest of bird's eye maple stood by the door to the bedroom. It was a beautiful piece, out of place among the otherwise plain furnishings.

"Come, Dominie, sit down here. Now what can I do?" Mina pulled out two chairs for her guests and took another for herself across from Janna.

"Mina, we have some business—" Roelof hesitated deliberately, glancing meaningfully toward Janna. "Oh, perhaps you don't know, this is Janna Korten, of Willem and Gertrude?"

"Ja, I recognize her." Mina smiled politely.

"She needs a place to stay for some time—"

"She can stay here, certainly." Mina's interruption was just as Roelof had expected. Even Janna seemed relieved by Mina's almost eager acceptance.

Vrielink sat back, relieved.

"But, I would like to know why, perhaps . . ."

"Ja, forgive me, Mina. Janna has had some trouble with

her parents, you see. She needs some place to stay until everything settles down."

"I am . . . I will have a baby."

Mina's smile broadened. "Ja, that's good, Janna. You should be happy."

"But my boyfriend—" Janna began to cry again, softly, restraining herself.

"Johnny Ver Steeg is dead." Roelof helped.

He watched Mina's face carefully, and saw her piecing everything together. She said nothing for a moment, trying quietly to understand. Then she rose and circled the table, coming to the girl's side. Still silent, she helped Janna to her feet and led her out to the kitchen, never looking toward the dominie.

She returned alone, carrying two cups of coffee. Roelof explained everything.

"Do you think she will return to her father's?" Mina asked.

"No, not unless Willem comes for her."

"She will not be taken by force, Roelof. I'll see to it. That man won't touch her unless she wants to go back to him." Mina's face changed slowly, hardening under a resolve that Roelof knew would be difficult to break. Her eyes winced when she spoke of Willem Korten.

"Korten was very confused when Janna left. He didn't know what he was saying, I am sure. The shock of it all—"

"That's no excuse for treating his own like that. He cannot say such things—even to his own child—not even this great *Christian*, Willem Korten."

Mina's words were typical of her. She was not considered one of the elect in Chandler, and Roelof had heard her use the word "Christian" with similar sarcasm many times in the past. He had first met her when he was given the assignment by his consistory: Mina had not been faithful in church attendance.

Roelof stood, looking towards the door. "I should be going now, Mina. I am happy that I brought her here."

"She will be taken care of; she is still a child." Mina

walked the dominie to the door. "Here now, button that coat. The spring nights get cold."

"It is still warm. Maybe I won't need it." Roelof stepped into the night air, still warm from the hot afternoon. Mina followed him to the porch.

"You look much better without it anyway. Now if those hands had some callouses, you wouldn't even look like a dominie."

Roelof watched her as she turned back toward the door; then he climbed aboard the wagon, slapped the reins across the horse's flanks, and waved a good-bye.

Mina's immediate concern and willingness had settled him. But the moonless spring sky seemed to echo Willem Korten's ringing words, and the dark night conjured the image of Johnny's bloodied body in too vivid detail. He thought of Janna; at least she was sheltered. He knew that she lacked assurance, that she probably wouldn't be sleeping, and that he was of little real help.

The six-mile ride back to Chandler took hours.

Roelof Vrielink stayed away from the Van Zee farm all summer. Korten, outraged by his daughter's living in with Mina Van Zee, had commanded Vrielink to stay out of his affairs. Yet it seemed that Willem was content to be rid of Janna for the interim; after all, he had told Isaac Brethhower, it would cost much more to send her some place in Sioux Falls.

He didn't see Mina again until Labor Day. By then, Roelof figured Janna to be quite far along, so when he saw Mina along the street with hundreds of other farm folk, all come to Chandler for the Labor Day Picnic, he wasn't surprised to see that Janna had stayed at home.

Ruddy-faced farmers and their wives brought long lines of children to town. The streets were full. Vendors peddled lemonade, peanuts, pop, and little bags of candy. The sharp smell of barbeque filled the summer air. Chandler's pool hall was overflowing all day long. Children and teenagers played games in the streets; and in the park, softball teams from Trosky, Hardwick, and other nearby towns squared off to determine the champion. The Edgerton band played in the afternoon and evening, and, as usual, everyone enjoyed the annual celebration. In the throng, it was quite possible to find an anonymity otherwise impossible on the dusty, vacant streets of the village.

Mina was speaking to a stranger when Roelof spotted her. He angled his way through the crowd until he stood beside her.

"Mina, how is it?"

"Well, Dominie—ja, good. And with you?"

"Fine."

She turned to her friend, a dark-haired farmer with a long mustache. "I must speak to the dominie, Frank; he hears my confession."

The tall man reared back and snorted. "You Hollanders got no confession, Mina. What are you talking about?"

She swatted him away with a left forearm. "You call me a Hollander? Come now."

He laughed again; the air filled with the tangy smell of liquor.

"Go now, I see you again later, maybe, Frank. Go—go to the bar there; you need some more." She turned him like a mother and pushed him in the direction of the pool hall.

Roelof looked away, laughing. "Many people again," he said.

"Ja, everybody comes to town for Labor Day."

Roelof came quickly to the point. "How's the girl?"

"She's big."

"How long yet?"

"Doc Saathof says no more than two months."

"She is healthy?"

"Ja, she seems fine. She helped with the work all summer. Never complained. Didn't seem to care."

"All is well then?"

Mina looked away, through the crowd, through the many people around her. Her skin was tanned by the summer sun, her hair brightened. She seemed oddly hesitant.

"No, Dominie."

"Is it her father—"

"No, no, he has not interfered." She laughed scornfully. "He hasn't lifted a finger. What is that man, Dominie? I can't understand such a person."

"He's bull-headed, Mina. I don't understand him either. But what isn't good about the girl?"

"Janna never smiles. I tell her that the Lord has given her the child to remember her Johnny. I tell her that the child will be one-half Johnny Ver Steeg. I try to cheer her. The neighbor children come over and try to help her laugh, but nothing works. Nothing. All day long she helps around the farm, but she never speaks, never smiles."

"She is so young, Mina. This is her first child. She has no husband. Do you expect singing?"

"Of course not. But I know, Roelof. I can see into the girl, and what I see makes me afraid."

Roelof glanced around the park. People talked happily in little groups while children darted in and out like mosquitoes. Roving bands of adolescent boys walked in regiment, their thumbs tucked behind their suspenders, looking far less grown up than they imagined, while the farm girls eyed them coyly like curious kittens.

"Can I do anything?" he asked finally.

"No, I'd like you to come out and try, but I don't think you or I can do anything."

It was all too plain. He leaned back on the only assurance he could muster. "We must pray then."

"Ja, Roelof. God would not reject this girl certainly—" Mina looked into Roelof's eyes, and he knew very well what she desired of him, and what he was really unable to bestow.

"No, no, certainly," he said, looking back toward the crowd as he visored his eyes with his hands.

"Ah, Mina, you good-looking woman," a voice sounded from nowhere, and suddenly a huge Swedish farmer was standing by her side.

"I will see you then, Dominie?" she asked quickly.

Roelof Vrielink smiled and departed.

Mina had focused Vrielink's pain. Certainly his God would not reject the innocent girl, he told himself. And yet He had done it before. Yes, He had. But for what purpose? No purpose?

When the last farmers left the Labor Day Picnic, Roelof Vrielink sat over an empty desk, staring into the flame of a dim lamp.

On a Saturday evening in mid-October, Roelof lit the gas lamp in his study. It was early, he thought, but the darkness seemed to settle comfortably into the village at an earlier hour each night. He hated to think of the winter, for as he grew older he felt each to be more severe than any before.

He opened the leather-bound Matthew Henry before him and started through the commentary on the Sermon on the Mount. Tomorrow afternoon's sermon would be the fourth in a series on Christ's words. The lamp dropped a soft glow over the old pages; he drew his special reading glasses from the desk drawer.

When he heard the knock at his front door, he was only too happy to respond. The house was silent—a knock brought promise of fellowship. He laid his glasses on the commentary and walked to the door.

"Dominie, you must come quick."

"Who's there?" he asked. The frontroom was dark and full of shadows.

"Kathy Sjoerdsma."

"Ja, Kathy, will you come in?"

"Mina says you must come quick—Mina Van Zee. She says it is time, and she says you must come quick 'cause it isn't good."

Roelof recognized the neigbor girl Mina had spoken of. He grabbed his coat from the hall tree as the young girl finally entered.

"Did you get Doc Saathof?"

"I tried, Dominie, but he isn't in."

Roelof Vrielink had lived through this scene countless times before, it seemed. He pulled the heavy black woolen coat around his shoulders, stepped out into the cold autumn evening, and shut the front door behind him. Kathy had already mounted her horse. Steam shot like smoke from its nostrils as it jumped and pranced.

"Kathy, listen!" He had planned it all before. "You go to Korten's, to Janna's parents. You know where they live?"

"Ja."

"Good, you tell them what is happening. And tell them to come. I will get Doc Saathof. Here, take the half-mile road; it is shorter." He pointed into the darkness, holding the reins of her horse, then slapped its thigh, sending horse and rider off into the darkness.

In a moment he had circled the parsonage and arrived at the church barn, where his horse was stabled. He handled the saddle and bridle like a jockey, mounted the mare, and left the barn, leaving the door open behind him.

Kathy was right. Doc Saathof's office was dark. He raced down Main toward the doctor's house, disregarding those who gawked as his horse galloped down the hard-packed street. He turned a corner and saw the house. Light streamed from the windows. Someone was home.

The mare stopped with a flurry of hoofs before the house. Roelof vaulted from the saddle and ran to the door. When no one answered his knock, he pounded the door with the butt of his hand until Mrs. Saathof finally appeared.

"Well, Dominie, I—"

"Evening, Mrs. Saathof. Husband in?"

"Why no, he—"

"Where is he?"

"Why, he's out on a call. I think Ed and Clara Hesselink's baby is on the way."

Roelof was stopped momentarily. His planning had not included anything like this.

"How long has he been there?"

"Since early afternoon."

"Clara's had, what—three now?"

"This is four, I think. What is it?"

He inhaled deeply. "It's Janna Korten. She has begun labor."

"When did she start? It is her first; it may be a long time yet."

"I don't know. But Mina Van Zee sent her neighbor to tell me. She just said that it wasn't so good."

"Well, you go, Dominie. I'll send word to Josef, and he will be on his way."

"Ja, thank you. It is all we can do." Roelof managed a smile at her deliberate manner, then turned and mounted his horse. By the time he was on Main, Mrs. Saathof was at her neighbor's door.

The cold October air splashed into his face and over his hands, numbing everything left uncovered. The moon was full and bright over the sloping hills, and the skies were filled with stars, lighting the road before him, making the country even brighter than the town. And as he rode, he gave thanks for the bright prairie night, and the bulky woolen coat that lay like a yoke over his shoulders, but kept the clear wintry air from penetrating, despite the six miles to Mina's farm.

Roelof didn't knock when he arrived. He flung his coat over an old wicker chair.

"Mina?" he called.

"Here, Roelof." The answer came from the bedroom.

He found Mina washing her hands in a china bowl. Janna lay white and almost lifeless in the brass bed.

Roelof was surprised at the tranquil scene. His heart was racing, for he had visualized the girl writhing in the pain of a savage labor. He had pictured young Janna in anguish, and Mina working to soothe her. But here he saw Janna lying very peacefully on the bed, her face emotionless.

"I'm glad you are here, Roelof. Is the doctor coming?"

"He will be, but he was out, Mina. His wife said he would be sent as soon as possible."

Mina Van Zee could normally strike awe in men. Her eyes were usually aflame with determination and strength. But this woman was not that Mina Van Zee. Her hazel eyes seemed soft when they reached for the dominie.

"I am afraid. I am afraid." She looked back at the bed.

"What's the matter?"

"It isn't good. She has been bleeding. She didn't tell me." Mina moved over to the rocker which had been moved from the parlor, and sat watching the girl closely. "She didn't even tell me she was in labor, Roelof. I don't know what's wrong. I have never seen a woman like this."

"Is she in labor now?"

"Ja, she moves occasionally. That's all I see. She doesn't scream or even talk, and the bleeding continues."

Roelof stepped around the bed and looked at the girl. Her deep-set eyes were closed, and her dark brows seemed to mar her light gray skin. He looked away, as if by instinct. He had seen death before, but this girl was too much an image of something he had never forgotten.

"Is she awake?" he whispered.

"I don't know, Roelof. I try to speak to her, but she does not respond." Mina rubbed her forehead. "I am afraid for her."

Roelof knelt by the bed. He leaned over to touch the girl's face and felt a coldness that chilled him. There was sweat on her forehead, but she seemed hardly alive. He closed his eyes for an instant and begged for strength.

"How did you know?" he asked.

"She doubled up before supper. I made her get into bed, and when I helped her change into nightclothes, I noticed the blood. She wouldn't say anything, Roelof. Then I went to her drawer and found more blood-stained clothes. And I think her water broke this morning, maybe even last night."

"How can that be?"

"I don't know."

"Can I do anything?"

"I don't know. I don't think anyone can do anything

really," she shook her head slowly as she rocked. She rubbed her eyes, then looked up. "But we must keep trying," she said, looking back at him. "One of us must watch her all the time. You can boil the scissors and some string. They're by the pot on the stove. Look in the kitchen. Then bring the iodine—it's in the cupboard." Mina got up from the chair and stood at the foot of the bed. "I don't know what will happen."

He left the room. He found everything in the kitchen—the water was already boiling. He found a pail by the door and filled it from the pump out back. He had been close to births before, but never had he found himself in this kind of position, for Doc Saathof usually handled the delivery with the help of a woman. The pump pushed hard in the cold night air, and with every rusty screech it made, Vrielink prayed.

"Roelof!" It was Mina's voice.

He grabbed the pail and ran to the kitchen, the icy water splashing against his leg and hands. He left the bucket and ran to the bedroom.

The covers were thrown back from the foot of the bed. Mina stood over the young girl.

"The baby is here. Is the water hot?"

"Ja."

He stepped closer and saw the purplish infant lying in a pool of blood between its mother's legs.

"So fast?"

"Ja, there was no warning. I just pulled back the blankets, and the baby burst out like a . . . like a . . ." Mina worked swiftly to control the bleeding. "She is ripped bad. Give me some hot water."

Roelof brought a steaming bowl to the bed and put the pitcher on the floor within reach.

"Is the baby alive, Mina?"

"Ja, I think he's fine."

"Praise God," he said softly.

"But the girl, Roelof, the girl." Mina pressed big wads of cloth into Janna. "I put some towels on the stove, in the front . . . and some bricks—they're hot by now. Bring them quickly."

Roelof's hands were burned by the hot bricks when he returned. But the baby was kicking on the bed. Mina had doused her hands in the scalding water and was rubbing the baby's back with her fingers. Suddenly there was a little bleat, and Roelof watched the tiny mouth stretch into a cry.

"Get the scissors and string. Bring the kettle."

Roelof's hands stung from the water and the hot kettle. When he returned, steam blanketed the window of the bedroom and hung like a cloud over the bed. Sweat poured from Roelof's forehead and ran from Mina's face and arms as she worked.

She wrapped the baby in clean warm linens, but left the cord jutting from its abdomen, still attached to its mother.

"We must cut it," she motioned for the scissors. "Quick, give me the iodine."

She doused the cord with iodine and poured ointment over the string. Then she tied it around the baby's lifeline, about one inch from the child, and repeated the action another inch from the first knot. The scissors cut cleanly through the cord. The baby continued to cry, but with every breath he seemed to turn a lighter pink. Mina spread more iodine over the cut ends of the cord. However, the blood still flowed from Janna Korten.

"Take the child away, Roelof. Keep him warm. Take him away quickly!"

He held the new life in his hands. The child's puckered skin, still changing into an even more radiant pink, looked beautiful. But although the child had been severed from its mother, Roelof knew the joy he held in his hands was still a part of what would yet happen in the bedroom. Here was life, and death, again. Vrielink's eyes closed tightly.

The front door slammed. Roelof turned. It was the doctor.

The doctor had no time for formalities. "Baby fine?" He took the child from the dominie without waiting for an answer, looked it over quickly and nodded.

"The mother?" He turned in an instant when he heard Mina moving in the bedroom. He placed the baby back in Roelof's arms and was gone.

Dominie Vrielink sat in a chair at the table, holding the child closely, infusing it with the heat from his own body. He grabbed his coat from the chair and wound it about the child, always holding it to his chest. The infant's eyes were closed, but as the warmth entered his tiny body, he stopped crying and struggled to open his eyes.

Still holding the child, Roelof rose and moved to the kitchen. He lifted the pail of cold water and set it on the stove. The fire still crackled within.

He heard the door then, and saw Willem and Gertrude Korten, well bundled against the cold, enter the house. Willem took off his black cap with his good hand, and removed his coat in an instant. Gertrude saw the child in the dominie's arms and reached out to take him, keeping the baby wrapped in Vrielink's coat.

"Well, where is my daughter?" Korten boomed.

Roelof quickly led him through the kitchen, leaving Gertrude and the child alone.

"She is not good, Willem." Roelof stopped before entering the bedroom.

Korten was red from the long ride. He wiped his runny nose with the sock on his maimed hand, sputtered and fidgeted as if no time had passed since their meeting in May. But he waited with the dominie.

Mina stepped out then, her face showing the strain. She looked at Willem Korten with contempt. Months of care and months of fear had kindled deep hatred within her, and Roelof saw it for a moment in her eyes.

"What now, Mina?" He broke through the hostility.

Mina looked back at Roelof, forgetting, it seemed, the anger and frustration, remembering only the sorrow she felt before Korten's arrival.

"She bleeds and bleeds. The doctor is doing all he can."

"What is the matter?" Willem broke in with the

question.

Mina's shoulders sagged as she shook her head again. "She doesn't want to live."

"My Janna?" Korten seemed almost offended. He marched past Mina, through the doorway to the bedroom. Gertrude sat staring at Roelof. She too had heard. Mina looked into the dominie's eyes, still shaking her head, then stared at the ceiling.

Roelof followed Willem. Doc Saathof worked rapidly, but it seemed that he was as helpless as Mina. "She bleeds from within and without," he was saying to Willem.

"It is too much?"

"No, she could live. But she doesn't want to."

Willem Korten spread his left hand over his daughter's forehead. He rubbed his fingers over her skin and pulled the dark hair back from her ears.

"Janna," he said gently, "can you hear me? This is your father."

There was no motion. The doctor blotted the blood that continued to flow from Janna's body.

"Janna, listen to me, I'm your father."

Her face was calm, almost serene; she did not respond in any way.

"Janna. Come now. You must come home with Mama and me." His eyes flashed at his daughter, but they glowed with repentance. "Everything is fine. Mama is holding the baby now, ja, she is, you should see it!" Willem's face nearly touched his daughter's.

"Janna, please, we will be happy, ja?"

His face darkened with the intensity of his pleading, but she didn't respond. There was no movement. He made no effort to stop his own tears.

"Janna, please, you must live! You must want to live!"

More bloodied rags fell to the floor as the doctor pressed clean towels into the girl. He held arteries with his hands, trying desperately to make the constant flow abate. Roelof wanted to run away, but he stood there, praying.

"Janna, please, I'm sorry, Janna, I'm sorry—please."

Gertrude appeared suddenly. She kneeled next to her husband, holding him with her left arm. His head dropped slowly, lower and lower until it rested on the bed.

"Janna, we love you." Gertrude tried to speak clearly as she held her daughter's arm.

Then there was movement. Janna's eyes remained closed, but her jaw quivered slightly, her lips moved, and they all heard her whisper clearly, "Forgive us," and her mouth closed.

It was only fifteen minutes later that Doc Saathof raised the sheet over her head. Roelof watched him from the door.

"What about the child?" the doctor asked as he walked by Vrielink.

"What do you mean?" Roelof was surprised at the question.

"I know a very good family in Edgerton who don't have any children. He is a good, healthy boy, you know."

Mina sat alone, holding the baby close to her, rocking gently. Gertrude tried to console her husband who sat, eyes downward, head in hands. Roelof had seen it again, the death of one so young, so innocent, and new life, here wrapped tightly in his own wool coat. Again his God had made a deal, swapping death for life. Johnny Ver Steeg was dead. Janna Korten was dead. Only a parentless son remained, swaddled in black wool. Willem Korten was defeated. Perhaps, he thought, it wasn't a trade after all, but a process—one's death for another's life. For him, for Korten, for all of them.

"Well, Dominie?" the doctor persisted.

Roelof nodded. "Willem, what about the child? The doctor says he knows a good Dutch family in Edgerton—they have no children—"

Roelof stopped suddenly, for Willem stared back at him strangely.

"That's right, Korten," said the doctor. "A young couple. She can never have children."

"We will take the child, Dominie," Gertrude said with resolution.

"Willem?" Roelof asked.

"He is our only grandson, this boy. He will be our only grandson. Janna and Johnny's boy."

Roelof saw the scars again beneath the flannel sock as Willem brushed his wrist over the corner of one eye and looked up into the face of the dominie.

He walked over to the table where Mina sat with the child. He bent over to take the child from her, but Mina moved her chair away. She held the baby tightly, but said nothing.

"Mina, this is right," he insisted, quietly, gently.

"To hell with what is right, Roelof. Is it good?" Her eyes burned into the preacher.

"Mina," he said. He turned toward the slumped and quiet figure of Willem Korten, then returned to Mina with the eyes of one who sees but dimly through an old window. "It's all right."

She too looked at Willem and Gertrude, then twisted back to Roelof slowly and very reluctantly gave him the baby.

Roelof held the sleeping child firmly and carried him across the room.

Willem raised his head but remained seated, his eyes following the child. He reached forward and carefully took the boy from the dominie.

"He is the Lord's, Willem." Roelof Vrielink stood over the old couple.

"Ja, Dominie." Willem and Gertrude bent to look at their only grandson. The child slept soundly in his grandfather's arms.

Through Devious Ways

John had seen the broken chain lying like a bullsnake on the bed of the wagon when the raw frost still gloved the leaves of the yellowed corn. He didn't mention it when De Regt had given him explicit instructions about the husking, because he knew the man, or at least his father did. After all, he told himself, Hermanus and his wife had coffee with the Van der Walls nearly every Sunday between the services at the church in Prinsburg. He just assumed De Regt had also noticed the chain and would fix it as soon as possible.

So he started snapping ears from the stalks and tossing them blindly off the bangboard and into the wagon. It had been nearly dark when De Regt left the field; the sun had only begun to lighten the eastern sky. A few down ears, covered by dirt and stuck by frost, made John's work more tedious, but De Regt was a proper farmer—he knew when to harvest his corn. The stalks stood high and proud in straight rows.

And John was proud of his abilities. He had acquired a reputation among the farmers for being a tireless and efficient worker. Many jobs were offered him during the harvest season. The frozen ears, the down ears, were all part of the job, and although their stubbornness wore at his nerves and fingers, he never thought of complaining, for he had picked corn in many fields more ragged than this one.

De Regt had left his son behind to pick the down rows. Henry was nearly thirteen, Hermanus's oldest boy, and he, too, worked hard to clean the ears from his row. But when dawn warmed into morning, when the sun quilted the Minnesota soil, melting the frost from the rows, Henry's head popped up more frequently from behind the wagon, signaling the boy's weariness, and John would wait, impatiently, to signal the horses to move ahead.

Little more than an hour had passed before John shed his overall jacket and hung it on the wagon. He glanced back and saw the boy chucking clods of mud at a meadowlark perched on a fence post.

"Here, *jongen!*" he commanded.

Henry glanced at him, then threw two more clods before the bird finally flew from its perch.

"Ja, ja. I'm coming. I'm coming," he grumbled.

John stood for a moment, allowing the boy to catch up, and looked into the wagon. Hundreds of nearly clean ears were piled unevenly against the right side, beneath the bangboard, but the bed was still visible near the left wall. Buried already was the chain that should have spanned and secured the sides of the wagon. Hermanus would be back to fix it soon, he told himself. His father always said that Hermanus De Regt was a good farmer.

"Giddap!" he signaled the horses and the work continued. The ripened ears cracked off the stalks easily and cleanly. Hermanus's gloves were old and worn, but John was an experienced picker. He had the right touch. Pull the hook back through the leaves, holding the ear with the left hand; jerk the ear and pull it away with the right, leaving a handful of leaves in the left, and toss it off the bangboard and into the wagon—all in one smooth motion. He had been at it for years, doing a man's share long before he was fourteen. He could barely remember picking the inside rows. On almost any day he could pick a hundred bushels.

The ears banged off the board—"clunk," "clunk," "clunk"—evenly, almost mechanically.

By mid-morning his fingers and wrists were loose and supple, warmed by the October sun and the constant jerking motion. He remembered other jobs when stubborn ears would stick to the stalks as if nailed there. Regular jerking wouldn't break them, and pain would flow through his hand and arm, and his wrist would pull itself out of joint. The pain would be so bad that he would be forced to quit; his wrists would swell as if they were infected. The Van der Walls couldn't afford any lost time this harvest. His father counted on the money that John made during the season.

When the sun stood nearly above his head, John Van der Wall noticed Hermanus returning to the field, straight as a poplar. By then the wagon seemed almost filled, its sides bulging abnormally. De Regt cut through the field behind the wagon, retracing its path. The team moved forward on command and the work continued, but John saw his employer emerge from the corn with a handful of ears and lay them down where John could reach them when the wagon passed that way again. De Regt continued cleaning up until he reached his son, some ten yards behind the wagon. Their muffled voices were barely audible over the snapping ears and the slow drone of the wind through the rows.

De Regt was tall and gaunt with a bony face and a long, Indian-like nose that arched from between two bulging eyes. His head seemed to bob like a crow's when he stepped carefully between the corn. His lips curled downward beneath a light mustache that grew like wild thistles down around the corners of his mouth, and his unkempt hair hung in little clumps around his ears. John remembered having once thought that De Regt looked like the portrait of George Washington that hung in the bank at Prinsburg.

When he reached John, De Regt turned and looked down the rows that ran straight as a taut rope. "How is the boy doing, John?" he asked.

"Good."

"Ja, he is a good worker."

John glanced back at Henry De Regt. The boy was barely visible, his back arched to the earth where he cleaned the ears from the inside row.

"You should get them all, John. Look at the piles I've picked there." He pointed a bony finger. "You're no child anymore—we can't just forgive such carelessness."

"Ja, I'll try." John continued to pick, looking up only when spoken to.

"Good day for husking here, ja?" De Regt removed his cap and brushed back his thin, graying hair. "The sunshine's warm, but the breeze is cool. And the field is dry."

"Ja, it is a good day." John looked up at his employer. There was a white ring about his forehead where the cap usually sat; otherwise, his face was as brown as the soil of his farm.

"Well, you are getting a load here, eh?"

"Ja, I think it is full. Do you want—"

"Oh, no, no, no. Plenty more will go in here yet. I can barely see the load above the box."

John stopped, surprised, but said nothing.

"No, you can get more on yet. I must fix the fence here. It is almost noon. I'll tell you when it is full. You can easily get in the rest of the row here." He pointed down the field, not even waiting for any response. He took three big steps back to the inside row, said something to his son again, and moved away.

"Mr. De Regt!" John could not let it pass so easily.

"Ja?" He turned back, his straight face above the corn, eyelids drooping over his swollen eyes.

"The wagon. You know about it?"

"What's that?"

"I say, the wagon, you know?"

"Ja, what of the wagon?"

"The chain is busted."

"Eh?"

"The chain—"

"Ach, ja, the chain . . . I forgot to fix it. Ja, sure, I will fix it. Sure, sure, sure." He waved impatiently, turned and left.

John looked at the wagon. The sides were bulging from the weight of the ears. He knew the wagon was full. But his father knew Hermanus De Regt. They had gone to the same church for as long as John Van der Wall could remember.

By the time he pulled the husking hook over his right glove again, he was angry. He had unloaded the entire wagon by himself—even the boy had not helped—and he was sure it held more than thirty bushels. Scooping out the load was hard work, it always was, hardly a relief from the monotonous hours of picking. But a sense of injustice kindled some new emotion within John Van der Wall, and his scoop worked constantly, even easily, moved by rising annoyance. When the box was empty, he looked again at the bin and was convinced that he was right.

Hermanus De Regt was still nowhere around. The boy bounded from the house when he saw the wagon empty, and vaulted into the box, picking up the reins on the way.

"Let's go, John. I'll drive."

"Where is your father?"

"I don't know." The boy seemed impatient.

John stood in the empty wagon, holding the broken chain. He scanned the entire yard, but nowhere did he see the man.

"Come on, John. We have to get another load."

John nodded, and the horses jerked the wagon forward, back to the cornfield.

De Regt's gloves were already reversed after many hours of work. The morning's husking had opened holes in the fingers, and John's nails soon wore down from the work. The balls of his fingers became tender, and each snapping ear sent pain searing through his hand. In the heat of his irritation, pain and exhaustion turned to bitterness. He felt a growing sense of injustice, despite his anger and fatigue.

But it made him work even harder. He became so swollen by his sense of outrage that the ears seemed to drop from the stalks. He picked faster and harder, exasperated by Henry when the boy couldn't keep up, but helping with the inside row to keep the wagon moving over the soft earth.

"Ja, John, you are doing better. I find only a few ears in

the rows."

He looked up quickly, surprised to see De Regt standing before him. He hadn't seen him approach.

"Are you thirsty?"

"No, sir." John kept working, the hard ears clunking off the bangboard.

De Regt said no more. He turned to his son and helped with his row. In a few minutes they were nearly at the back of the wagon. John moved even faster in order to keep ahead. Soon the sides of the wagon were bulging again, the wood curved like a buggy spring. But Hermanus kept working, talking occasionally to his son. John said nothing this time, his anger turning into hatred, his lips sealed by stubbornness.

"Hey, John, stop once!"

He heard the command and stood waiting like a tortured slave, his back to the master.

"You take all the rows down the field to the end there, ja? I need Henry to fix the fence. When you get to the end, take the load and put it in the crib. Then you can meet us back here."

John turned slowly to face his employer. The wagon was already full. He wanted to shout at the man, to tell him again about the chain, to scream about the full load, to remind him of Cornelius Van der Wall, his father, but his own stubborn hatred grew into a vicious delight in the injustice he felt himself suffering. He said nothing, but nodded slowly and turned back to the field.

In a moment father and son were gone and John was left to take all three rows. When he finally came to the end of the field, the load was heaped into a steep hill. Over 35 bushels, for sure.

When he returned to the field, John knew that suppertime was passing. The sun had fallen into the western sky, and the breezes which had kept the work cool through the morning and afternoon began to chill. Hermanus and his son awaited him at the point where he was to begin. He pulled the horses into the proper row and tied the reins securely, saying nothing.

"You work hard, John. Your father should be proud. You unloaded nearly 30 bushels faster than most men could."

John tightened his swollen hands into fists for a moment to control his rage. There hadn't been an ear less than 35. He pulled his overall jacket on once more, stepped into his rows, and began to pick again, accelerating the pace he had set earlier.

"John!"

He stopped and faced De Regt.

"Henry says he'll work until it gets dark and then have his supper. Is that good with you?"

"Yes, sir."

Hermanus left then, but he returned when darkness fell over the fields. Nearly a half load was already piled in the wagon, covering the broken chain again.

"Ja, boys, it's a good day's work," he said, hands on hips. "But it's time to stop now." He walked over to the wagon as both Henry and John began to remove their tattered gloves. "What's here—ja, 14 or 15?—plus 30 on the first, and 30 on the second. That's 75 bushels. Good work, eh, John?"

John threw the gloves into the box and jumped in himself. "Not so good, Hermanus. I've done much better."

"Better?" De Regt looked almost surprised.

"Ja, much better."

"Ach, 75 bushels is a good day's work for a boy like you. Not even some men can pick that much."

De Regt sat by his son, who drove the team back from the field.

In an hour John Van der Wall was home. Hermanus De Regt had invited him to stay for supper with his family, but John had quietly insisted that he would prefer to eat at home. As an afterthought, De Regt promised to have the wagon fixed by the next morning.

He told his parents nothing about what had happened,

ate very little, and went directly to bed. It was late, and tomorrow would be early again. He lay awake, quiet, sullen, his body tired, his fingers numb, his mind wrenched between two images of Hermanus De Regt, his own and his father's. He made no resolutions, no decisions about tomorrow, for he still believed that De Regt was a man of his word. His body, like his mind, seemed unsettled, for when he finally slept, he rolled on his bed as if he were sleeping on gravel.

"Morning, John."

The cold October air seeped through his jacket like water, but the frigid hour's walk was forgotten in a moment when he saw his employer.

"Morning."

"Well, let's get started. Two more days like yesterday and we might have it all in."

John walked slowly to the wagon and glanced over the side. The chain was still broken, buried beneath the corn picked late last night.

"What about the chain, Hermanus?"

"Eh?"

"I said, what about the chain?"

"Ach, ja, ja. I forgot about it." He snapped his fingers. "I will get at it today, sure."

"*Now*, Hermanus." John stood, looking straight at the taller man.

"What is that?"

"I said, fix it now, or I don't work."

The wind rushed through the corn. The men looked into each other's eyes.

"No! Get to work, Van der Wall." De Regt's eyes bulged with amazement.

"I will not work until the wagon is fixed. If you want me to work, fix the wagon."

"Why, your father, John—"

"My father isn't working here. *I* am your hired man. But I will quit—now—if you don't fix the wagon."

"But why? Surely you don't—"

"I picked more than 75 bushels yesterday, Hermanus, much more. You are not being fair with me."

De Regt rubbed his eyes nervously, saying nothing. He looked back at the morning sky to the east, then surveyed the remainder of his corn. Finally he stared back at his employee, looking stern and almost fatherly.

"I say you will work, Johannes."

Henry stood quietly at his father's side. His eyes moved uncertainly from the man at his left to John Van der Wall.

"I say you will go to work now, Johannes Van der Wall." De Regt lightened his tone, conscious of the boy at his side.

"I mean no disrespect, Hermanus. I just want what is fair." John's resolution gained strength in the confrontation. A full day of what-ought-not-to-be reinforced his belief in what he was doing now.

"I am the boss here." Hermanus put his hands on his waist. "You are here because I hired you. I will determine what is fair, what is just. How dare you?"

Henry stepped over to the inside row; dry corn stalks cracked as he walked.

"Well? Go to work!"

"When you fix the wagon, De Regt."

De Regt leaned over slowly and jerked at a broken stalk, then peeled the leaves slowly away. He glanced at his son.

"Very well then, you may go. I will find someone else in your place."

John walked down the field, his face lit by a small, unflinching smile.

"—and there are many others, Johannes," De Regt yelled. "There are many others who need to work, who need the money. Your father knows that, too."

John Van der Wall didn't stop to listen, but he heard each word clearly as he marched down the row toward the gate.

His tracks were still fresh across the dew on the forty

acres of pasture that he crossed to reach De Regt's farm. The sun rose in a blaze as he walked east across the meadow, face lifted. He stopped for a moment and stripped the overall jacket from his shoulders. He straightened it carefully, holding it by the collar. He had paid nearly a dollar for it in Willmar. His own money. Pa couldn't afford it, he knew. He threw it back over his shoulder, still holding the collar, and kept walking.

He was sure he could get another picking job. Ben Mc-Crory had talked to him just last week. Pa hadn't been able to afford much the last two years. Almost everything John needed for work was from his own earnings; even some of his little brother's things—shoes, a cap—were bought with his money.

Almost two years ago, he remembered, the crops had looked tall and strong in early July. The corn had stood more than waist high. His father had thanked the Lord as he asked His blessing every mealtime, it seemed. They had bought ten more acres four years ago, and John understood that a good crop would keep the creditors happy for at least another year. And then the hail. One night it was hot, hot and wet when they settled into their bunks. But the wind, a slashing wind that shrieked through the elm grove, lightning that made the yard as light as day, and thunder that shook the house, woke them all, and sent them into the storm cellar for at least an hour. John remembered his mother praying. And when the family came out, little cone-shaped piles stood by the downspouts, like little piles of salt. His father went to his field then, even though it was dark. John remembered seeing his dark figure melt into the night, as the sky flickered with lightning many miles to the east.

John walked through the field of corn where the Van der Wall's hope had stood so high just two years ago. Pa had to take a job then, with an implement dealer in Raymond. Everyone had to work much harder since then, especially his father. John respected his father. And when Pa Van der Wall expected more from his son, John tried his best to produce.

Their own corn was ready to be picked, but like everything else for the last two years, it would be done only when there was some extra time. He could start today. His little brother could help.

John Van der Wall was running when he entered the yard from behind the barn. The prospect of doing their own corn, plus the sustaining sense of righteousness he felt from his conflict with De Regt made him eager to begin.

His father had already left for work, and his mother was doing the chores alone when he walked up behind her and took the fork from her hands.

"John, what brings you home?" His mother's round face turned to him, her eyes showing surprise.

"I'm not going to work for De Regt again," he said, shoving hay through the chute.

"Well, why? You aren't done yet?"

"No."

"Well?"

"I quit."

"Why?"

"Hermanus was not fair to me, Ma." John stood the fork upright and leaned his arms over the handle. "He did wrong."

She untied the red scarf from her head and used it to wipe the sweat and chaff from her temples. There was anguish in her eyes. John saw it and winced as she spoke. "What do you mean?"

"The wagon was busted . . . the chain was broken. All day he promised to fix it, but he never did. He said I picked 75 bushels. He lied. The wagon held much more than 30, much more. You should have seen the box! The sides bent way out like this—" He made an exaggerated curve with his arm.

"Oh, John!" She brought the scarf to her face again.

"But, Ma, don't you see, it wasn't fair—"

His mother shook her head and exhaled hard.

"You finish the chores, John." She said no more but

climbed slowly down the ladder to the main floor of the barn.

John did pick corn that day—all day—and he didn't even break for dinner. His mother brought him lunch midway through the afternoon, but she made no mention of their neighbor. John knew that his father would return later; then the whole affair would be reviewed thoroughly.

The Van der Wall's corn was not as easy to pick as De Regt's. It had matured earlier, and the strong fall winds had taken a toll amid the rows. But John worked hard, even harder than yesterday, determined to get close to a hundred bushels in, despite his late start. His little brother Peter helped, but he was young and inexperienced, and John found himself helping with the inside row as often as he had when he worked for De Regt.

His father appeared silently late in the afternoon. There was no mention of the incident; both men knew that conversation would follow later at the supper table. They picked until darkness made the ears difficult to find; then John drove the wagon back to the crib and unloaded, while his father did the chores.

By the time John had cleaned up thoroughly, he was ready for the interrogation. He was surprised when the entire supper hour passed with no mention of his quitting at De Regt's. His father talked about a trip to Clara City that day to set up a self-binding reaper. He talked about some cousins of his, and his face brightened when he told of the huge farms he had seen.

Not until devotions were finished and Peter was gone into the front room was the incident between John and Hermanus De Regt even mentioned.

"Now, John," his father began, as his mother took the dishes from the table, "what is this all about—this business between you and De Regt?"

Both men sipped hot coffee.

"He refused to fix the wagon. I asked him to, and he didn't—he wouldn't." John felt nervous as his father's deep, brown eyes stared into him.

"What was wrong?"

"The chain was broken."

"Is that all?"

John swallowed the last of his coffee and set the cup back in the saucer.

"Ja."

"Well, I don't think I understand. His machinery is *his* business, John. You just work for him."

"He made me fill the wagon, Pa, fill it to overflowing. Twice the wagon was heaped up full—twice! And I asked him to fix it."

"How much did he pay you?"

"He didn't pay me."

"Then how did you know—"

"He told me I picked only 75 bushels. I know there was more. The wagon held 35 at least, probably 40. I know, Pa, I've picked before."

"Ja, ja, ja, you don't have to act smart. I know what you've done before."

Only the steady clink of dirty dishes and saucers interrupted the silence. His mother kept working, but listened closely, he knew.

"So you quit because it wasn't fair?"

"Ja."

His father scratched his temples. "Did you think of his side of it?"

"Pa, I asked him more than once—"

"He has to get his crop in alone now."

"He says he can get someone else easy."

John held his head high. His father called to his wife for more coffee.

"Ja, he's right, you know. Lots of boys your age are looking for work. Someone else will just make the money now."

"Pa, would you have kept working if you knew it wasn't fair?"

Cornelius Van der Wall shook his head. "Johannes,

Johannes, when the Lord sent the hail—not to Raymond, not to Clara City, not even to De Regt's fields, was He *fair?* Was that *just* of Him? Did I say to Him, 'Well, Father, I'm sorry, but I refuse to work with such injustice'?"

John looked away. His mother offered him more coffee, but he shook his head.

"When Verburg pays me two dollars for a job that he makes twenty on, do I yell and throw down my wrench? Do I quit and *zannik* about how it's not fair of him?"

John's mother removed her apron and sat down at the table between her husband and her son. She reached out to John as she spoke. "Everything is not always *fair* in this life, John. The Christian knows that, and he must learn to live with it, humbly and prayerfully. Doesn't Paul say too that we must be in subjection to the higher powers?"

"But I can get another job, Pa. McCrory asked me too, you know. Just last week."

"McCrory is not a church man, John."

"But he is a good man, Ma." John clenched his right hand into a fist. "I would rather work for Ben McCrory than Hermanus De Regt any day."

His father looked up quickly. "You are speaking of a brother in Christ, John!"

John trembled and swallowed quickly. He respected his father's argument, but he was convinced that there was more to all this than his father had yet seen. He laughed lightly, to himself, almost sarcastically, and shook his head. "Hermanus De Regt is no brother of mine. A man who will cheat you on purpose, then lie to you, is no brother of mine."

"John, I'm sure he didn't. . ." his mother tried to appease his anger.

"If he didn't mean it deliberately, Ma, then why didn't he fix the wagon like he promised? It wouldn't take him long."

"I can't answer for Hermanus. He will have to answer for himself." John's father spoke clearly and without emotion. "But you miss the point, John. We who follow

Christ must be humble and persevering. 'Blessed are the meek,' He said; 'they shall inherit . . .' But I see no meekness in you. Where is your love and forgiveness?"

John sat silently, looking from his mother to his father.

"It's De Regt who must ask my forgiveness, Pa. He wronged me." John had never spoken this way to his parents before, but he was prompted by a vigorous sense of what was right.

His mother looked up cautiously. "Perhaps he should go back tomorrow morning, Pa?" She looked uncertainly at her husband.

"I will not go back, Ma. I told him to fix the wagon or get someone else, and he told me to 'Get to work!' as if I was a slave. I will not be treated like that. I will not work for Hermanus De Regt again."

Cornelius Van der Wall was silent. Dina was astonished. "We will miss the money, John, you know that." She waited for her husband to speak.

"I can get other jobs, Pa." John was stronger now. His father's eyes had softened. John had not seen that look on his father's face before, but somehow he understood it, and he felt that he knew he had prevailed. "I'll go to Ben Mc-Crory tomorrow—at dinnertime," he said.

Cornelius nodded his head slowly.

"But, Pa—"

"Ja, Mama, the boy is right. Tomorrow morning he will harvest our corn again, then look for another job." He scratched his nose. "But remember what your mother and I have said, Son. You have to learn to take some things. You have to accept the Lord's will, humbly and graciously, even when it is hard. Then you will be blessed, otherwise not."

"Yes, Pa, I think I understand."

John rose from the table and went to his room. Through the heating vent he heard his mother crying later, but he heard also the deep, resonant voice of his father. He lay awake on his bed for a long time, confident in victory, but humbled, almost to the point of tears, by a sense of separation which was, to him, both exciting and fearful, and yet but dimly understood.

No one mentioned his quitting until after Sunday dinner several days later. Hermanus and his wife had stopped for coffee after the morning service, as was their custom, but John had no desire to sit around the table with them. He was not missed, however, for he had rarely sat with the adults before. But he knew that his parents would certainly raise the job issue with the neighbors, and he feared that the topic would arise again sometime after the De Regts had left.

Peter left the table quickly after prayer, but rather than begin to clean up the dishes, John's mother sat waiting for what she knew would be a continuation of their earlier discussion.

"Good sermon by the dominie this morning. Good sermon." His father's observation was obviously intended to provoke a reply.

"What do you think, Son?"

"Ja, it was good." He was surprised at the questioning; his father rarely spoke of the sermon to him, except to reiterate the dominie's points before Sunday's noon devotions.

"Do you believe what Dominie said?"

"Ja, oh, ja. It was a good sermon."

"And you disagree with nothing?"

The kitchen chair creaked beneath John as he fidgeted, looking desperately for something to add.

"No, I agreed with all that he said."

"Good, good." Cornelius looked stern. John knew that his father had caught him. "Ja, good," he said again. "Dominie spoke of the Lord's control over all things, didn't he?"

John nodded.

"He said that we have to recognize God's hand over us, and do His will—" he pointed to imaginary spots on the table "—in everything we do."

"Ja, but that's not easy," John mouthed familiar words.

"No, that's not. The Lord didn't say it would be."

His father stopped for a moment and lifted his cup. His mother's eyes moved from husband to son and back again.

"Ja," his father drew in a big breath. "Ja, well, we spoke to Hermanus today . . . about you. He said you worked hard." He nodded appreciatively. "He said you were a very good worker."

John breathed more easily for a moment. "Ja, I worked hard. I was angry with him, and I worked very hard."

"Ja, John, he said you were angry, very angry." He stopped again, shook his head slowly and continued. "He said that he fired you because of it."

John's mouth dropped open at his father's words. "He fired me? For what?"

"For being angry about the chain, and for swearing at him."

"Swearing?"

"Ja, he says you took the name of the Lord in vain."

John's mother watched him fearfully. His father's eyes held that strange new softness.

"Ach, he lies, Pa."

"John, don't cover up your sin." His mother pointed into his face.

"He says that you damned him with God's name."

"He lies." John shook his head quickly, a faint smile of disbelief spread across his face.

"Did you, Johannes?" His mother waited.

"Mother, I didn't. I tell you the truth. It all happened like I said."

She cried then, but John didn't know whether her tears were of belief or disbelief.

"I believe you, John." His father's voice was steady. "Hermanus lied, I'm sure of it." He reached over to his wife, pulling her closer to him. She cried softly in short, uneven breaths.

"Ma, go get us some coffee now. I will see De Regt later this afternoon. After church. It will be good, Ma."

She looked up at her son, walked to him and kissed him lightly on the forehead. Then she smiled and left the room.

"Does she believe me, Pa?"

"Ja, John, she believes you, too."

He held out his hand to his father. "Then why does she still cry?"

"For Hermanus."

John sat quietly for a moment, looking at his father. Then he pushed his chair away from the table and rose very slowly. He looked toward the bedroom where his mother had gone, then back to his father.

"John, how goes the work at McCrory's?"

"Good."

"That's good, and the pay?"

"Ja, Pa, good, too—all I need."

John turned away from the table, his mind still possessed by the image of his mother. "Excuse me, Pa?"

"Ja."

Peter bounded into the room just then.

"Time to get ready for church, Peter. We must go now in a little while."

"Ja, Daddy."

John was nearly out of the room when he heard his father's voice. "Will you be coming with us, Son?"

John looked back at his father, astonished. The question was new, but it was real. It was in his father's face.

"Ah, ja . . . ja, I will be going." He turned to the stairs, looked back once more at his father and younger brother, and climbed up the stairs to his room.

Reminiscence

"Why sure I remember Jake Bossen! Land sakes, who could forget him? Probably the ugliest cuss this side of the Missouri. Boy, that guy was ugly—worse'n a mud fence, that's sure.

"But every day he'd up'n walk through Harrison, not just once, but lots of times every day to ring those church bells. Any man as ugly as him you'd think'd be smart enough to stay off the street—lock himself up somewhere so he wouldn't scare the women and horses.

"But not Jake Bossen. Oh, no, why he'd be walkin'—we'd see him—three, four times a day through town, swingin' those long arms like a kinda ape, rolling along in the wind like Russian thistles. Why, you remember him too, don't you?

"Sure. Course, he'd walk monkey-like ya see, cause he had that humpback, you remember. Don't really know whether he was born that way though. He was kinda old already when I was growin' up. But I'm assumin' that he was. Least, that's the only way I ever knew 'im.

"Well, that old humpback would ride like a fat old muskrat up here, see, on his right shoulder, so when he walked, you know, that long left arm, why it'd be scraping the dust off the streets of Harrison. Sure! And his right, I suppose, got kinda jealous, maybe, of the left, what with hangin' way down there, bein' the first to pick up lost pennies and stuff, so the right just kinda growed down there, too. Boy, he was an awful ugly character! He just sorta loped along the street, you know, those lanky arms just hangin' there and swayin'.

"And then that beard! Why, I don't think he ever cut the darn thing. The last time I saw him, that old beard was hanging purdnear as low as his arms. Remember that? Boy, he was a queer-lookin' cuss! But he'd walk, what was it, three, four times a day down to the old church—every day 'cept Sundays . . . and even then, too, I guess, but at different times. All the way from the junky cabin he lived in, up there almost outside a town—all the way from there just to ring that darn bell. Even in winter, you know? Heck, he even did it in the rain!

"We all thought he was crazy, too, besides bein' so ugly. Remember thinkin' that? When we was little—Ed, you remember this, you was with us—we used to yell at him, 'Hey, Jake, what time ya got?' Sure! We'd yell at him from across the street even. And he'd stop rollin' along, look up, turn that ugly head a his to see who wuz callin' and then stick his right hand into his vest. Remember that, Ed, he always wore that suit, no matter how hot? Golly, we thought he was loony! Well, he'd reach in, pull out his watch, read it careful-like, and yell back the time. 'Ten to ten, kids,' he'd say, 'the Lord be wid ye.' All the time. Every time we'd ask him for the time, he'd say it. Then he'd keep right on rollin' down to the church, and sure enough if we didn't hear them bells in the next couple minutes. Pa always said you could set your clock to Jake Bossen.

"But he sure wuz awful lookin'! Don't really know if he was born that way, or if he got hit by the C & NW. That was jist the only way I'd ever known him.

"Sure, I remember Jake Bossen—who could forget him?"

"Oh, heck, remember the time that Johnny Vander Griest walked right behind him, actin' just like him? It was just after school got out, about '97 or so—something like that. We wuz walkin' down the road, comin' home, happy as larks that school was finally done. You, me, Hank De Boer, and who was the other one? Let's see—Phil Schuyler, sure it was Phil! Anyways, we was comin' home, you know, last day a school and all, and here if we don't find ol' Jake Bossen walkin' right in front a us.

"It was about noon, I know—we had only a half day that last day, remember? Anyways, Jim lets out the usual, 'Hey, Jake, what's the time?' Jake stops, turns around and glares almost—that guy was sure ugly—then he smiles when he sees us 'cause he thinks we wuz his friends. He grabs for his watch and says, 'Twelve twenty-five, boys, the Lord be wid ye.

"Well, there was no way we could just stop it there, you know, what with it bein' the last day a school and all, and just gettin' out for the summer like that. So Johnny Vander Griest—he was a character, that one—Johnny gets up behind him, right behind him, see, and he walks along just like Jake Bossen, and not a yard behind him.

"Did we laugh!! I remember layin' under a tree—them trees were just little ones then—just layin' and laughin' so hard my gut was ready to burst. I was sore for a day after! You 'member that, Ed, don't ya? Boy, that was funny! And Jake Bossen never seen him—he never knew. He never even turned around, and Johnny walked just right behind him. Man, that was crazy! Then he'd raise his right hand, like this, and scratch his ribs while he was walkin'—'member that? That was something, cause he looked just like a monkey, too. Oh, did we laugh.

"Yeah, I sure do remember Jake Bossen. Can't forget him, that's for sure.

"I remember goin' to church there and seein' Jake Bossen ringin' the bell. That was somethin', too, I'll tell you. The bell rope hung just inside the church door, but outside the ah, whotdoyou callit?—the ah, sanctuary. Right before the elders walked in, then Jake's time would come, and he'd have to ring that bell. I remember watching him. He'd raise those long arms a his, like he was reachin' for the sky, and grab that old rope as high as he could. Then he'd jump on the rope, yank it down with all his weight, and sure enough, bong! there'd go the old bell. But then remember how that bell'd swing back and he'd fly up like he was a cork bobber? Whoosh! up he'd go a coupla feet off the floor. His back'd be straight as a board when he was ringin' the bell—why you wouldn't even a know he wuz a hunch-back. 'Member that? Boy, I'd just have to think about Jake Bossen in church and I'd get the giggles. Ma would pinch me every time. But I couldn't help it.

"Yeah, that Jake Bossen was somethin'!—he really was!

"Ach, I almost forgot when them singers from Hull came one summer tryin' to get us to come to school there. Well, Ma put one up at our place for the night, you know. And when we was walkin' around the town, showin' this guy around, why here comes Jake Bossen just a rollin' along towards the church. The kid from Iowa stops like he wuz seein' Indians. He looks at 'im like this—eyes wide open.

" 'Who's that?' he says to me. So I tell him. That guy never saw nobody uglier, that's sure. I told him all about Jake, you know, about how I didn't know if he was born that way or not, and how everybody always asked him for the time. So here comes Jake.

" 'Jake,' I says to him, real serious-like, 'what time ya got?' Sure enough Jake stops, grins at us, lookin' at this new kid here while he's a reachin' into his vest pocket and pullin' out his watch. 'Five fifty-five,' he says, 'the Lord be wid ye, and wid ye scholars from Hull,' he says. Then he humps away just like usual, you know. That Iowa kid just about died laughin'. I swear he thought Jake Bossen was the ugliest man he'd ever saw alive.

"He was a strange one, that Jake Bossen . . . and he was some ugly man!

"I saw him hurt once, though. Least-wise if I'd a been him, I'd a been hurt—probably fightin' mad, too. We was older then. Ed, I don't think you was with us. We had some beer, must a been some holiday. Don't remember exactly when. But Johnny Vander Griest again—that kid could really be a stinker. Remember when he hung up Jay Pasma by his suspenders on the coatrack at school? That was Jay's first day, too, and him cryin' like a baby, but Johnny never got caught somehow—anyways, Johnny and me and some other guys had a couple, just a couple, but we was feelin' fine, eh? Anyway, Johnny spots Jake Bossen comin' out of his house and headin' like usual toward the church. There wasn't many people up that side a town—they was all down at the park at the barbeque. Anyhow, Johnny yells at Jake and asks him the time. Jake stops, like always, sees it's his friends, then checks the watch. 'Almost six,' he says, 'the Lord be wid ye, Johnny.' Well, Johnny didn't have enough yet. He was a tough one. Wonder what ever happened to him?

"Well, anyway, Johnny yells again. 'Jake,' he says. And Bossen turns around again. Nobody really asks him much more than the time, you know, so he's lookin' kinda surprised.

" 'Jake,' he says—let's see, how did that go again?—oh, yeah— 'Jake,' says Johnny, real serious-like, 'what's that thing on yer back, yer hinder?' We laughed, man, we laughed awful hard.

"Jake Bossen watched us for about fifteen seconds, smilin' all the time. 'The Lord be wid ye,' he says, and keeps right on a rollin' down toward the church. We just cracked up!

"Never really knew if he was mad or not. Didn't hardly seem like it. Boy, I'd a been hot if anybody had a said that to me!

"He was quite a guy, that Jake Bossen. Got a letter from the in-laws some years back. I 'member it well. Said that Jake Bossen had passed on. Said, lotsa people wuz at the funeral. Said, some even brought flowers. And it said that the people from the church just couldn't seem to find nobody around Harrison to ring the old bell nomore. Guess nobody wanted the job. Funny, eh?

"Yeah, how can ya forget somebody like Jake Bossen?"

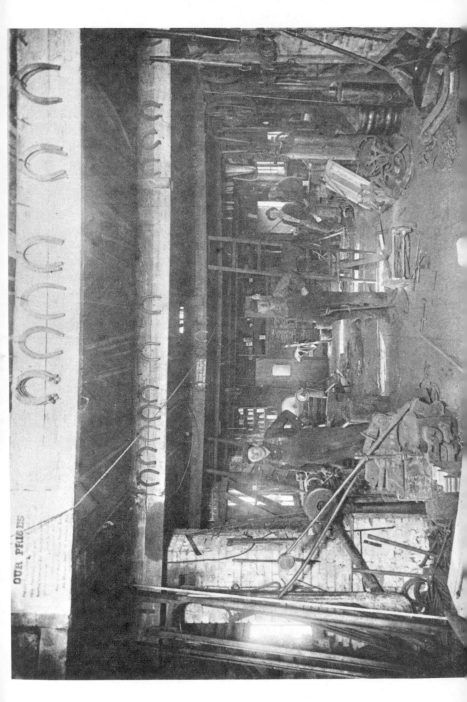

Second Cut

The only road east out of town was packed hard and dry by the heat of the July sun. Clumps of clover and awkward thistle stems jutted from the edge of the road into the dusty ruts which pointed to the summit of the hill. Edgar Hartman walked slowly, for he was in no particular hurry to arrive on the job. Jung's second cut would not go so easy as the first; the mid-summer heat and humidity made field work more oppressive. And, a healthy coat of dew still glistened on the roadside grasses, delaying, for a time, any thought of haying.

When he reached the top of the slope, he turned back to the little community of dwellings. The rectangular gray buildings all looked alike from here; they stood straight and square among the oaks and maples that shaded the village. And there was that kind of closeness in the town, the only home he had known in his fifteen years. Out of the face of a gusty west wind, he turned to the north to look over three-foot corn and several acres of alfalfa, then to the south and to already barren fields where June peas had been harvested. To the east lay more Wisconsin farmland, bordered finally by a belt of timber that underlined the gray-green horizon of water. As far as he could see to the left and right, the big lake touched the sky at the eastern horizon.

For several days now, winds from the west had turned this great body of water into a roaring king, and even from this point he could hear and feel, almost, the unusually powerful surf pounding on the heavy shore sand. All night, from his home a mile west of the shoreline, he had heard this relentless beating. But Edgar kept walking now; nothing had been done yesterday, so he knew there was much to be done today.

The roaring of the waves last night had been as disturbing as the day itself. All day long his father's blacksmith shop had been full of quiet business; few men had spent all day in the field; the funeral had brought entire families to town. Throughout the day the dusty main street was alive with subdued movement as farmers decided to use the trip to town to accomplish other purposes as well. Heels clicked all day long on the thick wooden sidewalks; horses and wagons moved constantly up and down the seldom-used streets, carrying a thick layer of dust into the shop.

His father had had work to keep him busy yesterday, of course, keeping the fire hot, and, when things were busy, sharpening blades and shares. But the steady clang of the hammer on the anvil was the only sound to break the unsettled order, for things were purposely hushed. The men of the village, usually brimming with talk of weather and fields and crops, were remarkably calmed on the day of the funeral. Even the usually spirited talk of the war in Europe failed to excite the contemplative atmosphere of shop and town.

Only the anvil spoke conventionally, as Henry Hartman's work proceeded, unhindered by outside events. Edgar's father was not a tall man, but his years as a blacksmith had molded his body into a straight, bulging stump of strength. He had seen his father working late into the day, the sun long set, only the jumpy rays of a noisy fire providing needed light. Late into warm, spring evenings his thick, muscular arms, wet with sweat, swung that hammer, always in the same monotonous beat, pounding, shaping, bending stubborn iron into implements for the farmers. But as much as he admired his father's strength, Edgar saw and knew him as a respected leader of the little Dutch community in which he lived, for Henry Hartman's impressive physical stature was equalled only by the strength of his character.

Men were drawn to his father somehow—family problems, church problems, financial problems; his father heard them all, it seemed, but Edgar heard none. Often, just as he was turning the glowing iron into an arc, he heard that quiet command, "Edgar, go to your mother," when some somber-looking man would enter the shop.

But last Monday things had been somehow different. Teunis Jansen had come in with the news: Gerrit Van Ess and Peter Blom were dead, drowned in the lake on Sunday afternoon.

His father had stopped his work; he had looked at Teunis. The shop had been very quiet, Edgar remembered.

The bodies already had been found, one close to where they had gone swimming, the other far up the beach near Amsterdam.

Edgar's father said nothing then; he glared, it seemed, at the anvil. The fire crackled and dimmed slowly. A few more words passed quickly, the funeral . . . the families . . . then Teunis left.

Quietly, his father motioned him to follow into the house. The wooden steps creaked under their feet. Edgar's mother greeted their unexpected entry silently, and, without asking, heated the coffee.

"The boy of Van Ess, and oldest boy of Blom. They are dead, Dina. In the lake yesterday."

His mother stopped moving momentarily, turning her face as if she'd been slapped. *"Och heden,"* she said, mumbling almost, then looked back to her husband. Saying no more, she continued her work, looking away again. His father rested his forehead in his hand; Edgar felt a cloud of anguish lying like lake fog in the steamy kitchen.

"On Sunday?" Mother asked.

His father replied softly. Silence returned.

Edgar watched his mother moving around the stove. He glanced at the bluish dishes hung from the wall and at the figure of the farmer on the shelf, all brought over from the old country. The chair creaked into the silence as he jerked up his hand to scratch his forehead. No one else moved.

"I must finish the shoe, Father." He rose unsteadily, and went back to the shop. All of this was new to him.

And he knew Gerrit and Peter, although they were older than he, for they too, he remembered, had sat here on these stools and barrels when they were younger, and waited with their fathers for shoes or shares. In recent years they had been well-known in the little town, for they were fine ball players, even heroes to the younger children. As they had grown older, the eyes of the village had seen their wagons standing outside the tavern across the street from the shop. It was no secret that they took out American girls. Their behavior had grown into something of a scandal in the otherwise settled community. Now they would never go to the war they had dreamed of. Edgar poked at the fire which had already lost its force.

His father returned. His silence was still conspicuous. He took up the hammer and returned to the anvil. With his left hand, he drew a piece of glowing iron from the fire, and began, at his usual pace, to shape it into a shoe. Finally he spoke, dropping the hammer to his side.

"Edgar," he said, "you know the boys. How do they live?"

Edgar kept pushing the wheel. "I don't know, Father."

Side by side they worked for several hours; they had spoken nothing else of Gerrit and Peter.

It was just after dinner that Monday when Cornelius Den Boer made his usual entrance at the shop. There was something different this time, Edgar realized, for the old man's thick white eyebrows were drawn low and deep, adding even more wrinkles around the corners of his eyes. Nor were there any stories of Holland, or of the immigrants who set first homesteads in the Oostburg area. He sat slowly on an empty barrel near the door, after the conventional nod of greeting.

"You know, Henry?" His voice was harsh and raspy.

"Ja." Edgar stopped his work, looking at his father who stared at the guest.

"The Lord took them, you know, for a purpose." There

was no spark of his usual jovial nature. He unbuttoned his black top coat as if he had just come in from the cold.

"Ja," came the reply, "He did."

"We can have little hope for their salvation." Den Boer pulled a stained yellow pipe from the pocket of his old black coat. He stuck the pipe somewhere in the thickly bearded jaw and struck a match across the rough cooling tank.

"We must teach our children to learn from this." The little flame illuminated the drawn face under the black, wide-brimmed hat. A huge mass of pale-gray smoke rose, then hung like a rain cloud about his head.

"We worship a righteous God, Den Boer, but we cannot judge these boys or the state of their souls so easily. We don't always know His will."

"There was no Christian life there, Henry. We know that, ja? They swam on the Sabbath. There is only hope for us if here we see the hand of the Lord."

Edgar, like his father, did not stop working. He expected to be excused from the shop at any moment, but as long as he did remain, he made a pretense of being quietly occupied at the wheel.

"Cornelius, the Lord always works in these mysterious ways." Edgar's father was slowly forging a wagon hitch. The pace revealed his respect for Cornelius Den Boer.

"Our children are losing the faith." Den Boer puffed gently at his pipe. "Ja, I been afraid more than once of things like this."

Edgar paused momentarily and listened intently. He did not face the old man.

"The Lord will punish us and our children for our sin. We do not obey the commandments as He wants us to yet. He shows us His wrath, and He has today, to teach us to believe in Him and obey His law."

Den Boer removed his hat and hung it on a convenient nail. Edgar knew his visit would not be short, and the conversation itself would continue for a long time. It seemed only a year ago that he had heard some of these things, for then, he remembered, it was the death of his niece, a little girl who had died unexpectedly of diptheria. But Den Boer mentioned very plainly that the boys were known to many women, and when Edgar heard such specific reference to sin, he worked even more intently to hide his embarrassment.

The old man did most of the talking, Edgar's father responding infrequently, trying vainly, it seemed, to restrain Den Boer. As time passed, the old man's speech slowed considerably, and each word was chosen more carefully. He sat and swayed evenly from side to side on the retired keg.

"People say that their teams led them home many nights after the tavern closed. But it is not only them, Henry, it is others too. Many others, they say, are spending their time in the ways of the world. These are our children. We pray daily for them, but it seems of no use . . . the children of the covenant . . . ." Edgar glanced up to see Den Boer slowly shake his head.

"These are new times, Cornelius," his father offered, slowly, the ring of the anvil underlining each phrase. "All the ways of the old country may not be taken so easily any more. We live here, in a new country. We covet the strength only the Lord can give us to see through the difficult times."

"Ach, Hartman, the Sabbath has not changed since we come to this country. My commandments read today the same like yesterday. We must change because of this new country?"

"The Lord's will is not always so easy to know." Edgar followed his father's gesture and forced a rush of air into the fire through the dusty bellows. Although the tempo of the work remained constant, the intense conversation finally began to wane, both participants wearying of the traditional arguments.

Cornelius sat silent; tiny whiffs of smoke rose like signals from the human statue. He was shifting and reorganizing himself, preparing for the last advance. His thorny hands moved slowly around the bowl of the pipe, withdrawing it, then placing it back within his tightly-drawn lips.

Henry pointed at the door, signaling his son to let in the air. Edgar pushed through the stagnant cloud of smoke and threw both doors open to the street, blocking them open with iron poles. The midday sun brightened the shop's interior, and the fresh lake air rescued the men from the strangulation of an atmosphere thickened by steam and smoke. Shadows that danced and leaped against the walls were erased by the sun's penetration; the light from the fire faded in the face of the afternoon sun. Cornelius shifted his position to look out on the town. The triangular hitch hissed wildly as Edgar's father buried it in the cooler.

"The dominie has to preach on these things. The people must understand that the Lord speaks to us in these things." Den Boer spoke through the open door as if addressing the street. His eyes stared into the little community, until, finally, his arms reached down to the rim of the keg and he lifted himself slowly from his seat.

"I must go now, Henry," he said, turning back to the shop and retrieving his hat. He buttoned his coat once again and stepped into the doorway.

"Tomorrow is the funeral."

The next morning Edgar realized very soon that the funeral would be an important event to the community. From all parts of the surrounding countryside, the staid farmers and their families descended on the village. The church was full of friends and relatives, coming to pay their respects and express their deep sympathy to the family. Edgar saw no smiles there. He heard the community's grief in the tolling of the bell and felt their mournful acceptance in the heavy rhythmical chanting of the Psalms. But no, as he walked east, he could remember little else from yesterday's funeral, for his eyes and thoughts had wandered from the caskets, to the families, over the large assembly of worshippers before him, and finally to Cornelius Den Boer, whose eyes stared at the pulpit.

But the funeral wasn't the end. Thinking back on it now, the atmosphere of the village was laden with emotion that day, as men acknowledged each other on the street but rarely paused to exchange conversation. The women spoke quietly to each other, congregating in little groups of two and three. The July sun beat down heavily, but only the corn profited from its strength.

Edgar kicked at a lump of dry clay along the road. Today was another day. The effect of the tragedy of last Sunday lessened, and while the drownings and their meaning would certainly continue to be heard in the dark blacksmith shop, Edgar knew that most people understood it was time to continue and overpower yesterday's agony.

Now he kept walking along the rutted trail. His father's business had brought contact with many farmers, and frequently he had been requested to help with work which had piled up beyond the control of one man. Today was such a day. One of his father's American customers had second cut of hay to do and needed some help.

The farm lay closer to the lake than the village and some distance to the north. The walk was pleasant this morning, the sun just beginning to breathe its warmth into the cool lake air which still lay over the lakeshore area. From scattered farms, all neatly kept, dairy cows wandered out to pasture, their morning milking over.

Eventually he saw Jung's farm. It appeared as he rose out of a natural crevice in the earth where a river used to flow to the big lake. Tall pines grew all around the homestead, giving it shade from the sun and a shield from the wind. He could already see his employer walking in front of the barn. Edgar had worked for this man before and was happy to return. Mr. Jung had treated him well in the past, and Edgar quietly enjoyed his jovial but salty tongue. Mrs. Jung always prepared massive feasts, and her husband paid as well as any of the farmers of the area, better than most Hollanders.

Jung waved as he saw Edgar approach. Edgar raised his

arm and waved a reply. The early morning sun had now nearly rid the ground of the dew which temporarily postponed the work, and Edgar knew he would spend little time talking.

"Ja, Hartman," he said, "are you ready to work?"

"Ja, Mr. Jung," Edgar replied. "Good to see you again."

Jung removed the faded black hat he wore for work and wiped the sweat which had already formed on his forehead. A thick-standing crop of gray hair stood proudly above a ruddy, red-nosed face, round and full, the kind of face that begged a smile. Edgar, despite his years, already stood above the man, but Jung's weight certainly surpassed the boy's. Packed into the shirt and pants he wore was a torso of lumpy and uneven bulk. He replaced the battered hat and looked back to Edgar.

"Hartman," he said, "let's go to Mama before we start."

Edgar willingly consented, and Jung put his hand on his shoulder to lead him to the house. They sat down on a step before the house, and the old man roared for service. The humid air provoked more sweat from his blue-lined temples, as the temperature rose with the sun.

"Mama," he roared, "I want a beer and one for Hartman too." The command had been given, and a graying woman returned to the kitchen after greeting the visitor.

"So tell me, Hartman, what do the Hollanders say about the two boys who drowned on Sunday?"

"Their funeral was yesterday, Mr. Jung. Many people were there."

"Yep, it's a terrible thing, what happened."

"Ja, terrible," Edgar repeated.

"The two boys were good boys. Van Ess, he worked here for me too. The other one I don't know. But they're too young, huh, to die already."

"Ja, they were only 18." Edgar was reluctant to talk about the deaths anymore, but the old man sat on the step, looking as if he had more to say. His belly hung over his thighs.

"The Hollanders send them to Hell, I suppose?" An

ironic smile spread across his face and grew into a belch of a laugh that exploded out of his round chest. He shook his head in mock disbelief.

Edgar didn't reply, as Jung continued. "They're good boys, Hartman. What does your father say?"

"My father is sad."

"Ja," the old man went on, "the lake, it's been rough, you know. Those boys shoulda bin more careful."

Mrs. Jung returned silently with two short glasses of beer, offering them to the men.

"Hartman, you drink a beer with me? Some of your people don't like it."

Edgar sipped the luke-warm beer and assented with a faint, sarcastic laugh. He was miles from Oostburg now.

"The lake was too dangerous, Hartman. Those boys, should not bin swimmin'. They shoulda known. They was born here."

When Jung's glass was nearly empty, he was back on his feet.

"We go now, there is much work today."

Edgar swallowed the heavy brew and rose to his feet. The sun was beating down on the Wisconsin countryside. The burly old farmer tipped his glass to the sun and the beer was gone. He walked to the barn, where his team waited.

Edgar watched Jung closely. He saw his father again and heard the rhythmical clang of the hammer on the anvil. He glanced at his own nearly emptied glass, then poured the remaining contents into the light dirt of the path to the barn.

The lake air was hot and heavy, and the day would be long and hard.

The Heritage of These Many Years

"She is awake now, Andy. Do you want to sit with her?"
My father closed the bedroom door behind him. I hadn't
seen my Grandma since Grandpa's funeral, so I nodded to
my father and walked into the bedroom.

I knew it might be my last chance. I had arrived in Gibbs-
ville earlier that morning, coming across the lake from
Michigan by ferry, just like two years ago for Grandpa
Roerdink. I remembered that well. It was raining in the
cemetery that day, and a cold autumn wind rushed off the
lake. I had helped Grandma to the coffin; she was already
frail and weak, past eighty years. She stared so long at the
coffin, and she cried as she smiled. Then she looked up at
my father. "He beat us there, Henry," she said.

Grandma Roerdink lay motionless on the bed, the
outline of her body barely visible beneath the heavy quilt.
Age itself had weathered her sallow face, and wrinkles
creased her cheeks and forehead. Her mouth was opened
slightly, and her breathing was audible, but regular. She
seemed asleep.

The room looked just as I had remembered. Off-white
curtains draped the only window, admitting a glow of
daylight. A curved-front dresser stood beneath the window. There was still no dust on the knick-knacks. And the
matching commode still stood perpendicular in the corner.
Two clean towels hung neatly from the rod above the por-
celain pitcher and bowl that stood on one of Grandma's
own doilies.

The room had always seemed dark and old to me; it
reminded me of wrinkled skin on flabby arms, of rimless

glasses and long, pointy shoes. But here was mystery too. Nameless faces lined the walls, and an old Dutch couple peered at me from an ornate oval frame hung above the headboard. I always loved this room, for there was excitement here, the fascination of experiences long past. I loved to sneak in as a boy, to sit alone on the bed and look around. I conceived heroic tales of the Civil War and Indian massacres, of romance and tragedy, of love and death. But alone.

"Who is it?" Grandma Roerdink's eyes winced, but didn't open.

"It's me, Grandma, Andrew."

"Ja, Andrew, all the way from Michigan, eh?"

"Ja, Grandma. Just to see you."

"Ja, ja, good . . . . You are still in school then?"

"No, no, I'm a teacher now."

"Ja, that's good, that's good. Stay in school, Andrew. Get a good education. The first Roerdink—Andrew will be the first Roerdink, Gerrit, the first to go to college—"

"Ja, Grandma, I'm out now—graduated."

"Ja, ja, my only grandson. To Hope College, ja?"

I saw the graveyard smile again. It was clear and radiant, and it grew.

"Andrew, will you be a dominie?"

"No, Grandma, a teacher."

"Ja, ja, a teacher. That's good. We need good Christian teachers."

Her eyes blinked rapidly, then opened slowly. They were dull and misty, but still blue. She stared at the ceiling. Then she turned her head and looked at me, smiling, but saying nothing.

"Grandma, you look good. How are you feeling?"

"Good, Andrew, good. I'm going home now. Then I will know."

"You mean with Grandpa, Grandma?"

"Ja, with Grandpa and the Lord."

She seemed wide awake now. I looked up at the picture above the broad oak headboard.

"Your mother and father, too, Grandma?"

"Ja, Andrew, and some day you too."

"Ja," I said.

"Come to the bed here once."

I rose slowly and stood at the edge.

"Sit here. Let me see you."

I sat gently at her side. Grandma's face was bright now. She seemed more alive than I expected. She looked at me in a strange way, a look that seemed to gather all of me in her gaze.

"My father was a good man, Andrew."

"Yes, Grandma, I'm sure. I never knew him, you know."

"I know. Ja, I know. I remember. I don't remember things good now, but the old days I still know good."

"Tell me, Grandma."

"Ach, Andrew always wants to know about the old days." She laughed very softly to herself. "Not all the young ones care anymore, do they?"

"Ja, I know."

"And the old days, they weren't always so good, ja?"

I felt for her arm beneath the blanket. She moved her elbow outward, still smiling.

"What was your mother like, Grandma? Like you?"

"Oh, no, Andrew. She was a good woman. A saint. It was hard for us in Holland, you know. But she never spoke of it."

"She was like you then, Grandma."

"No, no, she was so much better. When Pa said to leave, she didn't complain. With five children, me the youngest. She didn't complain."

"She was a good woman."

"Ja, Andrew, she died for me."

I knew the story. A burning ship—the *Phoenix*—here, off Sheboygan. Grandma's parents both died.

"On the ship?"

"Ja, on the ship."

Grandma Roerdink never spoke of the *Phoenix*. I had often asked her when I was a boy, but she would only turn away and shake her head. Even my father knew little about it. But I had always ached to know the story. I wanted so badly to hear it from her, for I could sense the excitement that must have been there. Huge yellow flames rising from the deck of a slowly sinking ship. And the lake, its waters deathly cold in late November. Gallant struggles, cruel deaths, the urgent prayers of my own ancestors, strangers in a strange land.

And now she was dying.

"You know the story, Andrew?"

"What's that, Grandma?"

"The story of the ship?"

"I have read about it, ja."

"But you weren't there. It's a terrible story, Andrew. A terrible story. Your Grandpa knew. I told him. But no one else. Not even your father."

"I understand."

Her eyes were clear now, but the smile was gone. She looked at me directly, into my eyes.

"I must tell you, Andrew."

"But Grandma, you don't have—"

"I must tell you."

"You shouldn't exert yourself now. You are weak."

"Ja, I am weak. The Lord will take me soon." She smiled again. "I will tell you. Someone must know." She turned her eyes away from me and stared at the ceiling.

"It is not an easy thing to say, Andrew. It is close in my mind for these many years, but it is not easy to say."

"Grandma, you shouldn't—"

"It was November, Andrew—I will tell you now—November of '47. We left Varssevelt. The farm was no good. Men were arrested when they worshiped. The new country seemed a dream to us. *Vader's* eyes—I can remember them now yet—they were bright when he spoke of America. How they shine yet, ja, I can see them." She swallowed hard and stopped. "Look at him, Andrew—he was a good man."

I glanced at the portrait. I had seen it often before. It had come from Grandma's uncle in Holland. He was seated on a chair as big as a throne, his wife's hand rested on his shoulder as she stood soberly at his side. He had a round face, a short wide nose, and close-cut hair. His shoulders were broad.

"You see him, Andrew?"

"Yes, He was handsome, Grandma."

"Handsome? He was not a handsome man, but he was good—a good *Vader*." She smiled at me then. "The picture, Andrew, you take it when I am gone. You must have it."

"Thank you, Grandma. Maybe you should sleep now."

"No, no, I will tell you. We sailed from Holland to New York. Then by train to Buffalo—there were Hollanders there. They told *Vader* to weigh all the baggage. I brought it to him. Sometimes the Americans would steal . . . Then we left from Buffalo, I think it was eleven, November . . . Thursday—to here, Andrew. We were coming here!"

She stopped again and looked at me. "We had come so far, ja, so far. And we were so close. All the way from Holland, Andrew. We were so close."

Her eyes turned back to the ceiling. "We stopped in Manitowoc. The lake was high and rough. The captain said we would stay in the harbor until it was safe. Some of the people cried then, I remember. Some even swore about that captain—we were so close, you know.

"Father stayed up that night with many men. They couldn't sleep. The rest of us went to sleep that night with dreams. I dreamed, too—dry land, a house, a sunny sky—I remember. The ship left the harbor late at night. I was only a little girl. I was sleeping, dreaming of the house. But *Vader* stood on the deck, I know, watching the shore lights with the other men.

"Then I remember him standing over me. He woke me. He woke all of us. He shook me softly. '*Opstaan*, Mina,' he said. But I knew. We all knew. We could feel something bad. His eyes blazed, ja, like the fire itself. But he spoke very soft. I remember it very well, Andrew, after these many years, for I saw him never again."

I looked up at the picture. The man in the picture had glassy eyes. They had been penciled in by a painter somewhere in Holland. I tried to imagine him as Grandma spoke.

"The hold was full of Hollanders. Many more than was right. In a moment, it seemed, everyone was awake—men yelled and children cried. Mother gathered us quickly in our night clothes. She didn't reach for any of her things. We hurried up on the deck. I remember trying to hurry up the ladder. Emma pushed me up. We were almost the first.

"Smoke was already in the air, Andrew. Mother pushed us, she even carried me forward to the side of the ship. She made us sit and kneel. Then she sat next to us and pointed to the shore. She spoke, in Dutch. '*Kijk,*' she pointed, '*daar is ons huis!*' People were screaming behind us, but mother kept us by the rail—she made us watch the lights on the beach. She wouldn't let us watch the people on the ship . . . . We were so close, Andrew. Do you understand? We were so close to our home.

"Emma asked her about Father. She said he would be here soon. She said he was fighting the fire. Mama watched for him, I saw her. There was fear in her eyes. I was a little girl, but I saw it. I knew.

"Then there was an explosion . . ."

She stopped talking and looked at me.

"Andrew you must not forget this now."

"No, Grandma. I promise."

"It has been with me for these many years, but it is not easy to tell."

"Grandma, if you think—perhaps you have said enough for now." I waited, silent.

"There is yet more." She didn't look away this time.

"The explosion blew up the middle of the ship. Fire went shooting up behind us. It made my back so hot. But the air was cold, Andrew—November, the twenty-first, Sunday morning—ja, that's something, the Sabbath, the Lord's Day . . .

"My mother cried then. She tried to stop, but she cried.

We knew too. She pushed us tighter against the rail. There was much more shouting—no, screaming. People ran like animals. They just had on nightclothes. And the fire grew. It was so hot. I cried too, Andrew. We all did.

"Wooden shoes banged on the deck. Men shouted and screamed. Mother understood no English. Some women went crazy, Andrew. They screamed so hard I couldn't stand it. Some laughed like witches. And everywhere there were children, Dutch children, my friends, separated from mothers and fathers. It was terrible, Andrew. No one should ever—"

Grandma Roerdink began to cry. I wanted it all to stop, and yet a strange fascination lured me. I knew there was more, but I tried to quiet her, to give her some peace.

"Please, Grandma, you shouldn't anymore. You are not strong." I squeezed hard on her elbow.

"There is more." She breathed deeply and smiled again. "You always liked the stories, Andrew. I remember. 'Tell me more, Grandma,' you would say. There is more.

"There was an American. A good man, like my father. He was handsome. A rich man. He played with us often on the ship. His name was Mr. Blish. He was there, suddenly, by Mother. '*Vrouw,*' he said, 'your man?' Mother took her hand from behind my neck and pointed to the fire. 'Come,' he said.

"Mother made us all hold hands. It was hard to walk—to stay together. People rushed all around us. I saw a woman with only a wool skirt on. She jumped over the side of the ship, screaming. Mr. Blish led us through. I had hold of Mother's hand. She squeezed it so tight. I cried because it hurt so. I can feel it yet, after these many years." She raised her elbow slightly. I felt it beneath the quilt.

"The flames grew behind us. You could hear them. They made a loud snapping noise. Then Mr. Blish stopped. 'Here,' he said—but Emma—she was the oldest—she was gone. My mother screamed out her name, but her voice . . . Emma was gone. Blish grabbed her arms and shook her hard. I remember hating him for that. I tried to kick him, to make him stop hurting her. He picked me up, above his head, and held me there. He pushed through the crowd. In a moment I was in a boat. There was a strange lady next to me. She took me in her arms. Suddenly I was cold, so cold. The boat was in the lake, away from the flames."

"Your sisters?" I asked.

"Mother stayed to look for Emma. I saw them never again."

"But your youngest sister?" I knew something of the story.

"Ja, Jenny. Mr. Blish put Jenny on another boat. I didn't know it then. I was alone. I was just a little girl, Andrew, and I was alone. I cried for my mother. I pounded on the strange woman's breast. She held me still tighter. *'Wees stil, Kleintje,'* she said.

"The little boat was filled with people. We could hold no more. Water was already coming in. Some men used their wooden shoes to scoop it out. A woman came up from the water and pulled herself up on the side. Her eyes were big, Andrew. But we could hold no more. A man pushed her away. She held to the side. I remember seeing the hand holding to the edge. Then, it was gone. My feet were in the water. It was so cold.

"And I can still see the ship, Andrew. It is so clear in my mind. The fire flew high from the water. So high. Another explosion. I saw bodies in the air. I saw them splash into the water. The flames were louder than the screaming, but I heard Dutch words, American words. Prayers. Curses. It was—I think of this often—it was something of hell, Andrew. I'm sure of it."

"It must have been, Grandma." I wanted to change it now, to remind her of her children, her life, the good things, but she continued quickly.

"We finally came to shore. Someone started a fire, another fire, to warm us. It raged upon the sand. I was still cold, so cold. The frost made the beach hard like clay. It was November, Andrew, late in November—close to Thanksgiving, and Sunday, a Sabbath morning.

"Still I watched the flames from the ship. They jumped up high in the darkness. I could cry no more, it seemed. The strange lady held me close, like I was her own.

"Could I have a drink, Andrew?"

"Ja, ja, I will get it." I stood at her bedside for a moment. Her eyes were closed. Perhaps she would sleep. I poured a glass of water from the pitcher on the commode and walked back to her bed.

"Grandma," I whispered, hoping that she was asleep.

"Ja, can you help me?"

I slid my fingers beneath her thin gray hair and raised her head slightly. She drank just one swallow.

"Thank you, Andrew."

I put the glass back on the dresser.

"You are in college now, Andrew?"

"Ja, I'm through—"

"Good, good. Hope College?"

"Ja, Grandma, Hope College."

"You are the first. Your grandfather was so happy. 'The first,' he said. We were both so proud."

I sat again at her side.

"I told your grandfather. He knew about the *Phoenix*. But no one else. Not even your father."

"Ja, Grandma. I will remember."

"Good. There's more though. The people from Sheboygan saw the flames on the lake. They came up the beach to get us in the wagons. The woman held me in her arms in the wagon. We moved slowly over the frozen sand. The light from the fires lit the way. I remember the hospital. It was warm and dry. Some time later Jenny found me. A long time. Three, maybe four months. We were the only ones saved. Everyone else, brother Pieter, sister Emma and Geertje, Mother and Father—all dead. Some families were all lost. Everyone. The Lord spared us."

"It's a terrible story, Grandma."

"Ja, it is. More than 200 of our people dead. It was horrible. For these many years I have tried to understand it, Andrew. So close. On the Sabbath. Why does our Lord take them like that? For years I have asked myself such things. And never can I get the answer!"

"Ja, Grandma." I could offer nothing.

She closed her wrinkled mouth, high beneath her nose, shut her eyes, and smiled once more. "Soon I will know, Andrew. Then I will understand. I will be with Him."

Five days later, Grandma Roerdink died. To the end her mind was clear, and I took my regular turn with her. Usually she would sleep, but occasionally she would tell me other stories of how it was years ago. Not once, however, did she mention the burning ship.

After the funeral I walked alone into the darkened bedroom and stood beside her bed. There were no wrinkles in her quilt, as if she had made the bed herself. I looked again at the ancient faces on the walls, and the oval portrait above the headboard. I studied it closely, trying to see Grandma's parents as clearly as she had, but my great-grandfather's eyes still looked strange, penciled in by some long-forgotten painter.

Glossary

afgescheiden kerk — the separated church (separated from the Dutch State Church, or the Reformed Church); in America, the Christian Reformed Church

Begrijp je dat? — Do you understand that?

Ben je gek? — Are you crazy?

broek — pants

Daar zou je mee naar bed willen, he! — You would like to sleep with her, eh?

Dat gaat te ver — That goes too far

Dat's Heeren zegen op u daal — approximately translated as "Jehovah bless thee from above," as in the Christian Reformed Church's *Psalter Hymnal* No. 280:3 (Psalm 134)

dief — thief

Dominie — the reverend

drommells — "shucks"; roughly equivalent to the American expletive "darn it"

duivel — the devil

duivels prentenboek — literally translated "the devil's picture book; meaning, however, playing cards

fijne — a sarcastic reference to an obviously pious person

gek — crazy

gekheid — foolishness

goed zo — very good

Getrouwe God de heid'nen zijn gekomen, en hebben stout Uw erfland ingenomen — approximately translated as "Faithful God, the heathen have come and have audaciously occupied Your promised land" (Psalm 79)

heilig boontje — a "little saint"

Hoe gaat het met je, dikzak? — How are you fatty?

Hou je mond! — Be quiet!

huichelaar — hypocrite

Huygens and Da Costa — Dutch Calvinist Poets

idioot — idiot

Ik ben Amerikaan — I am an American

in verwachting — expecting; with child

Je bent niet in de kerk geboren — literally translated "You are not born in the church"; meaning, however, "Don't leave the door open"

Je moet nooit over een andermans kinderen praten totdat je je eige schapen op't droge hebt — American Dutch expression meaning roughly, "Don't talk about other people's children until your own are safely grown!" The second clause, *je schapen op't droge hebt*, means to have accumulated enough money to be able to retire.

jongen — son or boy

Kijk, daar is ons huis — Look, there is our house

kippedief — chicken thief

kolonie — colony or settlement

Laat ons bidden — Let us pray

Laat ons lezen, vader — Let us read (the Bible for devotions), father

lieveling — darling

lompe boer — clumsy farmer

Loof, loof nu aller Heeren Heer, Amen — approximately translated as "Blest be His great and glorious Name" as in the Christian Reformed Church's *Psalter Hymnal* No. 280:3 (Psalm 134)

moeder — mother

Monden dicht! — Be quiet!

muur — wall; barricade

Neem dit toch mee! — Take this with you!

Nieuwsbode — Dutch newspaper, published in Sheboygan, Wisconsin, and edited by J. Quintus

Nu breekt me de klomp — literally translated "Now breaks my wooden shoe"; meaning, however, "I don't believe it"

Och, heden! — Oh, no!

opa — grandfather

ondergoed — underwear

opschepper — braggart

opstaan — get up

plaat — American Dutch spelling of *plat*: vulgar or course language

pruts — used in American Dutch to mean "cross," or "slightly annoyed"

rand — edge or perimeter

rotzak — a derogatory term roughly equivalent to "wretch"

schat — darling

Schiet op! — Hurry up!

Schiet toch op! — Hurry up now!

schrik — scare; *schrikken* means to scare

schurken — villains

slaapsok — sleepyhead

Spreek Hollands! — Speak Dutch!

Staten Bijbel — a 17th century Dutch Bible, heavy and large because it had such extensive explanatory footnotes

stommeling — stupid

Subiet! — Do it right away!

't Hijgend hert der jacht ontkomen — approximately translated as "As the hart is about to falter" as found in the Christian Reformed Church's *Psalter Hymnal* No. 74:1 (Psalm 42)

verdomd — cursed

verdorie — an expletive or curse

verdraaid — an expletive signifying disgust

verrek — a vulgarism

verrekte beesten — stupid animals

verrekte jongen — miserable kid

verschrikkelijk — terrible

vies — dirty

voorzanger — song leader (used in church services when musical instruments were deemed not fitting)

vrouw — wife

wablief — pardon

Wat benauwd! — How sultry! (denoting a nearly claustrophobic sensation)

Wat zeg je nou? — What do you say now?

Wees stil, kleintje! — Be still, little one!

zannik — American Dutch spelling of *zanik*: whine or nag

zondige — sinful

zwartrok — policeman, cop

Acknowledgements

Cover Photo — Family Portrait, Cornelius C. Schaap, approximately 1885; from the author's collection.

Frontispiece — Photography by Carl Vandermeulen.

P. X — Fiftieth anniversary reunion of the first Dutch settlers in Sheboygan County in Wisconsin; from the author's collection.

P. 8 — Photography by Carl Vandermeulen, Orange City, Iowa.

P. 16 — From the author's collection.

P. 40 — Civil War Veteran; courtesy of Mrs. Lucille Neuwerth, Sheboygan, Wisconsin.

P. 60 — Facsimilie of a sod house, Sioux Center, Iowa; courtesy of Katy Hansen, Orange City, Iowa; from the collection of the Sioux County Historical Society, Orange City, Iowa.

P. 82 — Photography by Carl Vandermeulen.

P. 98 — Photography by Carl Vandermeulen.

P. 110 — From the collection of Sioux County Historical Society, Iowa; courtesy of Katy Hansen.

P. 140 — Main Street, Hospers, Iowa; from the collection of Tom Huibregtse; courtesy of Katy Hansen.

P. 160 — Photography by Carl Vandermeulen.

P. 176 — From the collection of Sioux County Historical Society; courtesy of Katy Hansen.

P. 206 — Photography by Katy Hansen.

P. 226 — Photography by Carl Vandermeulen.

P. 232 — From the collection of Sioux County Historical Society; courtesy of Katy Hansen.

P. 244 — From the collection of Mr. John Van Gelder, Orange City, Iowa.

7762-10
5-44